SECRETS WE FIGHT

FORBIDDEN SERIES
BOOK 2

KIMBERLY KNIGHT

RACHEL LYN ADAMS

1

FALLON

I ARRIVED AT MY PARENTS' LUXURIOUS TWO-STORY HOUSE ON CAPE
Cod for their annual Fourth of July party. It had been a tradition in our
family as far back as I could remember. My entire family came, and
when I was younger, my siblings, cousins, and I would walk down to
the water to watch fireworks and drink until we couldn't think. I had
made a lot of memories over the years, and I realized it could all
change if my father was elected president in November.

As I stepped out of my blue Mustang Mach-E GT, the salty breeze
of the Atlantic Ocean blew through my hair, and the sound of laughter
and music drifted through the air. This year was special since my dad, a
U.S. senator representing Massachusetts, had led the Democratic
primaries and was expected to be confirmed as the party's nominee at
the Democratic National Convention the following month.

My gaze wandered over the meticulously manicured lawn and the
vibrant splashes of red, white, and blue decorating every corner,
reflecting the patriotic spirit. My parents had gone all out given the
circumstances surrounding my father. If he were to become president, I

wondered if our tradition would end, or maybe I or one of my siblings would have to take the reins for at least the next four years. My brother, my sister, and I were triplets, and if it came down to it, Faye would most likely host the party because she loved that shit. My brother, Finnegan, not so much.

Not bothering to go inside the house, I made my way around to where the party was held in the back and adjusted my sunglasses. It was a bright sunny day with no clouds in sight. That didn't stop everyone from standing around, sipping drinks, and shooting the shit. Despite their attempt to blend in, I also spotted my father's new security scattered throughout the property.

Before I could make a beeline for the bar, I noticed a striking man in a tailored suit, his demeanor exuding a sense of authority. While I'd never had a reason to speak to Agent Rhett Davis before, I knew who he was because the couple of times I had been in his presence, it had been hard to keep my eyes off of him. I couldn't help but feel a tingle of curiosity race through my body as our stares briefly met through our shades.

"Mr. Donnelley." He nodded curtly.

"Hey, there," I said with a mischievous grin, sidling up to him. He hadn't addressed me before, and because I thought he was easy on the eyes and I was in a flirtatious mood, I started a conversation. "If protecting my dad's life is the task at hand, you're doing a mighty fine job."

Agent Davis glanced at me, his expression focused, and all I could do was stare at his perfect sultry lips.

"Thank you, sir," he replied, his voice steady and unwavering. "My priority is ensuring the safety and security of your father and your family."

Undeterred by his professionalism, I chuckled at his response. "Well, Agent Davis, I have to say, you've got dedication down to an art. However, I can't help but wonder if there's room for a little excitement amidst all the seriousness." I knew I was taunting him, but I couldn't help it. Did agents have fun? Whenever I saw them, they were alert and focused on their jobs, but I had to imagine each of them had a carefree side, and I wouldn't mind spending time with Agent Davis when he wasn't on duty.

His lips twitched ever so slightly, betraying a hint of amusement. "I'm afraid fun and games don't fall within my duties. However, I'm sure you'll find plenty of entertainment during the party."

I leaned in closer, lowering my voice to a whisper. "You know, it's a shame because I have a feeling we could have a good time."

"I appreciate the sentiment, sir. But my commitment lies solely with my responsibilities. I'm confident you'll find someone equally charming to show you a good time tonight."

Was he flirting, or was that his way of letting me down easy? I couldn't help but laugh, though, appreciating his unwavering dedication to his job. "You know, you're absolutely right, Agent Davis. Safety first, I suppose."

He nodded, his gaze shifting back to the crowd. "Enjoy the party, Mr. Donnelley."

I sauntered away, feeling slightly rejected and ready for a cocktail. I knew there was no chance he would leave his post for a hookup. It was a far-fetched idea, especially since I wasn't sure if he was even into guys, but I'd broken the ice and enjoyed the little banter we had shared.

After ordering a vodka soda at the open bar, I scanned the crowd for anyone I knew. While my extended family was always in attendance, I'd also invited a few friends.

I spotted Tyler and Hayden as they stood off to the side of the pool. I'd expected to see a camera wrapped around Hayden's neck, but instead, it was Tyler's arms as they laughed and kissed and enjoyed the party.

"What's up, guys?" I asked as I approached. Tyler was my best friend, who I'd met in college, and Hayden was our professor he'd fallen in love with. It had been quite a shock when I'd found out, and even though they had broken up for a short period, they'd been back together for a little over a year and living together.

Without a response, Tyler lifted his left hand, showing a black band wrapped around his ring finger.

My mouth dropped open, and my eyes widened. "You're engaged?"

Tyler looked at Hayden. Both had huge smiles on their faces.

"Hayden proposed this morning," my best friend responded.

"Holy shit, guys. I'm super stoked for you two." I wrapped them both in a giant hug.

"Thanks, Fallon," Hayden replied.

We pulled apart, and Tyler said, "We don't know when and where yet, but I was hoping you'd be my best man."

"Absofuckinglutely. I'm going to plan the most epic bachelor party you've ever seen." I had no clue what it would entail just yet, but I was determined to make it memorable.

"Nothing that will require me bailing you two out of jail, right?" Hayden grinned.

Instantly, my gaze found Agent Davis'. He was staring at us from across the lawn, and again, my body tingled. Fuck, he was hot with his short dark blond hair and chiseled jaw, and as we stared at each other, I wondered what color his eyes were behind his sunglasses.

"Nah, nothing like that." I chuckled softly, still eyeing Agent Davis. "Don't think that would go over well with my father, but my brother is into poker. I'm sure I can find us a place to lose some money and have a great time with some beers."

"Who are you staring at?" Tyler asked.

I turned my attention back to my best friend. "Agent Hottie."

He snorted a laugh. "Who's Agent Hottie?"

I motioned with my head in Agent Davis' direction. "The one over there who I'm sure has muscles for days under his black suit."

Both Tyler and Hayden turned their heads, and when I glanced too, Agent Davis wasn't looking at us anymore. It was probably for the best.

"He's not bad," Hayden said. "But not as hot as a student I used to teach."

I snorted a laugh as Tyler tilted his head with an "aww."

Man, they had it bad for each other.

"Okay, you two. We need more alcohol." I downed my drink and went back to the bar.

———————

AS THE NIGHT WORE ON AND THE DRINKS FLOWED FREELY, I FOUND myself increasingly caught up in the celebratory spirit. The alcohol only fueled my desire for Agent Davis. I couldn't help it. I hadn't been in his presence for such a long length of time before, and I caught myself searching for him in the crowd the entire night.

With a playful smile on my lips, I stumbled over to where he was standing, his stare firmly fixed on the surroundings. "Hey, there, Agent Hottie," I slurred, leaning against a nearby tree for support. "Protecting democracy never looked so good!"

He turned his head to face me, a mixture of surprise and amusement flickering across his face. He was no longer wearing sunglasses, but I still couldn't tell the color of his eyes. He arched an eyebrow, his professional facade momentarily faltering. "You're quite something, Mr. Donnelley," he said, his voice tinged with a hint of laughter.

"Oh, you haven't seen the half of it," I replied with a wink, my words slightly garbled. "And let me tell you, you're rocking that suit, but I'd much rather see you out of it."

He chuckled, trying to maintain his composure. "Well, thank you for the compliment. But as much as I'd love to engage in playful banter with you, I have a job to do."

"Aw, come on." I pouted jokingly, leaning closer to him. "Don't be such a downer. Live a little. I promise I won't give you any more trouble …" I looked him up and down. "Well, maybe just a little."

He cracked a smile. "I'll keep that in mind, Mr. Donnelley. But for now, my duty is to keep you and your family safe."

"Nothing is going to happen," I stated as I eyed the crowd. Everyone was getting ready for the fireworks, and I was looking for my own, but in a totally different way.

"I'm on duty, sir."

I was tempted to reach out and touch him, but I refrained because I wasn't sure if he'd tackle me to the ground. *Then again ...*

Taking a deep breath, I said instead, "Fair enough, but remember, if you ever decide to ditch the suit and tie, I'll be here waiting to show you a good time."

His smile grew wider, and he inclined his head in acknowledgment. "I'll try to remember that, Fallon. Enjoy the rest of the party."

I pushed off the tree, a huge-ass grin on my face as I realized he'd called me Fallon and not Mr. Donnelley.

As the night continued, I danced and laughed, my thoughts occasionally drifting back to the enigmatic Secret Service agent who had momentarily succumbed to my charm. Maybe one day he wouldn't be protecting my father and I could make my move again. The question was: would it be as soon as November, or would it be in four years?

2

RHETT

Senator Donnelley's family and campaign staff filled the large hotel suite as they watched the election results pour in. When the polls had closed on the East Coast a couple of hours ago, everyone's sole focus became set on whatever information they could glean from the non-stop news coverage.

Senator Donnelley had a significant lead, and it seemed likely he would be the next president of the United States, which created an energetic atmosphere.

While I maintained my position between the kitchen and living room, every part of me stayed on high alert despite knowing all the people in attendance. Having been a Secret Service agent for almost five years and assigned to protective details for foreign dignitaries over the last three, I never let my guard down, and I prided myself on my ability to notice the smallest details in a crowded space.

I'd spent the entire night so far observing the senator's family, most of whom I'd only seen a handful of times over the last few months. Faye, Senator Donnelley's only daughter, had spent most of the night engrossed in her phone and taking selfies. Sitting next to her on the couch was her brother, Finnegan, who appeared disinterested in everything going on around him. His leg bounced up and down as if he was anxious about something. Then there was Fallon. He knew how to work a room and commanded just as much attention as his father as he laughed with almost everyone in the room during private conversations.

Fallon and I had only seen each other occasionally over the last few months since he was busy with law school and not involved with his father's campaign. But the few times our paths crossed, there was so much going on, he didn't approach me as he had during the Fourth of July party on Cape Cod.

Under different circumstances, I might have flirted back that night. Who didn't enjoy getting attention from an attractive person. And Fallon Donnelley was nothing if not good-looking with his chestnut-colored hair, striking greenish-blue eyes, and strong arms I'd noticed last summer. However, I always strived to maintain professional boundaries and made sure never to cross a line, so I couldn't allow myself to entertain the idea of flirting with someone the agency could be tasked with protecting even if I wanted to.

Besides, Fallon was almost six years younger than me and, according to what I knew, didn't seem to have serious relationships. It was likely he was a natural flirt and our previous conversation was an example of how he interacted with people. Still, I couldn't help but feel a small thrill when he stood and headed toward me.

"Agent Davis, fancy meeting you here," he said with a huge-ass grin on his face.

"Mr. Donnelley," I greeted.

"Ah, I see we've gone back to formalities."

The last time we had spoken, I'd accidentally called him by his first name. Clearly, my less-than-professional behavior months ago hadn't escaped his attention either. "Yes, sir."

Cheers erupted, and Fallon and I both glanced toward the senator's family and staff. From my vantage point I could see one of the many TVs set up throughout the room, and on the screen was a graphic declaring Patrick Donnelley as the next president of the United States.

I turned back to Fallon. "Looks like it's time to celebrate your father's win."

He smiled. "Yeah. For as long as I can remember, my dad has talked about running for president. This is all a bit surreal."

"Fallon, are you getting the champagne?" Faye huffed from across the room, refusing to leave the couch where she was flirting with Emilio, the campaign's social media director.

"On it!" he shouted back and grabbed a bottle of Dom Pérignon from the ice bucket on the counter. He lowered his voice when he addressed me again, "I'm guessing I can't talk you into a little celebratory drink?"

"That would be against the rules, sir," I replied.

"Rules are boring, Agent Davis." He winked. "Besides, you're missing out. My father always gets the good stuff." He popped the cork on the bottle, and several agents turned our way.

"Senator Donnelley, I have Senator Miller on the phone," John Chisholm, Donnelley's campaign manager, announced, drawing everyone's attention. "He's ready to concede."

While everyone silently listened to the president-elect's side of the obligatory phone call between opponents, Fallon walked around the room, passing out glasses of champagne, and I couldn't stop myself from tracking him. After the phone call was over, Donnelley hung up, handshakes were given, and Chisholm offered a toast for the president-elect.

When Fallon's eyes met mine, he flashed me a smile and lifted his glass. Knowing we were in a room full of people trained to notice every little thing, I quickly looked away.

A short time later, Senator Miller appeared on the TV. He spoke to the large gathering of his supporters and gave his concession speech. Once he was finished, the room we were in became a flurry of activity as it was time for Senator Donnelley to make his way to Boston

Common, where he was expected to also give a speech—although a much more upbeat one.

I watched as Fallon downed the rest of his champagne and followed the crowd out of the room. When he passed me at the door, his arm brushed mine, and judging by the smirk on his face, the contact was intentional.

He was going to be trouble.

THE FOLLOWING DAY, I WAS CALLED IN FOR AN UNSCHEDULED MEETING at 0600 hours with Assistant Director Monroe, who flew to Boston as soon as the election results were announced. While I waited for him in the conference room, my mind raced with questions about what could possibly warrant a meeting before I was expected to start my shift at the Donnelley residence at 0700 hours.

"Good morning, Agent Davis," Monroe greeted as he walked in with Agent Tanner, the detail leader I'd been working under for the last few months.

"Good morning, sir."

I stood and shook their hands and then sat back down at the large oak table. Monroe sat at the head of the table while Tanner took the seat across from me.

"I'm sure you're wondering why we've asked you to meet this morning," Monroe said.

I nodded. "Yes, sir."

"As you know, with the election over, we have deployed new teams to protect the president-elect's family. Agent Tanner will be moving to Fallon Donnelley's detail."

Providing security for immediate family members was standard procedure after an election, but I was surprised Tanner wouldn't be staying with Patrick Donnelley.

Tanner proceeded to explain, "I'm not sure if you're aware, but Fallon, code name Windstorm, is currently a student at Hawkins Law, and we have a need for agents on his team who can blend in with the students on campus. Unfortunately, one of the guys we'd selected was sent away for a mission overseas."

Instantly, I had a bad feeling about why I'd been called in, because at twenty-nine, I was probably close enough in age to the average law student to not draw too much attention.

He added, "Therefore, we're reassigning you to Fallon Donnelley's detail."

My stomach sank. Not only did it feel like a demotion to be moved from the future president's team, but I also didn't think being around Fallon all the time would be the best situation for me. He seemed quite determined to get under my skin whenever we were in close proximity, and the constant distraction could potentially hinder my ability to do my job. Yet, I couldn't tell my boss I didn't want to be a part of Fallon's detail because I was attracted to him.

"When do you want me to start?" I asked although it didn't matter. In my line of work, we didn't get much time to prepare for new protection missions.

"You and I will be heading over to the command post to join the rest of the team in time for you to escort Mr. Donnelley to class this morning," Tanner responded.

Monroe cleared his throat. "Agent Davis, you've made quite the impression on this agency. We know you have family connections here in Boston, and your reputation in the field office is stellar, so it only made sense to choose you as a replacement on the team."

Staying in Boston was the only bright spot about the detail change. It would allow me to live in the same city as my daughter, Poppy who I'd spent more time over the last three years video calling her than being with her.

He continued, "Additionally, it hasn't been announced yet, but Agent Tanner is retiring this summer, and we believe you would be an excellent candidate for the detail leader position on this assignment. If you're interested, I would like you to take this opportunity to prepare for the additional responsibility when the time comes."

Pride welled inside me at his praise while I maintained my

outwardly composure. "I wasn't expecting that, but thank you for considering me."

"We firmly believe you're the right man for the job," Agent Tanner added.

AT 0700 HOURS, AGENT TANNER AND I PULLED INTO THE PARKING garage of Fallon Donnelley's condominium building, where our command post was located as well. The agency had their ways of getting us what we needed to do our job in a short period of time. For this assignment we were renting a two-bedroom, two-bathroom condo next door to Fallon.

As we made our way up to the eighth floor of the high-rise, I took note of the surroundings to get a better understanding of the building's layout. When we stepped into the command post, the place was filled with agents who were packing up someone's belongings. Tanner motioned for me to follow him to where three other agents were waiting next to a table with monitors on it. I recognized two of them immediately.

"Davis, good to see you." Agent Colin Day came over and shook my hand.

We had met and become friends at the Federal Law Enforcement Training Center in Georgia when we first joined the agency. After that, we both began working at the Boston field office; however, once we began working protective missions in D.C., we hadn't been assigned to the same team, and then Day was transferred overseas for the last six months.

"You too," I replied. "Can't believe we're both back in Boston."

He grinned. "Should be a nice change of pace to stay in one place for a while."

According to the intel Tanner shared on the drive over, Fallon usually stayed in the area because he was busy with law school, and after going all over the country for political rallies, I agreed with my friend's assessment. Traveling with a detail required a lot more work to keep everyone safe.

"You gettin' soft, Day?" Agent Jones, the other guy I knew, teased.

"Says the guy who'll be sitting around watching camera feeds all day," Day jabbed back.

Brian Jones was another colleague I'd met while working in Boston. He was a hell of an agent and a whiz with computers. Knowing he'd be the one watching our backs while we were posted in and around the building was reassuring because nothing got past him. Plus, having two people I considered friends on the team had me a little more excited about my new assignment.

"Jones, how's it going?" I shook his hand.

"Just living the dream," he joked.

I turned and introduced myself to the only person I didn't know. "Rhett Davis."

"Justin Leigh." He grasped my hand.

With greetings and introductions out of the way, Agent Tanner showed us around. The living room was full of computers to watch the feeds from various cameras placed around the property that Jones would monitor. The condo also provided bedrooms for us to stay between shifts, especially if we were working overtime. Since I was rarely home while on the campaign trail with Senator Donnelley, I'd moved out of my place months ago, which meant I'd be staying at the command post until I found a new place to rent.

As we held a quick meeting to discuss logistics for our first day, I noticed movement on one of the cameras. "Who's that?" I asked, watching a man walk out of Fallon's front door.

"Name is Declan Rivers," Jones responded. "He arrived while we were setting up last night after Mr. Donnelley returned home from his father's speech. According to our quick background check, Mr. Rivers attends law school with Mr. Donnelley."

I'd pegged Fallon as a flirt, and I doubted a study partner would be leaving in the morning. Was he dating his classmate? A pang of jealousy hit me as I realized I might have to witness him hooking up with other people.

Why did that bother me so much?

3

FALLON

AFTER MY DAD WAS DECLARED THE WINNER OF THE PRESIDENTIAL election, I was hyped. I wasn't quite ready to go home, but it was almost closing time at the bars and clubs. So, when everyone was leaving after my father's speech, I texted Declan. We went to school together and had a standing Friday night Netflix-and-chill thing going on. It was a great way to relieve the stress of being a second-year law student at Hawkins Law. We both knew what we were doing was merely fucking, and we were okay with that.

He replied:

> It's Tuesday

> And I want to fuck

> All right. You don't need to twist my arm. I'll be right over

With one last glance at Agent Davis, I left Boston Common.

Declan showed up about thirty minutes after I arrived at my condo. We fucked, we got off, and passed out. When we woke to my seven thirty alarm, he left so he could get ready for school. I was tempted to skip class since I'd only gotten a few hours of sleep, but missing even one day would set me behind, and I didn't want the added stress.

After a quick cup of coffee, I headed to the bathroom for a shower. Just as I was almost to my living room there was a knock on my door. Looking through the peephole, I found the man I thought I'd never see in my condo—even though I'd fantasized about it a few times—standing on the other side.

I raked my hands through my disheveled hair, licked my lips, and opened the door. To my surprise, Agent Davis was dressed in a light gray sweater and jeans, and he wasn't alone. Why was he in street clothes? Not that I was complaining because he looked good enough to eat.

After a quick perusal of Agent Davis, who was staring at my bare torso, my gaze flicked to Agent Tanner's, another man I knew from my father's security team, and I greeted them. "Gentlemen."

"Good morning, Mr. Donnelley. May we come in?" Agent Tanner asked.

I eyed Agent Davis for any clue as to what was happening, but he adverted his stare. "Sure." I stepped to the side and let them pass.

Agent Tanner turned to face me as I shut the door. "We know it's early, but we need to speak with you regarding your security detail."

My shoulders sagged slightly because I knew they would show up eventually; I just didn't think it would happen so early in the damn morning. With my father elected to the presidency, our family's lives were all about to change.

While I wouldn't be living at the White House with my mom and dad, I was aware I would have bodyguards with me. My brother wasn't going to like it much, given he frequented underground poker clubs weekly, if not daily. My sister probably wasn't going to be thrilled being shadowed either, since she enjoyed going to clubs to hook up with guys. Hell, who was I kidding? I wasn't going to like it either.

Unless, of course, Agent Davis being in my condo meant he was going to be assigned to me.

I could have fun with him.

Hopefully, in more ways than one.

"Sure, but I need to get to class," I replied.

"We're aware of your schedule, sir. Agent Davis will accompany you to school."

My eyes found Agent Davis', and I hid the smile tugging at the corners of my mouth because whatever was happening meant I was about to see a lot more of him, and that sent a little tingle of excitement through my body. "What do you mean he's accompanying me to school?"

"I'll be sitting in your classes with you." There was no hint of enthusiasm in Agent Davis' tone. He probably had his sights set on continuing with my father's detail, and what Secret Service agent wouldn't want to protect the president? I guess I couldn't blame him, but the elation I had felt about him being there for me took a slight blow.

"Okay ..." I waited for more to be said and realized that was why he was in street clothes and not the black suit he usually wore. Like the one Agent Tanner was wearing.

Agent Tanner continued taking the lead. "We know you need to get ready, but we wanted to come next door and—"

I balked. "Next door?"

"Yes, sir." Agent Tanner nodded. "Our command post is in the condo next to yours so we can monitor the surroundings and be close by."

"What happened to Mrs. Ruff?" I wondered. It had been a few days since I'd seen my elderly widowed neighbor, but I didn't think she found a new place to live—or worse.

"She moved," he simply replied.

I looked at Agent Davis for more details, but he didn't speak.

"She moved ..." I repeated Tanner's words in disbelief as I leaned against the back of my couch. I hadn't seen anyone coming and going from her place. Mrs. Ruff and I crossed paths several times a week when I would stop by to take out her trash or ask if she needed anything, so she'd had plenty of opportunities to tell me she was leaving. I didn't even get to say goodbye.

"Yes," Agent Tanner confirmed.

"You made her move? How the hell did that happen so fast?"

"We're Secret Service, sir," Agent Davis stated. "We can make anything happen."

"What does that mean?" I challenged. It wasn't even eight in the morning, and they had kicked an old lady out onto the street? I was pissed.

"Mrs. Ruff is staying in a suite at a very accommodating hotel until we can find a suitable place for her to live for the next four or so years. I promise the agency is taking good care of her," Tanner advised.

"You better, or I'll have someone's head."

"Understandable, sir." Tanner nodded. "We need to review your schedule and then let you get to class."

I snorted a small laugh. "My schedule? It seems you already know it since you know I need to get to class."

"We know of your law school schedule, but we would like to be briefed daily if you plan anything other than attending class and coming home."

I crossed my arms over my chest. "If you know my school schedule, then you know I don't have much time for a social life."

Agent Davis grunted, and both Agent Tanner and I turned our attention to him. What the hell was that about? Had he seen Declan leave my place? Since they were stationed next door, they probably knew, but why did Agent Davis react that way? Could he possibly be jealous? Was Agent Hottie gay?

Agent Tanner turned back to me. "Yes, we are aware of your heavy course load, but we also know you like to have fun. We ask that if you have plans, to please let us know so we can do whatever is necessary to ensure your safety."

"And what if I don't know in advance?" I questioned.

"As you're probably aware, we will be with you twenty-four seven from this moment forward. We'll always be there to protect you, but we ask for a heads-up so we can conduct security sweeps and anything else we might need to do beforehand," Agent Tanner explained.

"All right. I can do that. I have no plans today except for school."

"Great. Agent Davis will be with you in class, and we will have two other agents on campus as well. When you're home, someone will be inside your condo while other members of the team will be in and around the building as well as manning the command post."

I stared at the two men as I let Agent Tanner's words sink in. For the next four years, I wasn't going to have any privacy. While I expected to have protection, I didn't realize how invasive it would all be. "Why does someone need to be *in* my condo?"

"For your safety, sir," Agent Tanner replied.

"I get that, but why inside my place? What if I want to walk around naked and shit? Have friends over? Have someone stay the night?" My eyes moved to Agent Davis' to see if he had another reaction, but he remained stoic.

"We know this will be a change for you, sir, but we aren't here to cause you distress. You can live your life normally and certainly have people over, but know we will be with you. It's our duty."

"Are you going to watch me fucking sleep?"

Agent Tanner shook his head. "Of course not. The agent will stay in your living room unless he is needed somewhere else. The agents assigned to you, of course, will be laxer than those with your father, unless we learn of a direct threat to you."

"Right, you won't need to watch me pee. Got it." I pushed off the couch. "I need to jump in the shower."

"Yes, we'll let you get to that."

I started toward the hallway but turned back. "Do I get to drive myself, or do you have to escort me now?"

"You can drive yourself," Agent Tanner replied. "Your team will follow you in an agency vehicle, and Agent Davis will walk with you to class."

"Great," I clipped, and my eyes moved to Agent Davis'. "I hope you're ready to be bored out of your fucking mind for the next year and a half."

I turned back around and headed to my room without another word from Agents Tanner and Davis. The more I learned what was involved with having a bodyguard, the more I didn't fucking like it. I slammed the door, not caring if they left or not. They were taking over my space, and they could do whatever they wanted. Instead, I turned on my stereo and the shower and stripped out of my gray sweats.

With "I Ain't Worried" by OneRepublic blaring through the speakers, I sang at the top of my lungs, trying to shake off my bad mood. At first, I had been looking forward to Agent Davis being on my detail; now I wished I could live on a deserted island for the next four years and two months.

With the music still pumping, I got out of the shower, brushed my teeth, and dressed in a long-sleeved T-shirt, jeans, and a Bruins sweatshirt. I'd had a full-on concert in my bedroom while I was getting ready, which had certainly lightened my mood. But when I walked out to my living room, I stopped dead in my tracks. Agent Davis was standing near the front door. Instantly, my cheeks flushed. Had he heard me singing?

"Ahhh …" I stammered.

Agent Davis swallowed. "Are you ready to leave, sir?"

"Yes, but can you just call me Fallon? This whole *sir* thing isn't necessary."

"Yes, sir."

I snorted and shook my head slightly.

"Sorry. Force of habit."

"We'll work on that since we'll be spending so much time together." I grabbed my wallet and keys near the door. "So, are you ready to go *21 Jump Street* this bitch?"

Agent Davis laughed. He actually fucking laughed and then opened the door. "I'm not really a student."

"No?" I asked, stepping into the hall and seeing Agent Tanner and two other guys in black suits waiting.

"No, sir. Your school has been informed I'm part of your protective detail and will be sitting in on your classes."

"Mr. Donnelley, these are Agents Day and Leigh," Agent Tanner advised. "There is another agent on this shift who will be staying behind to monitor the camera systems we have set up. You can meet him when you return home."

"Great. We'll be one happy family here soon. We're going to have a shit load of fun, guys. Maybe later we can braid our hair and order pizza."

All four agents smiled, and we walked down the hall.

Agent Davis pressed the button for the elevator, and we stepped inside. It felt weird to be surrounded by four men with guns who could probably kill a man with their bare hands. But it also intrigued me, and I decided to make the best of it. Sure, I would love to say goodbye to them at my door and lock myself inside my condo each night, but I understood they were doing a job. They were sworn to protect me in case some asshole had an issue with my father becoming president or some other threat, but I still wanted to have fun with them.

"Since Agent Davis will attend classes with me, does that mean he'll be my study buddy?" I winked at him.

"That can be arranged if you'd like," Agent Tanner stated.

I smiled wide at Agent Davis. "I think that would be best since he'll also be listening to the lectures."

We reached the bottom floor in the underground parking garage, and I walked to my car. I half expected Agent Davis to slide into the passenger seat of my Mustang. Instead, Davis, Day, and Leigh got into a black Chevy Suburban parked in Mrs. Ruff's old spot and waited for me to back out of my space. Tanner stayed behind.

They followed me to the Hawkins Law campus, and when we arrived, Agent Davis slid out of the SUV and walked with me toward the school.

"You know, you can ride with me next time," I said to him.

"I think that would be best." He smirked after using the words I'd said back at my condo building.

I chuckled. I was learning he loosened up a little when he wasn't in front of his colleagues, and that was an Agent Davis I could get used to.

We strolled into the lecture hall for my first class, and Declan was there already. He and I usually sat next to each other, and since Agent Davis was to act like a fly on the wall, I let him do his own thing while I went to sit next to my friend.

"Who's that?" Declan asked.

"Secret Service."

"Damn, that was fast."

"Yep, but you know"—I eyed Agent Davis as he sat in the row behind me and looked around the room, assessing the place—"with Agent Hottie following me most of the day, I'm not going to mind at all."

4

RHETT

IT WAS LATE AFTERNOON WHEN FALLON AND I SLIPPED INTO HIS Mustang after class. After he'd suggested I ride with him, I had teased him that it would be best, mainly to give him shit like he'd done when asking me to be his study partner. However, from a logistical stand-point, it made the most sense because anyone who worked for the Secret Service had heard endless stories about First Children trying to ditch their security detail. Not that I expected Fallon to pull a stunt like that, but anything was possible.

"So, Agent Davis, how was your first day of school?" Fallon grinned as he pulled out of his parking space. Day and Leigh followed close behind.

"As dull as I thought it would be." I tried to hide my smirk.

"Are you saying Constitutional Law wasn't riveting?" His eyes gleamed with amusement.

"Pretty sure I zoned out when Professor Lunden started lecturing about fundamental liberties."

He gasped and clutched his chest. "You zoned out? What if someone used that moment as an opportunity to take me out?"

"I wasn't listening to your teacher drone on; that doesn't mean I wasn't watching you."

"Can't keep your eyes off me, can you, Agent Davis?" He pulled onto the main road.

I sighed and shook my head. "Gotta stay alert for those scary law students lurking in the halls."

"You never know. There could be a couple of admirers out there who might want to get close to me. You need to be prepared to protect my honor," he teased.

I chuckled. "Noted. I'll be on the lookout for those who can't resist your charm and ready to fend them off if need be."

"Ah, you admit you find me charming. Good to know."

"I didn't say that."

"Sure you didn't."

We both laughed.

I knew our lighthearted moment was highly inappropriate. Jokes that bordered on flirting with someone I was sworn to protect could quickly blur the lines of professionalism. It didn't matter how easy the conversation flowed between us, or how much I enjoyed our banter, I needed to focus on my job.

As our laughter died down, I took the opportunity to change the subject. "What do you usually do after class?"

"You don't already know? I assumed you guys had a file full of information about my life."

"I can neither confirm nor deny the existence of any such intel." I winked. What the hell was wrong with me? Why couldn't I control myself? I cleared my throat. "But we haven't had you under surveillance, if that's what you mean."

"If there's a file, I doubt it would be very exciting."

"Not sure I believe that."

He shrugged and glanced at me. "Despite what you might think, my life is quite boring."

I arched an eyebrow.

"What? I'm serious. Most days, I go to school, study, and maybe work out for a bit."

My ears perked up when he mentioned working out. That sounded a hell of a lot better than listening to lectures all day. "Do you use the gym in your building?"

"How'd you know there was a gym? You haven't even been there a day yet." He stopped at a red light.

I'd studied the building's blueprints while Tanner had driven us to Fallon's condo, but I couldn't resist messing with him. "That's classified."

He grinned and stepped on the accelerator when the light turned green. "Okay, I see how it's going to be. But yeah, during the winter I work out at the gym on days I'm not doing indoor training and circuits for rowing. Think you'll be able to keep up with all the exercising I do?"

"Is that a challenge?"

"Absolutely. Need to make sure you're in good shape if you're responsible for my safety."

I threw my head back and roared with laughter. "My stamina is quite high, thank you very much. You should be the one worried about keeping up with me."

"Is that so?" He smirked. "Unfortunately, we'll have to wait until Friday to find out. I've got a ton of studying to do today and tomorrow for an exam. The election last night threw off my entire schedule, and I'm behind on some classwork."

And your hookup last night probably didn't help, either.

I shook my head to rid it of the intrusive thought that felt too much like jealousy.

Fallon pulled into the underground garage of his building and parked in his space. "I meant to ask earlier how all of this works?"

"What do you mean?" I asked.

"Well, I assume you work in shifts. What time do you leave? Do you get days off? That kind of thing."

We unbuckled our seatbelts as I responded, "Typically, there are three shifts: days, mids, and nights. Since you're in class during the day, the hours for those three shifts have been altered a bit. For now, the day shift will start about an hour before you leave for school and end around 1700 or 1800 hours."

"You're going to make me use military time now?" He rolled his eyes.

"Sorry, habit." I grinned and continued. "Under normal circumstances, agents rotate through the various shifts every two weeks, but I'll stay on days during the week, at least until the end of the school year. We want to avoid drawing too much attention to your detail in class if we can help it. However, you'll see most of us nearly every day during various shifts because we work a lot of overtime based on the agency's needs."

"Sounds complicated."

We climbed out of his car.

"It can be, but you don't need to worry. You'll always have protection around you."

MY SHIFT ENDED AT 1800 HOURS, AND AFTER TELLING FALLON I'D SEE him before class the next day, I left his condo and walked to the one next door.

"There's our star student," Agent Jones called out as I stepped inside.

"Very funny," I huffed. "At least I'm not stuck in this place all day."

"I prefer watching camera feeds over trying to blend in on campus."

He had a point.

"I hear you, and I've got to do it again tomorrow, so I'm going to go chill for a bit." I walked toward the bedrooms and took the first twin-sized bed that didn't have anyone's stuff on it, yet. I kicked off my shoes and lay on the bed. Finally being off shift, I couldn't wait any longer to find out when I could see my daughter since I was back in the city and off the campaign trail. I pulled out my phone and sent Alexis, Poppy's mother, a message:

> Hi there. I'm in town, and I've got some news. Are you and Poppy free to meet for dinner on Friday?

It didn't take her long to reply:

> Hey! We're actually going away for the weekend to visit my parents. Do you want to come over tonight instead?

Not wanting to wait until the following week, I answered:

> Sure. I can be there in thirty minutes

> Great. See you soon

Alexis and I had never been an actual couple. We'd gone on a few dates more than three years before, and it hadn't taken us long to figure out our busy schedules weren't compatible since I'd just started working in the protection division, and she was finishing up her master's degree.

We parted on friendly terms, and I thought that was the end of things until she called two months later to tell me she was pregnant. The timing wasn't ideal, but we'd managed to make it work.

She continued to support my career, even though it caused a lot of the day-to-day parenting to fall on her shoulders. She often rearranged her schedule to ensure I could spend time with my daughter, and I was extremely grateful we had found a way to co-parent.

Slipping my phone into my pocket, I put my shoes back on and checked out a set of keys for a black Chevy Tahoe. The agency provided us with vehicles to use during our non-work hours because when we were off-duty, we were still expected to be on-call in case there was an emergency requiring more agents than those who were on shift. Because of that, a few cars had been dropped off for us.

I made my way down to the parking garage, where the SUVs were parked. Agent Tanner had explained that an agreement was made with the building's management to use some of the guest parking spaces for our fleet. Any additional personal-use cars we had were given residential permits for street parking. When I told Fallon the Secret Service could make anything happen, I meant it.

After climbing into the Tahoe, I made the twenty-minute drive to Alexis' house in the suburbs. I made a mental note to add the area to my search for a new place to live so I could be closer to my daughter.

As I strolled up to Alexis' door, anticipation and excitement filled my chest. I hadn't seen Poppy in two months because I'd been traveling across the country with Senator Donnelley. It was the longest my daughter and I had been apart, and I couldn't wait to hug her again.

I knocked, and Alexis smiled when she opened the door. "Hey, it's good to see you."

"You too." We hugged briefly before the pitter-patter of my three-year-old's little feet echoed through the entryway.

"Daddy!" Poppy squealed, her blonde curls bouncing as she ran onto the porch.

I knelt, and she jumped into my outstretched arms. "Hey, sweet pea. I missed you."

She wrapped her tiny arms around my neck and squeezed as tight as she could. "Want to see my dollies?"

"Of course, I do." I chuckled as I carried my daughter inside. When I set Poppy down, she immediately grabbed my hand and pulled me toward her bedroom.

"I'll give you two some time to catch up," Alexis said.

I gave her a small smile before she turned toward her kitchen, and I followed my daughter down the hall.

"You sit there." Poppy pointed at the purple area rug in the middle of her room.

Before I knew what was happening, I had a doll in one arm, a plastic toy bottle in my other hand, and received strict instructions on how to feed her baby. It was those moments, spending time with the most important person in my life, that I lived for.

We played for a while before Alexis came into the room to let us know it was time for Poppy to get ready for bed.

I helped her brush her teeth and change into pajamas with little unicorns, which I learned was her current favorite. At her age, it changed daily, and it was hard to keep up, especially being away for so long.

"Will you read me a story?" Poppy asked.

"Absolutely."

She grabbed a book from the shelf in the corner of her room and climbed onto the bed. I did all the voices as we read about a princess who had to rescue a prince from a dragon. I loved seeing a children's book turn traditional gender roles on their heads.

"Mama says the princess is a hero like you."

My chest tightened. It would be easy for Alexis to hold my job against me since it kept me away a lot, and while I didn't consider myself a hero by any means, it meant a lot to me that she put a positive spin on what I did for our daughter.

"I want to be a hero too," Poppy added as her ocean-blue eyes that matched mine grew heavy.

"You can be anything you want to be." I tucked her in and placed a kiss on her forehead. "I love you, sweet pea. I'll see you again soon."

Walking to the kitchen, I joined Alexis. She was waiting for me at the small dining table, and I sat across from her.

"Thank you for letting me come over tonight."

She nodded. "Of course. Poppy was so excited when I told her you were on your way."

"Hopefully, I'll be around more often now."

She tilted her head. "Really?"

"Yeah, I've been assigned to a detail here in Boston."

"That's great news."

While I hadn't initially been happy about my new assignment, I couldn't help but think things were working out as they should.

"I'll still be working a lot and will probably have to travel occa-sionally, but living locally should make spending time with Poppy a lot easier," I explained, knowing a regular visitation schedule wasn't possible due to my job.

Alexis reached across the table and squeezed my hand. "We'll figure it out. The important thing is for you to be a part of her life. Everything else will just take some flexibility on our part."

I couldn't help but feel grateful our unconditional love for our daughter allowed us to work together to provide Poppy with the best life possible.

ON FRIDAYS, FALLON FINISHED CLASS EARLY, SO HE DECIDED HE WAS going to hit up the gym after we got back to his place. Tanner relieved me so I could race next door to change into my workout gear. When I returned, Fallon was waiting in his living room, eager to head downstairs.

"Windstorm is ready," I said into the microphone attached to my tank top.

"The room is all clear," Agent Day's voice came through my earpiece.

"Let's go." I opened Fallon's front door to leave.

We walked down the hall and stepped into the elevator. He pushed the button for the second floor, where the gym was located, and after the doors closed, we started to descend the six floors.

"Time to prove you can keep up with me," he teased with a playful glint in his eyes.

I grunted a laugh. "Are you always this cocky?"

"I thought you said I was charming."

The elevator doors opened, saving me from having to respond. Fallon and I walked toward where Agent Day stood at the glass doors of the gym. Once inside, Fallon pulled off his Hawkins Law hoodie, leaving him in a tank top and a pair of gray sweats similar to the ones he had worn two days before.

My eyes scanned his body, admiring his broad shoulders and well-defined arms that I'd noticed the other day in his condo when he'd opened the door shirtless. When our stares met in the mirror, he smirked.

"Like what you see?" he provoked.

I shrugged. "Just sizing up the competition."

"Let's go, then. I usually do some light cardio before hitting the weights, and then finish with a longer run."

I nodded and followed him over to the stair climber, where we spent five minutes warming up. Nothing was said between us, but we shared occasional glances. I was well aware of Day's presence near the door, so I was careful to maintain some decorum with Fallon.

Once we finished with the cardio, we moved on to the weights, where he added a few plates to the barbell and lay on the bench. "You wanna spot me?"

"Sure." I stood by his head, ready to assist him if he needed me to. His biceps tensed and his chest tightened as he completed his reps.

We switched positions and continued to egg each other on as we moved to other arm exercises. The energy between us intensified as the workout progressed, or at least I felt as though it did.

Working out together was going to test my resolve to keep things professional between us because, like he had observed in the car a couple of days prior, I couldn't seem to keep my eyes off him.

Which, lucky for me, was my job.

After our run, we were both drenched in sweat.

"I need a shower," Fallon said, rubbing his face with a gym towel.

"Me too."

We headed back to his place, and while he grabbed a shower, I downed a bottle of water and waited in his living room for my relief to show up.

Fifteen minutes later, Agent Bernard walked inside to take over. After giving him a brief rundown of the day, I made my exit.

As I was about to enter our command post, I heard the elevator ding. Despite another agent standing nearby, I turned to see who was coming, and was caught off guard as I watched Declan Rivers, Fallon's hookup from election night and classmate, step into the hall.

Maybe Fallon did have more stamina than me.

And the thought annoyed the hell out of me.

5

FALLON

THE HOT WATER CASCADED DOWN MY BODY, SOOTHING MY MUSCLES and washing away the sweat from the intense workout with Agent Davis. I replayed the gym session over in my head and the genuine camaraderie we were developing. His contagious smile flashed through my mind, and I imagined that slip of his expressionless demeanor was for me and only me. He was impassive with the world around him, and I had to admire his dedication to his job, but I wanted to be more than his assignment.

The way he looked at me, with a mixture of intrigue and *something else*, made my heart skip a beat. It felt as if the connection we shared extended beyond his duty to keep me safe.

Sure, we had our little banter, but was it flirty on his part? I was 100% flirting, but I worried I was reading too much into things and he only tolerated me because of his job. For all I knew, he wasn't single or even gay. Did he have a partner waiting for him at home? Where was home? Was he married with kids?

I couldn't stop the questions as they swirled in my head, but knew one thing for certain: I was crushing on him hard. Before I realized it, my hand slid down my body and fisted my hardening dick.

Closing my eyes, I remembered the way his shorts revealed the sweat glistening on his powerful thighs, and how I almost let go of the lat pull-down bar when he lifted the hem of his tank top to wipe his forehead and exposed his chiseled abs. I'd caught a glimpse of his six-pack, and the memory made my mouth water. My hand rapidly pumped my shaft as I pictured myself licking a trail from his pecs down his stomach to his cock.

It was easy to indulge in my little fantasy behind closed doors, and the mere thought of him walking into my bedroom and catching me jerking off was enough for me to groan my release in minutes. Bracing myself with my free hand, I shot my cum in spurts down the drain with the warm water.

Quickly, I lathered myself with body wash and finished my shower. Once I stepped out, I dried off and dressed in a T-shirt and sweats. My stomach grumbled, so I walked out of my room, ready to ask Agent Davis if he wanted any pizza because I was going to order some. Except, as I entered my living room, I saw he wasn't there. In his place was Agent Bernard.

"Good evening, sir."

"Oh … Hello." I glanced at the clock hanging in my dining room and saw it was a few minutes after six o'clock. Damn, I didn't even get to say good night to Agent Davis, and why did that make me sad? "Is it cool if I order pizza?"

Before he could respond, Agent Bernard held his fingers over his ear and then said to me, "Mr. Rivers is here to see you."

Shit. I had forgotten he was coming over because working out with Agent Davis was enough to make me forget my own name. It had slipped my mind that Declan and I usually hung out on Friday nights to let off some steam and mess around. It was a way for us to forget the daunting amount of studying we had to do each night and whatever else our classes threw at us throughout the week. And quite honestly, I firmly believed blowing my load was the best kind of stress relief—

and Declan certainly knew how to fuck—but I'd already relaxed in the shower.

"Oh, right. Do I get the door or what?" Having Secret Service around was still new. Did Declan get frisked? Should he be on some sort of approved list? I'd gone over scheduling with Agent Davis, but I supposed everything else was a learn-as-I-go type of thing.

"I'll get it," Agent Bernard replied, and since he was standing next to the door, he turned and opened it.

Declan's gaze moved from Bernard to me, and I grimaced. It felt as though we had a chaperone and weren't free to chill like we normally did.

"Hey. I was about to order pizza. Want some?" I asked as I pulled my phone from my pocket.

"Ah, yeah," he said and watched Agent Bernard close the door after he stepped inside.

Yes, Dec. This is going to be awkward.

And it was.

I ordered the pizza, and while we waited for it to arrive, Declan and I played Call of Duty. We usually watched TV and messed around, but that wasn't possible with someone in the living room with us.

We ate the pizza and then moved things to my bedroom, all while Agent Bernard sat in an armchair near my front door. Yet, when it came down to me and Declan fucking, I couldn't do it. Not only because of Agent Bernard in the other room, but also because I couldn't stop thinking about Agent Davis.

———

I WASN'T USUALLY ONE TO WAKE UP EARLY ON A SATURDAY IF I HAD nothing to do. But I jumped out of bed and freshened up in my connecting bathroom before eight o'clock.

Even though I'd seen Agent Davis the last three mornings, I found I still had a little pep in my step as I walked down the hall to my living room. I was trying not to seem too eager, but damn, it was hard. I hadn't been so smitten with anyone since—well, ever.

"Good morning, Agent Davis." I smiled as I walked into the room and headed toward my kitchen. "Would you like a cup of coffee?"

"Sure."

Him accepting the offer surprised me because I half expected him to tell me drinking a cup of coffee was against the rules. "Cream and sugar, or are you a psychopath?"

He balked slightly and then walked toward where I stood in the kitchen. "A psychopath?"

"You know. They say psychopaths drink their coffee black."

He chuckled. "Is that so?"

I lifted a shoulder and then placed a mug under my Nespresso. "That's what some shit on the Internet told me."

"Do you believe everything on the Internet?"

I rolled my eyes. "No, but you still haven't answered the question."

He leaned against the granite countertop and crossed his arms over his broad chest. Unlike the other mornings when we had class, Agent Davis was dressed in a black suit with a white shirt and black tie like his colleagues wore. The fabric of the arms tightened around his biceps and made me swallow hard at the naughty thoughts running through my head.

"No, I'm not a psychopath."

I plopped a pod into the machine and started brewing the coffee. "Right. You had to take a psych eval and all that shit, huh?"

"I did, and obviously passed with flying colors."

"Good to know." I grinned. "So, cream and sugar?"

"Just cream if it's sweetened already."

I pulled the vanilla creamer from the fridge. It was sweetened, of course. "Does this work?"

"Perfect."

The Nespresso finished brewing, and I handed Agent Davis the cup and creamer. "Spoons are in the drawer behind you."

He took the items from me and added creamer to his coffee while I grabbed another mug and made my cup.

"So, you didn't have any coffee this morning before your shift, or do you need more caffeine to tackle the day?" I asked.

"Agent Jones was the first one up this morning and made a weak pot. Since you offered, I took you up on it for a chance to have a second cup."

I cocked my head to the side. "Agent Jones was the first up? You two live together?"

Agent Davis stirred his coffee. "It's only temporary. I was traveling the country while on your father's detail, and the others worked on missions elsewhere. We were kinda in limbo until the election. I thought I'd be living in D.C. once your father won, but instead, the agency assigned me here for the next four years. About half of us are looking for places to rent."

"And the other half?"

"The evening and night time shift guys have all found places, but since I work days like Day, Leigh, and Jones, it's been hard to go apartment hunting, so we're all roomies until we can find our own places."

"I had no idea." I grabbed the creamer off the counter and poured a good amount into my mug.

"It's just a transition stage." He took a sip.

I leaned on the counter across from him. "You were hoping to be in the White House, huh?"

He stared at me for a beat and then said, "At first, of course. That's what we all want. But then ..." He looked off to the side.

"Then you found out you got to protect the president's handsome son, and you knew you'd won the lottery?" I grinned.

"What? No. I'm not protecting Finnegan."

My eyes widened and my mouth dropped open. "We're triplets! I look exactly like my brother and sister." More so my brother, because we were identical.

Agent Davis smirked. "I'm just messing with you, but yes, I wanted to work at the White House. However, my daughter is here, so this works out even better."

I blinked. "You have a daughter?"

"I do. Her name is Poppy."

Do you have a wife? I wanted to probe. I didn't think he was married since he was staying next door, but had he been married before? Instead, I asked, "How old is she?"

"Three."

"Wow, she's young. I bet it'll be nice to have more time with her."

"For sure, but I work a lot of hours, so I'm not sure how much that will be."

"We'll just have to find ways for you to see her."

"Really?"

"I mean, I'm not going to adopt a kid so mine and yours can have play dates or anything, but I'm sure we can figure something out."

"Like what?"

We both took sips of our coffees, and it didn't go unnoticed that we were having a casual conversation in my kitchen over a cup of joe. This open and easygoing guy was definitely the Agent Davis I preferred.

"I don't know yet." I thought for a moment. "Does she like hockey? My cousin's kids like sports, and they are around your daughter's age."

"I … I don't know. She likes purple and unicorns and dolls and all that stuff."

"Then we'll have to take her to a Bruins game to find out."

"I'm not sure we can work it out with your detail."

"Oh. Right." My shoulders sagged. How would it work if I wanted to see a game? Would it be like a school thing where I had one agent with me and the rest waiting outside in case something happened? An arena would be much different than on campus.

"I'm not saying you can't go to games," Agent Davis said. "I just don't see it working with my daughter involved, is all."

"Yeah, that would be weird."

He reached out with the hand not holding his mug and cupped the side of my arm. "It was a nice thought, though. Thank you."

"I'd still like to make something work because I know what it's like to not have a father around much because of his job." I frowned.

My dad was great, but he worked long hours as an attorney, and I rarely saw him growing up. We had weekends together, but sometimes those would be cut short if he had to prepare for trials. When he became a senator, I saw even less of him. That didn't mean I didn't admire him and the work he did as a criminal lawyer. It was partially why I was attending law school. I wanted to follow in his footsteps, but not entirely. I would never run for the Senate or even be president one day. I wanted to forge my own path and my true passion was to become a civil rights attorney and help members of the LGBTQ+ community.

"That's sweet of you, Fallon. We have time to work out a plan."

A smirk spread across my face. "First, it was charming. Now you think I'm sweet? What's next? Sexy?"

"I—" He stopped and placed his fingers over his ear and then spoke into his cuff. "Roger that."

"What?" I asked as our eyes met.

"Looks like we're spending the next sixteen hours together. I'm with you until the night shift."

"Really?" My eyes lit up. "Now I wish I had plans other than studying all day."

AFTER COFFEE, I MADE SOME EGGS—AGENT DAVIS DECLINED THE food—and then set myself up in my bedroom with my books and note-cards and did what I had to do. It sucked knowing he was only a few feet away, and I had him for the entire day, but school came first. It wasn't like he was my boyfriend or anything, anyway.

A few times, he checked on me to see if I needed anything, but for the most part, Agent Davis sat in my living room. I'd tried to warn him that being on my detail would be boring.

For dinner, I took a break, and we ordered Chinese. We got enough for all the guys on shift, and after we ate, I took a shower. I felt restless and wanted to do something. It had been a while since I'd been to Chrome—the gay nightclub my friend Tyler introduced me to—and I was itching to go out and dance. To let loose.

Maybe it was because my time with Declan the night before had been a bust, but I felt as though I needed some sort of release. Not necessarily fucking, but something to burn off my energy.

While I could easily go to the gym, I was curious to see if Agent Davis and the others would go to a gay club or try to talk me out of it.

Walking back into the living room, I sat down on the couch next to Agent Davis and stared up at the ceiling as I leaned my head against the back. "So, am I supposed to ask you if I can do things, or do I just tell you?"

We turned our heads to face each other.

"You just tell me."

"Great." I jumped up. "We're going to a club."

"Wait. What?" He stood.

"It's almost eleven, and the club is just getting busy. We're going dancing."

"Fallon ..."

"Rhett ..."

His name hung in the air as we stared at each other, but he didn't correct me. "Are you serious right now?"

"I am."

"Okay." He headed for the front door. "Let me tell the guys and we'll make it happen."

"Thank you."

Just before he reached the door, he faced me again. "I don't mind you calling me Rhett, but don't do it in front of the other agents, okay?"

"Okay." I beamed and turned on my heels toward the bedroom to change.

AGENT VANCE DROVE, AGENT SHEA RODE SHOTGUN, AND AGENT Davis and I sat in the back of the black SUV. It was the first time I was driven somewhere in a Secret Service vehicle with my security team, and it really sank in that I had bodyguards. It almost made me feel like a celebrity, which, I had to admit, was pretty exciting.

Once Agent Vance pulled up in front of Chrome, I was told to stay put while Agent Davis and Agent Shea did whatever they needed to do to make sure I could get into the club safely. After they gave the all clear—whatever that meant—Agent Davis returned to the vehicle and opened the back passenger door.

I slid out, and with him by my side and Agent Shea following us, we walked into the club. There was no showing the bouncer at the door my ID. Instead, we were waved through, people looking and whispering and probably wondering who the hell I was. Or maybe there was a small chance they knew, given my dad was the next president of the United States.

"Do you dance?" I hollered over the music as we walked toward the bar.

Rhett's eyes widened, and he shook his head. "Don't you dare."

"But what if I'm in danger on the dance floor?"

"Trust me. Nothing is going to happen to you."

We stopped at the bar and waited for someone to step aside so I could move up and order. Agent Shea stayed near the door, his eyes scanning the place.

"But I can dance?" I asked.

"Of course."

"But what if I want to dance with *you*?"

Before he could respond, the person in front of us stepped back and bumped into Rhett. He looked him up and down and then turned to me before looking back at Rhett. The guy quickly muttered he was sorry and scurried away.

"Great. You're going to scare off all the guys." I wrinkled my nose playfully and moved into the empty space.

"Good," Rhett stated.

"Long time no see."

I turned toward the bartender to respond, but I realized he wasn't talking to me.

He was speaking to Rhett.

6

RHETT

WHEN FALLON TOLD US THE NAME OF THE CLUB, I INSTANTLY WENT ON high alert. Not because of my job, but because I knew there was a good chance I could run into someone who would recognize me from the many nights I'd spent at Chrome when I lived in the city, and I was apprehensive about him learning something more intimate about me than I'd planned to share.

It wasn't that I wanted to be deceitful about my sexuality—plenty of people knew I was into both men and women. But the chemistry between Fallon and me was undeniable, and not telling him I was bi allowed me to maintain some boundaries because I was finding it harder and harder not to give in to temptation.

Unfortunately for me, Perry, the bartender, blew my cover right away, and it felt as though the protective wall I'd built around myself when it came to Fallon was about to come crumbling down.

"Hey, Perry," I said, wondering if he'd just started his shift since I hadn't seen him when Shea and I completed our sweep.

"You working tonight?" Perry asked, looking between me and Fallon.

The black suit and earpiece were a dead giveaway, so there was no point in denying it. "Yep." The agency didn't have a rule about us telling people what we did for a living, and I'd told Perry I was part of the Secret Service before I left town for the campaign trail.

He turned to Fallon and smiled. "I guess that means you're the only one drinking. What can I get you?"

"Sam Adams in a bottle."

A few seconds later, Perry placed the bottle in front of Fallon, who then slid some cash across the bar.

"Let's sit over there." Fallon nodded toward a table in the corner.

Although the club was busy, most people were dancing, which made it easy to find an open spot.

Before we stepped away, Perry called out, "Hey, Rhett, give me a call sometime when you're not working."

I didn't want to be rude, but that ship had sailed, so I just smiled and followed Fallon to the empty table.

He picked one of the seats facing the dance floor, and since I couldn't sit with my back to the crowd, I pulled out the chair next to him and sat. The music wasn't as loud where we were, which meant I heard him just fine when he asked, "So, how do you know the bartender?"

I rubbed the back of my neck. "We may have hooked up a few times."

"Interesting."

"Is it?"

"Well, yeah." He took a sip of his beer. "After you told me you had a daughter, I sort of assumed you were straight."

"Definitely not straight, but I am bi."

It appeared as if he wanted to say something else, but two guys walking our way caught his attention, and a broad smile spread across his face.

"Do you know them?" They looked familiar, but I couldn't quite place them.

He nodded. "They're friends of mine."

"Hey," the shorter of the two men said when they reached our table. "Didn't expect to see you here tonight."

"Last-minute decision. I was getting restless at home." Fallon stood and hugged the guy before shaking the hand of the other one. "You two want to sit with us?"

"Sure," the taller one replied.

They grabbed the seats across the table, and Fallon took a second to introduce us. "This is Tyler, my friend from college, and his fiancé, Professor Foster. Guys, this is Agent Davis."

Professor?

"I've told you a dozen times to call me Hayden," the professor huffed.

Fallon smirked. "I know, but it's fun to watch people's faces when I introduce you that way."

Hayden rolled his eyes while Tyler chuckled.

Tyler studied my face. "You were at the Fourth of July party on Cape Cod," he mused, and then a look I couldn't decipher passed between him and Fallon.

"Yep, and now Agent Hottie's my bodyguard."

Somehow, I'd forgotten about the nickname he'd given me at the party, and I shook my head at his ridiculousness. "We don't refer to ourselves as bodyguards," I retorted.

"Sorry. Agent Hottie is part of my protection detail." Fallon looked at me. "Better?"

"Much." I smirked.

"So, they already set you up with Secret Service? That didn't take long," Hayden said.

"I know. The morning after the election, a whole team swarmed my condo building."

"It wasn't that dramatic," I grumbled, which caused the three of them to laugh.

"Man, I feel for you," Tyler said to me. "Trying to keep this one in line won't be easy."

Fallon clutched his chest in mock indignation. "I have no idea what you're talking about. I'm a model citizen."

"I've got four years of stories that say otherwise," his friend teased.

"Maybe I need to take another look at your file." I winked.

Hayden grinned and said, "Sounds like you won't be able to keep any secrets from here on out."

"I don't have secrets," Fallon huffed.

Everyone laughed.

I was certain Fallon Donnelley had a few secrets no one knew.

Just like I had my own.

The conversation quickly switched to the wedding Hayden and Tyler were busy planning. They made an effort to include me in their chat, which was a nice change of pace from the formal discussions I had to sit in on when working for politicians and other dignitaries.

When "Replay" by Lady Gaga came over the speakers, Fallon got up and said, "Let's dance."

Tyler seemed eager to get out on the dance floor and pulled Hayden up to join him. Fallon glanced at me, his eyebrow raised, and I shook my head.

"Go have fun. I'll stay here."

He shrugged and followed his friends.

I stood so I could keep a better eye on him and those dancing nearby. Agent Shea was standing on the other side of the club, and even with the lights dimmed, I could tell he was also scanning the area.

It didn't take long before some guy approached Fallon and leaned closer to say something in his ear. Fallon smiled, and they began to dance together. My fists clenched when the guy's hands grabbed him by the waist and pulled him closer so the man could grind against him.

I hadn't been able to stop thinking about Fallon's perfect body since watching him work out the day before, and I was tempted to rush over and rip the stranger's hands away. Given my job was to protect him, I could probably get away with it, but there was no law against dancing, and he didn't appear to be in any danger.

A few seconds later, Fallon peeked over the guy's shoulder, and our gazes locked. With my arms crossed over my chest, I maintained eye contact as they continued to move to the beat.

For the duration of the song, we watched each other while I wished I could be the one with him in my arms, dancing close, our bodies pressed together.

Despite what some might think, I liked to cut loose and have a good time. Unfortunately, with my job, I didn't get to do it as often as I would like. And it made me a little sad that Fallon would likely never see that side of me since it would be difficult to let my guard down around him, especially with the watchful eyes around us.

A little while later, Fallon said something to Tyler and Hayden, who each hugged him, and then he made his way back to me. "I'm ready to call it a night."

"Already?" I questioned because I'd expected him to want to stay until closing.

"Yeah. It's not as much fun when I can't dance with the person I want to."

I shouldn't have let his words affect me, but a slight flutter burst in my chest because I felt the same disappointment watching him with someone else. Still, I couldn't say or do anything to change the situation we found ourselves in, so instead, I spoke into the microphone on my wrist and told Shea and Vance we were ready to leave.

Once outside, Fallon and I climbed into the back of the SUV, and as Vance pulled away from the curb, our knees brushed against each other. It was only a slight touch, but it was enough to send a spark of electricity through my body. Fallon must've felt it too, because his head turned in my direction before I quickly looked away.

The smart thing to do would have been to move my leg, but the back of the dark SUV was the only place I could allow myself to act on the small crush I'd developed over the last few days. I avoided glancing in his direction again during our drive because, despite my training to keep my emotions in check, I worried my face would betray how attracted I was to him. And that could only cause problems for me and my job moving forward.

When we finally arrived at his building, we took the elevator up to the eighth floor and I followed him to his front door, where the next shift of agents were waiting to take over.

With nothing left to do, I said, "Have a good night, Mr. Donnelley."

"Later, Agent Davis." He winked.

I glanced at my fellow agents to see if they had seen what Fallon did, but they said nothing.

Fallon and I were playing with fire, and yet I couldn't help but look forward to the next time we were alone together.

WHEN I ENTERED THE COMMAND POST, JONES AND DAY WERE SITTING at the dining table. It wasn't unusual for any of us to stay up late, even when we weren't working. Our bodies got used to operating on only a few hours of sleep at a time, and it was often difficult for us to transition from being on alert to relaxing and trying to grab some shut-eye.

"Did you have fun at Chrome?" Day questioned playfully as I grabbed a bottle of water from the fridge.

It wasn't a surprise he knew where we'd gone tonight because it was hard to ignore whatever the other agents were up to since we were living in the command post. Having been my friend for years, he knew Chrome was a place I had frequented when I'd worked in Boston before.

"It's definitely not as fun going there while on the job." I rubbed a hand over my face. "Crowds suck, and the dim lights made it even worse."

"And you don't even get laid at the end of the night," he teased.

His words had me thinking about Fallon, who was just on the other side of the wall. The desire I'd felt watching him on the dance floor had been undeniable, and I couldn't help but imagine what it would be like if I had followed him inside his condo instead of saying goodbye at the door.

Would he lie in his bed shirtless in nothing but a pair of boxers and ask me to join him? How would his lips feel against mine as we kissed for the first time? Would he explore my body with his mouth and hands, touching every inch of me until I was a trembling mess?

"Dude, you must be exhausted," Jones said. "You totally zoned out just now."

Fuck. I needed to get my shit on lockdown. I couldn't have these guys suspect anything.

"Yeah, I wasn't expecting to work a double, and I barely got any sleep last night. I think I'm going to crash."

"Are you still going apartment hunting tomorrow?" Day asked.

I nodded. Agent Tanner had given a couple of us the day off so we could try to secure housing. "That's the plan."

"Mind if I tag along? Marissa is relocating to Boston, and I told her I'd get a jump start on finding a place."

Day and his girlfriend, Marissa, had met in D.C. when he first started working there and had been doing the long-distance thing over the last few months while he was out of the country. I couldn't help but feel happy for my friend that they'd finally get to live together.

"That's awesome news, man. I haven't had a chance to start searching online yet, so we may just drive around until we find some apartments to check out. We can grab breakfast first and then get started."

"Works for me," he replied.

I chugged the rest of my water and headed toward my room where I fell asleep fantasizing about everything I wanted to make real if only my circumstances were different.

7

FALLON

THE DESK IN MY LIVING ROOM WAS FILLED WITH STACKS OF LAW textbooks, legal pads, and highlighters. I'd written out numerous flashcards to quiz myself and was making progress until Rhett cleared his throat. A small smile tugged at the corner of my lips as I spun in my chair to face him sitting a few feet away on my couch.

"Yes?" I asked, still smiling.

His eyes twinkled with a mischievous glimmer, and I couldn't help but feel a flutter of excitement in my chest.

"Need a study buddy, Counselor? I may not be a *real* law student, but I can certainly help quiz you."

A surge of enjoyment washed over me, and I leaned back in the chair. "You want to help me study?"

He lifted a shoulder. "Sure, why not?"

"Didn't you say you don't pay attention in class?"

"I have nothing else to do, so might as well help you."

"All right, then quiz me, Rhett." I grabbed my flashcards and settled down next to him on the couch. The close proximity sent a delightful shiver down my spine, and I remembered how, a few nights before, we had sat in the back of the Secret Service SUV, our knees pressed together, and how neither one of us had made a move to break the contact.

He leaned in close, his voice laced with a subtle flirtatious tone. "I like it when you say my name."

I swallowed, no words making it past my lips as I stared into his blue eyes and handed him the flashcards.

"Ready?" he asked.

I nodded, still not able to say anything. Agent Rhett Davis was flirting with me, but I was at a loss for words and couldn't flirt back.

"Relevance – Basics."

I cleared my throat. "Evidence is relevant if it has any tendency to make a material fact more probable or less probable than would be the case without evidence."

"Correct." He smiled and flipped to a new card. "Privileges – Attorney-client privilege; elements."

"Privileges apply to: 1. Confidential communication; 2. Between attorney and client; 3. Made during a professional legal consultation; 4. Unless privilege waived by the client; or 5. If an exception applies."

He nodded and continued through a few more cards until my stomach grumbled.

"I think I need a break," I said.

"Of course."

I stood and asked, "Hungry?"

Rhett got up and placed the cards on my desk. "I am, but my shift will be over soon, so I'll grab something next door."

Other than the day I ordered Chinese food for everyone, I'd been having dinner after Rhett left, but for some reason—even though I wouldn't consider myself a superb cook—I found myself saying, "That's not for another hour. Let me just make something for both of us."

"Are you sure?"

"I am if you like salmon."

"I do." He nodded, and we walked toward my open kitchen.

"Asparagus?"

"Yes."

"Then dinner will be ready in less than thirty minutes." I nudged my head for him to sit at the island.

"Fallon ..." He took a deep breath.

"What?" I grabbed the foil from a drawer.

"We're crossing a line."

"It's food. Not like we're fucking."

"Jesus, Fallon." He stood abruptly. "Don't say that."

"Why? Because you want to?"

He started to pace, and it was the first time I'd seen his resolve crack to the point he was having a hard time hiding his emotions. I didn't wait for him to respond. Instead, I turned the oven on, pulled the ingredients out of the fridge, and got started making the dinner I had at least once a week.

Growing up, we'd had a chef who had fixed us meals, and during undergrad, the fraternity house where I had been president had employed one. I hadn't learned how to cook until after graduation when I started living alone. I'd thought I would have Tyler to cook for me because he'd moved in after we graduated, but that didn't last long since Hayden asked him to live with him a month later.

At first, I'd ordered takeout since the only thing Tyler had taught me in the short time he'd lived with me was four ways to make eggs. But then I searched the Internet for simple recipes and voilà, I could cook a few things to keep me alive that weren't just breakfast and sandwiches.

Rhett finally sat back in his seat, and I continued filling the foil packets with the salmon, asparagus, lemon, spices, and hot sauce.

"You don't have to eat it, you know? I'm just being nice since you're on shift. I don't want to eat in front of you, knowing you've been with me all day and probably just as hungry as I am," I said.

"I know, but the issue is I want to eat it. I've never been in a position where all the fucking lines are blurred, but they are, and I don't know what to do. I worked my ass off to get a job with the Secret

Service, and in less than two weeks on this assignment, I've fucked up."

"You haven't fucked up." I closed the packets and placed them on a cookie sheet. "Does it say in your handbook or whatever that you can't eat while on duty?"

"You know it isn't since we ate lunch together." He rolled his eyes.

"But it isn't the food we're talking about." I put the cookie sheet into the preheated oven.

"Exactly."

I leaned on the island, my elbows resting on the surface and my face only a few feet from his. "There's no reason for Agent Day to come inside, right?"

"Only if there's an emergency."

"The only emergency around here is we haven't kissed yet."

Rhett's eyes moved to my lips, and I licked the bottom one before sinking my teeth into it.

"Fallon," he groaned.

"No one will know. We're both consenting adults."

"I'm assigned to keep you safe."

"Yeah, and I don't see any big scary guys coming to get me."

He continued to stare at my lips as though he was fighting with himself. I knew just by the way he hesitated to close the space between us his resolve was crumbling. But what was wrong with two guys who were attracted to each other sharing a little kiss? Would crossing the line really hinder Rhett's ability to keep me safe if something were to happen? I would think it would make him want to help me more because feelings were involved.

Without a word, he stood and came around to my side of the island. I pushed off the countertop and spun to face him. Stepping in front of me, he used his body to cage mine against the island. My breath caught, and I waited to see what he was going to do.

He leaned in, and all hesitation was gone as his lips locked with mine. His kiss was soft yet full of passion, and I felt myself melting. The scent of lemon and spices wafted from the oven and lingered in the air, but all I could focus on was the intoxicating taste of Rhett's lips on mine, which sent shivers down my spine and made my knees weak.

When he finally pulled away, I was breathless. His bright blue eyes locked onto mine, searching for a reaction, but I couldn't think or move. He'd kissed me. Agent Rhett Davis had actually kissed me.

His hand reached up to caress my cheek gently, and I could feel myself flush with heat.

"Is that what you wanted?" His voice was low.

"Yes." I wrapped my arms around his neck and kissed him again.

I never thought a kitchen could be so exciting, but as Rhett and I continued our make-out session against the island, it felt like the most romantic place on Earth. Our bodies pressed against each other, and every touch sent sparks through my veins. While I was desperate for more, I knew it was too soon, and I didn't want to push him to the point where he put a stop to what we were doing.

His hands cradled my face, pulling me closer, as if we were both trying to meld into one another. "Fallon," he whispered against my lips. "No one can know."

"Of course not."

One of his hands gripped my hip firmly, tugging me to press against him, while the other tangled in my hair. I moaned softly against his lips, and the sound seemed to fuel his passion even more. In a sudden burst of determination, he lifted me effortlessly onto the granite counter. I wrapped my legs around his waist and dragged him toward me, still kissing him as though my life depended on it.

In the midst of our heated kissing, the delightful aroma of the dinner I was baking filled the air. It barely registered since I was so lost in the moment with Rhett. But then, the scent started to change, smelling slightly burnt. I pulled away from the kiss, my eyes meeting his with concern.

"Wait. Shit!" I jumped off the counter and raced to the oven, but it was too late. Smoke billowed out as I opened the oven door, and the loud beeps of the smoke detector echoed throughout the kitchen.

In a flash, the front door burst open and Agent Day rushed in.

"It's okay," Rhett called out. "Fallon burnt the dinner he was cooking."

Agent Day nodded and spoke into his two-way radio. "Stand down. Windstorm burned his dinner. All clear." He turned to Rhett and asked, "You got this?"

"Yeah. Can you open a window before you leave?"

I pulled the tray from the oven. The charred salmon and asparagus were inedible. How the hell did it start smoking? Pressing the off button for the oven, I found my answer. I had the temperature up way too high, and while losing myself in Rhett's kisses, I'd completely lost track of time since I hadn't set a timer.

He waved the smoke out the window while I threw everything into the trash.

"Guess I'm ordering out."

"Okay." His response was almost cold, and I wanted to pry and ask him what he was thinking about, but if I had to guess, he was beating himself up for kissing me.

And that hurt.

8

RHETT

I STOOD IN THE SHOWER THINKING ABOUT THE NIGHT BEFORE.

The kiss in Fallon's kitchen had thrown me for a loop, and I didn't know what to do.

Trying to pinpoint when things had changed for me, I narrowed it down to the night we'd gone to Chrome. That was when Fallon and I moved from what I considered harmless flirting to me longing for things I had no business wanting. Then a couple of days later, I could no longer fight the attraction I felt and kissed him.

When I'd started my shift the day prior, I had been determined to push all my desire for Fallon aside and focus on the job I was assigned to do.

Unfortunately, I couldn't help but stare at him while he worked on some assignments for school. The way he bit his lip when he concentrated on whatever he was reading had me imagining other things his mouth could do. Or when he ran his fingers through his hair in frustration, messing it up just a little, I pictured it was the same disheveled look he'd wear after a long night of rolling around in bed.

I thought if I offered to help him study, it would give me something else to focus on besides how damn hot he was. The problem was, Fallon wasn't only attractive, he was smart as hell too. Good looks and intelligence were a lethal combination, and I had felt my self-control slowly slip away.

By the time he'd offered to cook dinner for us, I was hanging on by a thread. And when he said, "The only emergency around here is we haven't kissed yet," it had felt as though I only had a split second to choose whether to fight against our connection or finally take what I wanted.

The moment our lips touched, I knew I was in trouble. That kiss conveyed the emotions and chemistry we weren't free to speak out loud. Every reason I'd had for why we couldn't indulge in our fantasies flew out the window when his tongue met mine, and in an instant, everything had changed.

When the smoke alarm blared, I knew Day would rush in, which served as a reminder that we couldn't act so carelessly because other agents were always nearby.

As I stepped out of the shower and began to dry off, I decided the best thing to do was to tell Fallon the kiss had been a mistake, and we couldn't let it happen again. It wasn't what I wanted, but I believed professional boundaries were needed if I was going to do my job effectively.

At exactly 0800 hours, I walked into his place to relieve Agent Meyer, who had been working nights. "Anything to report?" I asked.

"No. All was quiet last night," Meyer replied and then headed out.

I could faintly hear the shower running down the hall, and my mind conjured up images of Fallon naked beneath the spray of water. I quickly pushed the inappropriate thoughts out of my head.

After what felt like an eternity, Fallon walked into the living room with a towel wrapped around his waist, giving me an eyeful of his toned chest and abs. My pulse raced, and I had to remind myself I was there to protect him, not flirt with him. But it was hard not to check him out.

My perusal of his hot-as-fuck body didn't go unnoticed, and he teasingly said, "You might as well take a picture if you're going to keep staring at me."

I cleared my throat before quickly averting my gaze from the temptation in front of me. "You should probably get dressed."

"Am I distracting you from your job, Agent Davis?"

"Fallon …" I sighed, looking back at him.

"Fine. I'll be right back." He spun around and walked to his room.

I paced as I tried to think of how to say what I needed to without sounding like a jerk. The last thing I wanted to do was make Fallon feel as though I regretted kissing him, because if things were different, I'd be rushing to his room for another taste. But I couldn't risk my job just because I had the hots for the man I was tasked with protecting. The Secret Service would consider our situation a conflict of interest and more than likely move me to another team if they found out about us. And if they moved me out of Boston, I would see Poppy less often.

A few minutes later, Fallon returned, tugging a Hawkins U Rowing hoodie over his head, and walked toward the kitchen. "Coffee?"

"No, but we need to talk." I followed him and leaned against the island while he made his cup.

"You can't stop thinking about that kiss either?" He smirked.

I shook my head. "No. I mean yes, but it can't happen again."

He crossed his arms and glared. "Why not?"

"Because Day or any other agent could have easily caught us in a compromising position—"

"But they didn't." He turned to grab the creamer from the fridge.

I ran a hand down my face. "It doesn't matter. I'm supposed to protect you, not make out with you in your kitchen."

He closed the refrigerator door. "Fine. We'll just go to my bedroom to make out, then."

"Fallon," I growled.

"Like I said last night, we're both adults. We should be able to do whatever we want."

"The agency won't see it the same way," I snapped.

"Whatever. You've clearly made up your mind. If you say it can't happen again"—he closed his eyes and drew in a breath—"then that's the way it's gotta be."

"Fallon—"

"Look, there's no point discussing it any further. We can go back to you just being another agent and forget anything happened between us." He grabbed his to-go mug and poured creamer into it. "We need to leave before I'm late for class."

Even knowing it was for the best that we pretend I was nothing more than his protector, it didn't mean the decision hurt any less. And Fallon accepting my choice without much of a fight made it even worse.

A COUPLE OF WEEKS LATER, AGENT DAY AND I WERE TAILING Fallon's Mustang as he drove to his parents' house for Thanksgiving. We were the only two in the car because Patrick Donnelley's house was already bustling with Secret Service and most of the other agents on our team had the day off to spend with their families.

I'd chosen to ride with Day because things continued to be strained with Fallon. We still rode to school together every day, but not much was said when we were alone in his car. He'd also started studying at the library after class when he didn't have rowing practice, so we rarely returned home before the end of my shift.

Part of me thought the distance between us was a good thing because I could go back to maintaining professional boundaries with him. However, I missed our flirty interactions and how easy it was to talk with him. I missed the way we playfully challenged each other, and how he managed to bring a smile to my face even when I tried to keep my emotions in check. I just plain missed him, but I didn't know how to fix things.

"Does something seem off to you?" Day asked as we pulled onto the interstate.

"What do you mean?"

"I'm not sure exactly. Fallon's been more subdued lately. Normally, he talks to everyone and jokes around, but he's been keeping to himself a lot. I'm just wondering if we're missing something we should be aware of."

Since I couldn't admit to my friend I was to blame for the change in Fallon's demeanor, I said, "He's got some tough exams coming up that are stressing him out."

"That makes sense." Day's easy acceptance of my lie made me feel even guiltier.

Ten minutes later, we took the exit toward the Donnelleys' house in Weston, just outside of Boston. When we turned onto their street, the familiar stone wall surrounding their estate came into view. I'd spent some time there when I worked for Fallon's father, and I was in awe every time I saw their sprawling whitewashed brick home. The property had rolling lawns and trees as far as the eye could see, and the inside was even more impressive. I couldn't imagine what it was like growing up in such a beautiful place.

We followed Fallon as he drove down the winding driveway and stopped near the garage, where several other vehicles were parked. He got out of his car, and without a glance in our direction, made his way up to the house. Day and I quickly climbed out of the government SUV and caught up to him just as one of Patrick Donnelley's agents opened the door.

I greeted him with a nod and then moved inside. The Donnelleys had a large extended family, and it appeared everyone had descended on their home for the holiday. Children played and laughed while the other guests milled around the first floor and engaged in various conversations. I watched as Fallon kissed his mother's cheek and shook his father's hand before bypassing everyone else and making his way to the bar. He filled a glass with amber liquid, tossed it back in one gulp, and then poured himself another.

With his drink in hand, he walked over to where his siblings were seated on the couch. Both of them had their faces buried in their phones and seemed more interested in whatever they were looking at on the screens than the activity surrounding them.

When it was time to eat, Mrs. Donnelley made sure the chefs

prepared plates for all the agents, and we decided amongst ourselves to eat in shifts; that way, we could continue to provide security while also enjoying the delicious meal.

Day and I each grabbed a plate and joined a few of the agents who chose to eat outside. With so many bodies in the house, the crisp autumn air felt refreshing. Day knew two of the agents, so he made the introductions.

"You guys are on Fallon's detail, right?" asked Agent Ramos, one of Finnegan's agents. "How's that going?"

"Easiest detail I've been on," Day replied.

Agent Pederson, part of Faye's detail, snorted a laugh. "Yeah, you're with the golden child."

I tilted my head. "What do you mean?"

"Just that you're protecting the responsible kid who goes to law school and doesn't get himself into trouble," Pederson elaborated.

"You havin' trouble with Faye?" Day teased.

Pederson shook his head. "You don't know the half of it. I don't think she's spent more than ten hours at home this last week. I've gone to more nightclubs since joining her team than I did throughout my entire twenties. That doesn't include the countless shopping trips I've accompanied her on. They should change my job description to 'official bag handler.'"

We all laughed.

Ramos chimed in and said, "At least you haven't had to travel to some seedy poker clubs. I swear Finnegan has to be the worst poker player ever. He says it's just an unlucky streak, but I'm not convinced he knows what he's doing."

"Wow. I guess we do have it easy." Day nudged me with his elbow.

If only he knew.

Throughout the night, I kept watch over Fallon while he did everything he could not to look my way. When the festivities were over, he drove home while Day and I followed him again. The two of us were on duty until the night shift started, which wasn't for another hour. Fallon parked his car and headed for the elevator before Day pulled into our spot.

As soon as Day turned off our vehicle, we hopped out and rushed over to Fallon just as the elevator doors opened. Day gave me a questioning look as we stepped inside, and I shrugged, pretending I had no idea what was going on with Fallon.

The ride to the eighth floor was silent, and it killed me that I was the one who had created a situation where we barely spoke to each other anymore.

Fallon looked around as we walked to his door. "Where are the other agents?"

"Since it's a holiday, you're stuck with us until the night shift starts," I replied.

He unlocked his door, and I completed a quick sweep of the condo. When Fallon entered, he walked toward the kitchen to put away the leftovers he'd been sent home with, leaving me to decide if I should follow him or give him space.

Assuming he didn't want me to hover, I took a seat on the leather couch in the living room. When he came back, he had two plates in his hand. "Thought you might want another slice of pie."

I took the piece of pumpkin pie he was offering. "Thanks. I can't remember the last time I've had a meal as good as the one today."

We ate in silence for a few minutes, and then he asked, "What do you normally do for the holidays?"

I swallowed a bite. "For the last few years, I've been scheduled to work, but before that I would fly out to Arizona, where my parents live."

"What about Poppy?"

I sighed. "She spends the holidays with her mom, and then we get together when I have time off. My parents try to plan their visits around my schedule so we can celebrate as a family, but it doesn't always work out."

Fallon looked at me with a hint of sadness in his eyes. "I can't imagine not seeing my family on Thanksgiving or Christmas."

I lifted a shoulder. "It comes with the territory. If I'd planned things out, I would have probably waited to have kids because my job isn't very conducive to a family life, but I wouldn't trade Poppy for anything. It just takes a little more planning to spend time together." I took the last bite of the dessert.

"I'm guessing your schedule makes it harder to date too," he pondered and then shook his head. "Sorry, I shouldn't have brought that up."

"It's fine."

He stood and grabbed my empty plate. "No, you made it clear there are boundaries we need to abide by, and asking about your dating life crosses a line. I'm going to stick these plates in the dishwasher and then go to bed."

"Wait—"

"I'll see you tomorrow, Agent Davis."

THE FOLLOWING DAY, I HEADED OUT TO SIGN THE LEASE AGREEMENT for my new place. I'd already made arrangements with Agent Tanner to switch to the mid shift because the leasing office was closed for the holiday weekend, but the property manager was making an exception for me and offered to meet in the morning.

When Day and I had gone apartment hunting a couple of weeks before, I'd found a perfect two-bedroom, one-bath place only a few blocks from where Alexis and Poppy lived, and couldn't wait to have my daughter over as soon as possible.

As I drove away from the apartment complex with my new keys in hand, I passed a retail store and decided to stop so I could pick up a few things before heading back to the command post. Besides needing to grab some toiletries, I wanted to get an energy drink because I was operating on very little sleep.

The night before, I'd gone straight to my room after Agent Meyer relieved me. I tried to fall asleep, but I ended up tossing and turning the entire night as I thought about Fallon.

Our conversation, while not our usual light-hearted bantering, had left me conflicted because I really did enjoy spending time with him. My head told me to leave things as they were and focus on my job. But my heart—and other parts—begged me to give in to my desires and see what could happen between us. It was like one of those classic cartoon characters with an angel on one shoulder and a devil on the other, each trying to convince me what path I should take.

I found a parking spot near the entrance of the store and headed inside. I grabbed the items I needed, and as I went to check out, I passed a display of prepaid cell phones, and divine inspiration hit. Maybe there was a way Fallon and I could explore things with each other as long as we were careful.

Of course, I needed to get him to forgive me for pulling away first.

AFTER MY SHOPPING TRIP, I DROPPED OFF MY STUFF AT THE COMMAND post and then made my way to Fallon's to start my shift. When I walked into his condo, he was sitting at his desk and didn't bother to look my way, even though I knew he heard me come in.

"See you tomorrow, Fallon," Agent Bernard said as he left.

"Later." Fallon waved over his shoulder.

When the door clicked shut, I moved toward him and tossed one of the cell phones I'd purchased onto the desk.

"What's this?" he asked, pushing it off his papers with the eraser end of his pencil.

"Your new phone."

His head snapped up, and he gave me a questioning look. "I already have a phone."

"I know. This one is so we can text each other."

"They have apps for that, you know?" he sassed.

I stared at him for a beat. "Right. I didn't think of those, but I saw the phone and figured this could be our secret."

"Our secret, huh?"

I spun his chair around so he was facing me and knelt in front of him. "I messed up. Big, okay?"

He leaned back and crossed his arms over his chest but didn't say anything.

"I'm sorry for freaking out after our kiss. I should have handled things better."

He let out a breath. "That doesn't change anything, Rhett. We're still in the same situation."

I placed my hands on his knees and was relieved when he didn't push them away. "True, but I decided the risk is worth it."

"You decided?" He grunted a small laugh. "So, does that mean I don't get a say?"

My shoulders slumped. While dealing with my own issues, I hadn't considered the possibility he might have changed his mind about us. "Of course, you do."

He lifted my chin with his finger. "Are you sure about this? You're not going to get scared again?"

"I wasn't scared," I huffed.

He quirked an eyebrow.

"Okay, fine. I was. And I've regretted it every single day. I won't lie and tell you it will be smooth sailing from here on out. I still have my career to consider, and we need to be careful. But I'm tired of pretending there is nothing between us."

"I am pretty irresistible." He smirked.

"Cocky too," I teased before turning serious again. "So, did I totally fuck things up, or do you think you could give me another chance?"

He leaned forward and cupped my face with his hands. "Yeah, I can do that."

Fallon pressed his mouth to mine, and the kiss was tentative at first, but when I traced his lips with my tongue, he slid his hands from my cheeks to the back of my neck and pulled me closer. My heart raced as his lips moved in sync with mine. For just a moment, I let go, and I didn't focus on anything other than him. I didn't worry about the forbidden nature of our relationship or what might happen if anyone found out about us.

I just enjoyed getting lost in his kiss.

His tongue tangled with mine as he explored every inch of my mouth. I moaned softly, and it seemed to spur him on. My body felt like it was on fire, and I couldn't believe I'd been stupid enough to consider denying myself more moments with him.

Eventually, he pulled away and rested his forehead against mine. "I've got to get to practice."

"Can't you skip it today?" I kissed my way down his throat.

"Nope. We have a mandatory meeting after."

I sat back on my legs. "So, not only did you get me hot and bothered, but I have to watch you work out for the next couple of hours?"

"Consider it your punishment." He winked, and after one last peck on the lips, he stood to get ready for rowing.

9

FALLON

THE BED DIPPED, AND MY EYES FLUTTERED OPEN. RHETT WAS FULLY dressed in a hunter green long-sleeved Henley shirt, the top button undone, and jeans.

"If you're going to crawl into my bed, the least you could do is be naked," I teased, moving closer. Was this how things would be since our talk on Friday? I'd gone to bed happy, knowing I would see him soon and our situation would no longer be awkward. I could get used to him in my bed, that was for sure.

He kissed my throat, working his way down to my collarbone. "I would be if we had time."

I pulled back and gazed into his eyes. "I can make time."

"You have class, baby boy."

A zing went straight to my dick at his use of a nickname. "Yeah, but we can be quick."

"There will be nothing quick about our first time."

He kissed my neck again, and I rubbed my aching cock on his crotch.

"But you know, I'm good at multitasking."

He groaned. "Fallon …"

"Shower with me." I continued to rub myself on him, and I could feel his erection stiffen in his pants. It was clear he wanted it as much as I did.

"And what if Agent Day walks in?"

"You're my man on the inside. He has no reason to come in here."

"Except when the smoke detector goes off," Rhett teased.

"I'm not cooking, but I do need some protein." I grinned and rolled on top of him. He stared up at me as though he was really struggling with giving in to me. I glanced at the clock. "We have a little more than an hour before we need to leave for class. That's plenty of time."

"If anything were to happen—"

"The only thing that's going to happen is I'm going to suck your dick and you're going to fuck me."

"Jesus," he groaned. "I meant if there was an emergency."

"What the hell do you think is going to happen? There's no reason I would be in danger."

"It's not just you." He brushed a piece of hair off my forehead. "If there's a threat to your father or some kind of national security issue, our protocol is to get you to an undisclosed secure location as soon as possible."

"My dad isn't even sworn in yet."

"Doesn't matter. Someone who's not happy he's the president-elect could take it to the extreme."

I knew there were people in the world who thought killing someone would solve all their problems, but the chances of anything happening before my father was president were slim. At least, I hoped.

"So, you're saying we can't have sex ever?"

"No."

"Then what are you saying?"

"That we need to be careful."

"Of course."

"And"—Rhett nudged me so I slid off him and he climbed out of the bed—"get your sweet ass into the shower, and I'll be right there."

He didn't have to tell me twice, so I quickly stripped out of my pajama pants and walked into my bathroom. While the shower heated, I gargled some mouthwash and then moved into the glass-encased stall.

A moment later, a naked, well-endowed Rhett stepped inside. My mouth watered as I ogled his nude form. I was kicking myself for saying we were only going to have me suck his dick and Rhett fuck me because I wanted to take my time as I explored every inch of him.

"We need to hurry," he advised.

"What did you do?"

"I made it appear I was in the other bathroom in case someone does walk in." He backed me up until I was flush with the cold tiled wall. "And I found your condoms and lube."

I swallowed. It wasn't like I hid them; everyone kept their shit in the top drawer of their nightstand for easy access. But it made me wonder. "Anything else in there you liked?"

A slow grin spread across his face, and he reached down and fisted my hard erection. "Definitely, and once I think of other ways for us to be discreet, we're going to have a lot of fun with your collection."

"Or I can use them while you watch."

"Yeah, I'd like to see that." He pumped my slick cock.

My knees wobbled slightly, and I had to brace myself against the wall.

Since getting my own detail, I hadn't been with anyone. Declan and I had called off our weekly hookup because I couldn't mess around with anyone with ears in the next room. There was no way for me to tell whoever was on duty to leave or to ignore what was happening in my bedroom because it was literally their job to watch my every move. But with Rhett on the inside and the only one I wanted to hook up with, I was sure we could make things work.

Like we were in the shower.

"Now, less talking," he ordered. "We gotta hurry."

"Right."

Even though my dick was aching, I lowered to my knees and grabbed Rhett's shaft. With no hesitation, I licked the underside of his crown and flicked his hole a few times before engulfing him in my mouth.

"Jesus Christ," he moaned. "It's been way too long. Keep going."

No chance in hell I would stop before he was shooting his jizz in my mouth. I wanted to taste every fucking inch of this man. The bit of pre-cum I had tasted confirmed he was sweet and delicious, and that only fueled me more.

I licked and sucked his shaft, head, and balls while I peered up at him. We stared into each other's eyes, and while I bobbed up and down, I grabbed his firm ass and pulled him closer. His tip hit the back of my throat, and I kept going as I took all of him into my mouth. He moaned and fisted my hair, keeping me from pulling away as I deep-throated him.

"Yeah, just like that, baby boy."

The shower beat down on my back as I went harder and faster. With the water making my entire body slick, I fisted my cock and tugged in rhythm with my sucking.

"That's it. I'm going to come." He held my head still and took over as he fucked my mouth with rapid drives of his hips.

Within seconds, his body went taut, and he blew his load down my throat. I drank all of his sweetness and then stood.

Rhett backed me up against the shower wall again and claimed my mouth in a scorching kiss. "You're something else, you know that?"

"Is that good or bad?"

He spun me, my chest meeting the tiled wall. "Good. Now I know that sassy mouth of yours has other talents."

"Just wait until you see what I can do with my dick."

He leaned in and whispered into my ear, "Yeah, but me first."

I jutted my ass out and spread my legs as I waited for Rhett to grab the condom and lube. Looking over my shoulder, I noticed he was still hard. "So, you do have a lot of stamina, huh?"

He chuckled as he rolled the condom onto himself. "Guess we'll really find out who has more."

Squirting the thick substance onto his fingers, he stepped closer and went straight for my hole. I moaned as he rubbed the lubricant around my puckered rim and then pushed a digit inside.

"Damn. You're so tight."

"Don't you worry. You're going to fit nice and snug. Now, I thought we had to hurry?"

Rhett slipped his finger out and then went back in with two. "I really wish we didn't have to. I want to take my time with you."

"But we can't," I panted.

"But we can't," he agreed.

Getting more lube, he coated his latex-covered shaft and then stepped fully behind me. I spread my legs even farther, and he nudged his tip against me. Slowly, he slid in, and my entire body ignited. My hand grasped my aching cock, and I pumped it. I needed to come so badly, and since we were in a hurry, I didn't waste any time as I worked myself while Rhett slid to the hilt.

"Fuck, you feel so good," I gasped.

"So do you, baby boy."

He held on to my sides as his hips rocked into me and his pace quickened. With one hand on the wall, I braced myself and continued to slide my other hand up and down my shaft. My knees felt as though they might buckle, but I stayed strong, riding the high he was providing.

"You gonna come for me?" he asked.

I nodded and breathed out, "Yeah."

"Let go, then."

Within seconds, I moaned my release as I milked myself. My toes curled, and I could have fucking sworn I saw stars. With a few more thrusts, Rhett stilled and groaned his release. I didn't want to move. Didn't want to leave our private moment and face the day.

As he pulled out of me, I wished things were different. That we could crawl back into my bed and forget school and the Secret Service and all the shit that came with it. I wanted to take his hand and walk with him outside. I wanted to grab the snow that had recently started falling since the season had changed and make snowballs to toss at him. To have a friendly competition before I raced over and kissed the shit out of him.

But none of that could happen.

I wouldn't say I was feeling melancholy about the sex we just had, but in the wake of it, reality hit me because I knew as soon as we stepped out of the steamy shower, Rhett was no longer just Rhett.

He was Agent Davis.

"Hey." He lifted my chin. "What's wrong?"

"Nothing." I grabbed my shampoo and squirted it into my palm.

"Something is wrong."

"I just don't want this"—I waved my hand between us—"to end right now."

He lifted his brow. "It's not ending."

"I just mean returning to reality."

"Yeah." He sighed. "I get it, but we'll be together after class and tomorrow morning and every morning that follows. With my shift starting an hour before you have to leave for school, we can make that *our* time."

"I want all the time, Rhett." I lathered my hair.

"Me too." He cupped my cheeks. "But I'm willing to make this work if you are."

"Of course, I am."

"Good." He kissed me quickly. "Now, finish getting ready so you're not late."

"I can't wait for winter break. Then we won't have to rush off to class." I tilted my head back under the spray and rinsed the shampoo out.

Rhett said nothing, and when I straightened my head, he was looking down at the tiled floor.

"What?"

"I haven't had a chance to tell you I won't be here for winter break."

I sucked in a small breath. "What do you mean, you won't be here?"

"Usually, we work sixty days on and thirty days off, but since I'm assigned to be in classes with you, we had to change things up. Agent Tanner is giving me the three weeks of your winter break off."

"Oh," I whispered. "That's going to suck."

"Yeah, but we can text."

"You know that's not the same thing." I grabbed the conditioner and squirted some into my palm.

"I know, but we have to work with the schedule we're given."

I fingered the conditioner through my hair. "What are we going to do this summer when I don't have school and you're off for the entire thirty days?"

"I'm not sure, but we'll make it work."

"Promise?"

"I hope so."

I nodded and picked up my bottle of body wash and soaped up my body. Rhett stepped out, grabbed a towel, and dried himself off.

After I finished my quick shower, I shut off the water and got out too. We both dressed, and while I finished getting ready, he left the room to deal with the decoy bathroom.

What the hell was I going to do while he wasn't around for three weeks during winter break? It wasn't as though I could sneak him in or slip my detail and drive to his place. I was back to hating that I had a security detail, but then a thought occurred to me.

"Hey, Rhett," I called.

A few seconds later, he stuck his head into my bathroom, where I was putting toothpaste onto my toothbrush.

"Yeah?"

"My mom organizes a Breakfast-with-Santa thing every year for Christmas. I can get you the information, so you can bring your daughter."

"Really?"

"I mean, I don't have to meet your daughter if you don't want me to, but at least we can see each other for an hour or something."

He stepped into the room and kissed my cheek. "I would love that."

10

RHETT

FALLON CURLED INTO MY SIDE AS WE LAY IN HIS BED, BOTH OF US sweaty and panting after an intense round of sex. It was how we'd spent most of our time before school the last couple of weeks, but this morning was different. We were trying to savor every minute because, after my shift, I would begin my time off and likely not be alone with him until I returned to work after winter break.

Fallon rested his chin on my chest. "So, you got any big plans while you're off?"

We'd avoided discussing winter break since I'd told him I wouldn't be around until school started again. I didn't know his reasons for not bringing it up, but I'd wanted to focus on getting to know him better and enjoy the moments we spent together rather than worrying about something we had no control over.

"Well, I need to finish setting up my apartment because Poppy's going to spend a few days with me."

"I'm sure you're looking forward to that."

I smiled. "Yeah, it's been months since I've had her overnight and even longer since she's been able to stay with me several days in a row. I'm just glad her mom didn't already make plans for the holidays, so it all worked out."

"When did you and her mom break up?"

"We didn't." Fallon and I hadn't talked much about our dating histories, and since I had a kid, it was likely he'd assumed I had been in a serious relationship with Poppy's mother.

"What?" He lifted his head and glared at me.

Answering that way had been a dick move on my part, but I couldn't help but chuckle. "Alexis and I were never together. We went out a few times and quickly realized a relationship between us wouldn't work. It was quite a surprise when she told me she was pregnant a couple of months after we'd gone our separate ways."

"Do you two get along?"

I shrugged. "It's not like we're BFFs or anything, but we're on friendly terms. She's a great mom and has been nothing but understanding regarding my work schedule. I can't ask for much more than that."

"I can't believe you said BFFs." He grinned.

"Yeah, my younger boyfriend must be rubbing off on me."

"First off, twenty-nine isn't much older than me." He rolled his eyes. "Second, and more importantly, you just referred to me as your boyfriend."

"I did."

He sat up, and I followed suit. "I didn't realize you thought of me in that way."

We hadn't had a conversation about what we were to each other, and I suddenly worried I was moving too fast for him. I grabbed his hand and laced our fingers together. "I know we can't really be together in public, but I'd like to think we aren't seeing other people while we explore things in our private bubble."

"I haven't had a boyfriend before," he murmured, looking down at his lap.

"Are you serious?"

He nodded and lifted his head slightly to meet my stare. "I've had guys I've gone out with, but none of them ever got promoted to boyfriend status."

"Not even Declan?"

He snorted a laugh. "I wondered if you would ever bring him up because I was pretty sure you saw him leave my place the morning after the election."

"Yeah, the two of you act pretty chummy in class too." I huffed.

"Someone sounds jealous." He winked. "But no, Declan and I didn't date. We had sex to blow off some steam, but it was never more than a casual thing. We haven't been together since that night."

"Not even when he came over after our first gym session?"

"Nope. Agent Bernard was here, and I didn't feel like fucking with an audience."

Knowing they were no longer *blowing off steam* together was a relief, but that didn't mean he wanted more with me. "That makes me feel better, but listen, if it's too soon for us to label this—"

"I didn't say that. It's just the boyfriend thing is new to me."

I leaned forward and pressed my lips to his. "Me too, but we'll figure it out together."

Our moment was broken by the alarm on his phone going off. At least that one wouldn't send agents rushing in, but it did mean it was time for us to get ready for the day and go back to pretending we had a strictly professional relationship.

FALLON AND I DIDN'T GET ANOTHER CHANCE TO BE ALONE AFTER class because he had indoor training with his rowing team, and when we returned to his condo, Agent Bernard was already waiting to start his shift.

It sucked, but it was the reality of our situation. At least I'd thought to buy us prepaid phones, so we could text each other whenever we wanted without any identifying information in case they fell into the wrong hands, and we'd been putting them to good use the last few days we'd been apart.

I received one from Fallon:

> Hey! I got those Breakfast with Santa tickets for you and P. You just need to give your name at the registration table if you still want to come

It was baffling how attached I'd become to those messages, but my heart raced each time I heard the notification ding.

> Thanks! I think P will like that

> You're welcome. What have you been up to today?

> Nothing much. Just getting ready for poker night with some old friends from the field office

> So you're home alone right now?

> I am

> Okay. Give me a sec

Excitement coursed through me as I wondered what he was up to. I didn't have to wait long because the phone rang a minute later.

"Hello," I answered, and I could hear music playing in the background.

"Hey, handsome." Fallon's smooth voice filled my ears.

"Where are you?"

"In my room."

"What's with the music?"

"I didn't want Agent Brown to hear me. I told him I was going to take a shower, but I was hoping you'd help me get dirty instead."

I groaned. "I do like it when you're dirty."

Rushing to my room, I stripped, leaving a trail of clothes behind me, and climbed onto the bed.

"God, I wish I could video call you right now."

"Me too, baby boy." My dick twitched as I imagined him naked, waiting for me. "But this will have to do for now."

"What are you wearing?"

"Is that the best you got?" I teased, even though I was already palming my aching cock.

"Well, if you're not into it, I can stop," Fallon replied with a laugh.

"No," I grumbled. "Keep going."

I heard some shuffling on the other end of the line and pictured him lying naked in his bed. The image filling my mind had me letting out a groan.

"Is your dick hard?" he asked. "Do you have beads of pre-cum ready for me to lick off if I were there?"

"Jesus, baby boy." I slid my hand up and down my shaft, wishing it were his hand instead.

"You didn't answer me, handsome. I can't see you, so tell me how hard you are for me right now."

"It's hard as fucking steel," I growled. Phone sex was new to me, but I couldn't deny what hearing his voice was doing to my body either. "And ready for your wicked mouth."

"Oh yeah? You want me to suck your big dick? Gag on it? You want to watch my eyes water as I swallow you whole?"

"God, you're naughty, aren't you?" I moaned, pumping myself.

"You know I am."

"If I were there, I'd have you on your knees, taking all of me down your throat. My hands in your hair, controlling how fast you move," I said, stroking myself even harder as I imagined Fallon kneeling in front of me. I closed my eyes, my balls drawing up as I thought about his warm mouth engulfing me.

"Tell me more. Make me come all over my stomach while I talk to you," he breathed heavily.

"Are you touching yourself right now?"

"Yes, and I'm so fucking close," he rasped.

"I want us to come together. Imagine my dick filling you up. Your perfect ass tightening around me as I thrust into you over and over." As the words left my lips, my cock swelled. I shut my eyes tighter, listening to his labored breathing through the phone.

"Yes." His breathing quickened. "Fuck yeah."

"You going to come?" I gasped, ready to blow.

"I'm coming," he groaned.

I came too, hot spurts of cum shooting onto my stomach, and sighed, "Damn, baby boy. Now I need to go shower before the guys get here."

I HAD JUST ENOUGH TIME TO SHOWER BEFORE DAY AND OUR OLD coworkers were supposed to show up. When I worked in the field office, we got together regularly for poker nights, and I was looking forward to catching up with friends I hadn't seen in a while.

As soon as I was dressed, I heard someone knock. When I opened the door, Day shoved a case of cold beer into my arms and said, "Let's get this party started."

Party was a bit of an exaggeration. Neither of us would drink more than one beer because we had to be prepared to respond to an emergency at any given time. But I appreciated his enthusiasm for having a good time.

"Well, you're the first one here, so you can help me get the snacks ready." I led him to the kitchen.

"Man, I've been looking forward to this night off for a while."

I arched an eyebrow. "C'mon, things haven't been that bad with this job."

Both of us had worked in stressful situations, and Fallon's detail was a piece of cake compared to some of the high-profile officials the agency assigned us to.

"True, but the amount of overtime I've been working has been a killer on the home life."

"Yeah, I'm surprised Marissa let you out of the house tonight," I teased.

"I made it worth her while before I headed over here." He smirked.

"TMI."

"Probably." He chuckled. "I don't know how you do it. I remember how hard it was trying to meet new people and date with our schedules, but you gotta make sure you go out and have some fun."

Little did he know how much *fun* Fallon and I had shortly before he had shown up. The sounds Fallon made when he came were seared into my brain, and the memory would likely replay in my head as soon as I was alone again.

"What's with the goofy grin on your face?" Day asked, pulling me from my thoughts.

"I don't know what you're talking about." I opened a bag of potato chips and poured them into a bowl.

"You're seeing someone, aren't you?" That was the problem with being friends with people trained to notice the smallest detail. "Why didn't you say something before?"

I could lie, but there was no point. Day knew me too well and wouldn't hesitate to call me out. "It's new. Who knows what will happen."

Before he could interrogate me further, the other guys arrived and pulled Day into other conversations.

While we sat around the table playing cards, I worried that admitting to my friend I was seeing someone might backfire if he noticed a change in the way I interacted with Fallon.

HAVING A CHANCE TO RELAX WAS A NICE CHANGE OF PACE, BUT NOT seeing Fallon every day was starting to take a toll on me. Thankfully, Poppy was coming over, and I would be able to focus on her instead of feeling sorry for myself.

When the doorbell rang, I headed to the door and found Alexis and a smiling Poppy standing on the other side.

"Hi, sweet pea." I knelt to hug my daughter.

"Hi, Daddy. Mommy says I get to stay here with you."

I smiled up at Alexis and then looked back at Poppy. "That's right. I have a lot of fun stuff planned for us the next few days."

Her eyes widened. "Like what?"

"Let's get you and all your stuff inside." I eyed the two bags Alexis held and the backpack Poppy was wearing. "And then I'll tell you."

"I know I packed too much," Alexis said as I led them to Poppy's bedroom. "But she kept grabbing stuff she wanted to show you. She was so excited, and I didn't have the heart to tell her no."

"It's not a problem. I don't have a lot of toys for her yet, so at least she'll have things from home to play with."

"This is my room?" Poppy shrieked and ran to the twin bed covered in unicorn sheets and stuffed animals.

"It sure is. Do you like it?"

"Yeah. I love unicorns." She picked up the purple one and squeezed it tight.

Alexis placed the bags next to the dresser. "Poppy, do you want to help put your clothes away before you start playing?"

"Okay." She opened the bag closest to her and pulled out a red velvet dress. "This is my favorite. Can I wear it now?"

I chuckled. "Actually, you should wear it tomorrow when we have breakfast with Santa."

Her face lit up. "We're having breakfast with Santa?"

"Yep, and then I thought we could buy a Christmas tree, and you could help me decorate it."

She bounced up and down and began chanting "Santa" over and over.

"Maybe you should have waited until tomorrow to tell her." Alexis laughed. "She's going to be hyped the rest of the day."

"Probably," I agreed, but seeing the excitement on my daughter's face was worth it.

11

FALLON

Every year, my mother hosted the Breakfast with Santa charity event for children and their families. I never had much interest in the event, but that was before I was dating someone who had a kid.

Holy shit.

I was dating someone, and he had a kid.

When I'd told Rhett I hadn't really dated before, that was true. I'd never had the desire to be with someone long-term before because school and rowing kept me busy. But Rhett was different. I wasn't exactly sure why yet, but something about him made me weak in the knees and also drove me to want to jump his bones at the same time. He was smart and funny, and I wanted to spend every waking hour with him. Lucky for us, we basically got to do that.

Before winter break, that was.

I was counting down the days until we were in my condo alone and sneaking around again. Of course, that meant I would be back in school, so it was a catch twenty-two. At least I could see Rhett for a few hours at my mom's event. I wasn't sure if I would get to speak to him since he would be with his daughter, but I had to hope.

Snow was falling as I exited the building with Agents Day, Leigh, and Meyer. There was no need for me to drive myself because I only did that for school to give me and Rhett more alone time. So, I slid into the black SUV and, as Leigh drove, I pulled out the prepaid phone Rhett had given me and sent him a text:

I sighed.

When Leigh pulled up to the children's museum where the breakfast was being held, I noticed another SUV like the one I was in ahead of us. It stopped, and we pulled up behind it. Was it my brother or sister? My parents were more than likely already inside because the event had started a couple hours ago. In order to accommodate everyone, breakfast was served across several time slots, and my mother insisted on being present for each one.

Once I got outside the vehicle, I looked over to see my brother step out of the other SUV. I walked to him, and we hugged.

"Know if Faye is here yet?" I asked him.

"Nope, but, uh"—he rubbed the back of his neck and eyed his security detail—"I need to talk to you."

I blinked. "Okay?"

He nudged for me to follow him, and I glanced at Day, who was to be the man on the inside with me since Rhett was on leave. He nodded his head as though he understood to give me a moment with my brother, and I followed Finn to a spot several yards away.

He lowered his voice. "I need to borrow some money."

"What?" I snorted. "You have money."

Our parents paid for our housing, all utilities, and any other living expenses. They also took care of our schooling, but Finn and my sister had finished college and weren't pursuing anything beyond their bachelor degrees like I was. In the almost two years since Finn had graduated, he had yet to get a job. It didn't bother me that he lived off our parents, but why was he asking me for money? They gave us extra cash each month for anything additional we wanted, so what the hell was he spending his on?

"I spent it."

I chuckled. "On what? Hookers?"

"No."

"Blow?"

"No," he clipped. "Just, can I get a grand, and I'll pay you back next month?"

"A grand?" I balked. "Why the hell do you need so much?"

"Just"—he threw his hands in the air—"forget it. I shouldn't have asked you."

He stormed past me, and I turned to tell him to wait, but my eyes collided with the baby blues I wanted to get lost in. Rhett was standing with a little girl next to the other Secret Service agents on my detail.

"Everything okay, sir?" Day asked.

"It is. Thanks." I bent down to Rhett's daughter's height. "And who do we have here?"

The three-year-old moved behind Rhett as he said, "Mr. Donnelley, this is my daughter, Poppy. Poppy, this is Fallon, the man I work for."

"The one you keep safe?" She peeked around him.

"Yeah, sweet pea."

Among other things.

"It's so good to meet you, Poppy. How about we go inside? I heard Santa has hot chocolate."

"Really?" Her blue eyes lit up as she moved to his side.

I stood and asked, "Is it okay if I take her inside and get her a cup?"

"Sure." He smiled warmly, and I grabbed Poppy's hand. The agents followed me inside, and Poppy squealed as she took in all the decorations.

My mother went all out, transforming the museum into Santa's village. Every square inch was decked out with lights and ornaments. Elves worked on fake toys in an exhibit as though they were making the presents Santa would bring on Christmas Eve. Seeing how excited Rhett's daughter was made me realize the amazing work my mother did for the event, and then it hit me that she would be in D.C. the next four years, and likely hosting events at the White House instead.

I stopped at the entrance of the room where the breakfast was being held. "Why don't you and your dad find your seats, and I'll get that hot chocolate?"

Poppy let go of my hand, and Rhett held out his phone with the barcode on it for the staff to scan his tickets. Just as I walked away, I peeked over my shoulder, and he winked and mouthed, "Thank you." My heart swelled, and even though I didn't have much experience with kids, I thought meeting Rhett's daughter went well.

If only he could have introduced me as his boyfriend and not the man he works for.

STANDING OFF TO THE SIDE, I WATCHED RHETT AND POPPY EAT THEIR waffles and bacon. Poppy sipped her lukewarm cocoa while Rhett drank coffee. I'd already said hello to my parents and my sister. Finn was nowhere in sight. I wondered if he left, or maybe he was making his rounds and asking everyone for money. I razzed him earlier about why he was broke, but deep down, I knew. My brother had always had a gambling problem. I wasn't sure if my parents knew, and if word got out the president's son had an addiction, there was no telling what would happen. Maybe it would be eye-opening for Finn, and he could get help.

My phone buzzed in my pocket, and when I pulled it out, I realized it wasn't my regular phone, but the prepaid one.

> Can you sit with us?

My gaze moved from the screen and locked with Rhett's. He nudged his head to the empty chair next to him.

> Are you sure?

> Yes, if you can

I had no reason not to. His table was open, and I could eat anywhere I wanted, given that my mother ran the show, but what would the agents think? If anything, I would play it off and say something about Poppy.

I made my way over to Rhett's table, and Poppy beamed.

"Hey, little lady. Are you having a good breakfast?" I smiled warmly.

"When is Santa coming?" she asked.

It was like the man himself was listening because suddenly, the door opened and we heard, "Ho, ho, ho!"

The kids went nuts, and with all eyes on the man in the red suit, Rhett reached under the table and squeezed my knee. I tried to show no reaction as I glanced at the agents standing in the back of the room, but I felt movement below my belt. Luckily, everyone was distracted by the man of the hour.

I took out the prepaid phone again and sent Rhett a text:

> I want to kiss you so badly right now

He quickly sent a response:

> Me too baby boy

> I still want to go to the bathroom and make out

I would if we could

Santa came to our table before I could reply. "Well, hello, Poppy. Are you enjoying your waffles?" he asked.

The little girl's eyes widened as she looked at her father. "Santa knows my name?"

"Of course, I do," Kris Kringle replied. "I have my naughty and nice lists, remember?"

Each table had assigned seating. When the parents purchased their tickets, they entered their child's name. It was an added touch my mother had the great idea of doing, and over the years, I'd watched children react with awe when Santa addressed them by their names.

"Am I on the nice list?" Poppy wondered.

"You'll find out on Christmas morning." He winked and moved on to the next table.

"Daddy, how is Santa going to leave my presents since you don't have a fireplace?"

This girl was too smart for her own good. I turned to Rhett to see what he would say.

"Mommy has one, and he will leave presents there for you."

"But we're still getting a tree?"

"Of course. I need to decorate my apartment, don't you think?"

"I hope we get a really big tree." Poppy took the last bite of her waffle.

"You guys are going tree shopping?" I asked.

Rhett nodded. "Yeah. I had to rent a car because she's still in a car seat and I don't have my own vehicle, so after this, we'll stop by a tree lot and get a tree while I have a way to get it back home."

"That's cool. I've never had a tree in my condo."

"You haven't?"

I lifted a shoulder. "My parents always go all out at their place, and when I was at Hawkins U, we had one in the fraternity house, but since living by myself, I've never seen the need."

"To be honest, I haven't had my own in years because of my job. I had to buy all new ornaments and everything, but I want to make memories with Poppy as we hang each decoration."

I gave him a soft smile as I nodded. "I get that."

"Do you … Do you want to join us?"

My eyes widened. "Really?"

Rhett shrugged. "Sure. You can buy one too, and the guys can tie it to the roof of the SUV to take it to your condo."

"But I have no one to help me decorate." I frowned.

"Then come over to my place and help us."

"Okay." I breathed. "But won't the guys be suspicious?"

He looked over to where Day was standing next to one of my sister's agents. "We'll just tell him it's for Poppy."

RHETT WORKED OUT THE DETAILS WITH DAY AND THE OTHER GUYS TO follow him to the nearest tree lot. I slid out of the SUV and waited for Rhett and Poppy to park. Day stood next to me, and it was on the tip of my tongue to ask him to wait in the vehicle for me. I knew that wouldn't happen, but I wanted to feel some sort of normalcy with Rhett as we walked around while he and Poppy picked the best tree.

Once Rhett unbuckled his daughter's car seat, she jumped out of the car and raced through the open gate. Rhett was quick on her heels, and I followed. The little girl ran up and down every row, looking at the different trees.

"Can we get this one?" Poppy asked, looking at a tree that had to be nine feet tall.

"That one's a little tall for my ceiling," Rhett said.

She took off again and then said, "What about this one?"

Rhett assessed the limbs and then shook his head. "Has a big gap in the back. We need a pretty one."

As we moved around the lot, it hit me that even though I was included in the little adventure, it wouldn't normally be that way. My relationship with Rhett was a secret, and he had a life outside of protecting me.

One I couldn't be a part of.

12

RHETT

Before we left the Christmas breakfast, Fallon went to say goodbye to his parents while I approached Day to tell him about our plans. "Hey, Fallon's going to go Christmas tree shopping with me and Poppy and then come over to my place to help decorate."

A puzzled look crossed his face. "Really?"

"Seems he and this one"—I nodded toward my daughter—"hit it off after she found out he got us these tickets to meet Santa."

"And he gave me hot chocolate." Poppy beamed, unintentionally making my lie more believable.

My friend smiled down at her. "Uh … okay. Are you heading out now?"

Day seemed a little caught off guard by the change of plans, but if he thought it was weird, he didn't say anything. It was probably my own fears causing me to worry that someone might figure out what was going on between me and Fallon.

"Yeah, but we'll meet you outside so you all can follow us to the tree lot."

Once in the rental, I pulled in front of the museum and waited until Fallon slid into the SUV. Poppy chatted excitedly in the backseat as I drove to our destination with Day following close behind.

"We can't get a super big one. It has to fit in my apartment, sweet pea."

"How big can we get?"

"With a star on top, we should probably get one that isn't more than six feet."

"How tall is that?"

"About my height."

She squealed. "That's super tall."

After pulling into the lot, I got Poppy out of her car seat, and she took off for the entrance. I was quick on her tail, not able to see if Fallon was following or not, but after a few rows, I saw him hanging back just a little as my daughter asked about each tree.

"What about this one?" Fallon asked Poppy as he inspected a six-foot Douglas fir.

"Daddy, Fallon found a tree!" she shouted excitedly.

It would definitely fit in my small living room.

"Do you like it?" I asked her.

"I love it."

"Okay." I smiled at my boyfriend. "I think this is the one."

WHEN WE ARRIVED AT MY APARTMENT COMPLEX, I PARKED IN MY assigned space, and Day found an open visitor's spot. Being outside the city made parking so much easier than when we were in Boston.

While I helped Poppy out of the car, Fallon and the other guys came over to help with the tree tied to the roof of my rental. I used the keypad to let us into the lobby of my building, where Meyer stayed to stand guard while I led everyone else to the stairwell. Leigh helped me get the tree up the three flights of stairs.

"Do these guys need to do a sweep of your place before I can enter?" Fallon teased as I unlocked my door.

Day chuckled. "Might not be a bad idea. Hate to see the headlines if anything happened to you in a Secret Service agent's home."

While I wasn't worried about those types of headlines, Day's words made me think about the risk Fallon and I were taking. Sure, we had a valid reason for him to be at my place, but we needed to be careful not to put ourselves in situations that drew attention. Especially when he was so close and I was having a hard time keeping my hands to myself.

"Do you need a broom?" Poppy asked as we walked inside.

I tilted my head. "What do you mean, sweet pea?"

"Fallon needs to sweep. I help Mommy sweep."

Everyone laughed at how adorable my daughter was. "That's just a word Daddy and his coworkers say when we go into a new place to make sure it's safe for Fallon."

"So, where are you going to put this thing?" Leigh asked, looking around the small apartment from the doorway.

Luckily, I didn't have much furniture and didn't need to move anything around to make space. "Probably next to the couch?"

Day placed the stand on the floor and then lay down so he could tighten the screws while Fallon and Leigh held the tree in place.

Once it was set up, Leigh left to post up in the hallway outside my apartment while Day stayed behind.

"Can we decorate now?" Poppy ran over to the bags of Christmas décor I'd bought earlier in the week.

"Of course. We should start with the lights. Do you want to use the white ones or the ones with different colors?"

"Different colors." She bounced around the living room while I took them out of the packaging.

I glanced at Fallon, who stood next to the tree while watching me and Poppy. He was quieter than usual, and I wondered if something was bothering him. The last time he became withdrawn was after I tried to put a stop to things between us. He'd seemed fine at the breakfast event, but had something happened since then I wasn't aware of?

"Day, I need an extension cord for the lights. I have one in the hall closet. Could you grab it for me?" I asked, hoping for a second to speak with Fallon.

"Sure thing," he responded.

When he was out of sight, I walked over to Fallon and whispered, "You good?"

He gave me a small smile. "Yeah. It's just weird with Day here because I don't know how to act without it looking suspicious."

"Yeah, I wish I could tell him to hang out in the hall, but he'd think something was up for sure. I already let it slip during poker night that I was seeing someone, and I don't want to give him a reason to think it's you."

His eyes widened. "You told him you were seeing someone?"

"It's not like I planned to say anything, but Day started talking about relationships and because we're trained to be observant, he noticed something was up with me."

It seemed like Fallon wanted to say something, but Day returned with the extension cord in his hand, and I took a few steps back.

"Found it. Now let's get these lights up."

While Fallon and Day began stringing the lights, Poppy and I searched for a Christmas movie to stream. We settled on *Rudolph the Red-Nosed Reindeer* and Poppy moved back and forth between wanting to help with the lights and watching the movie. With Day on the opposite side of the tree from where Fallon stood, I took advantage of being out of his line of sight and ran my hand across Fallon's back as I walked around him.

He whipped his head around and mouthed, "Behave."

I winked at him.

Once the lights were in place, I told Poppy she could plug them in.

"It's so pretty," she squealed when they turned on. "Fallon, you like?"

He nodded. "I do. You did a great job picking out the multi-colored ones."

Watching the two of them interact made me look forward to the day I could have a normal family life. I'd worked hard to get to where I was with my career, and I couldn't see myself doing anything else. But I also wanted a future where I could enjoy the holidays with Poppy and someone I cared about. It was too soon to know if that would include

Fallon, but most agents didn't work on protective details much longer than six years. When I returned to the field office, I'd have a more normal schedule, which would allow me to have more time with Poppy, and possibly Fallon.

We spent the next thirty minutes placing the ornaments on the tree. At some point, Poppy had become engrossed in the movie, leaving the rest of the work to us. When we were finally done, Poppy was sound asleep on the couch. Alexis had warned me she didn't nap very often anymore, but I guess the excitement of our day had worn her out.

"I should put her in bed," I said as I lifted her into my arms.

Fallon stood. "Okay, I'm going to use the bathroom real quick."

He followed me around the corner from the living room and down the hall, where I pointed out the bathroom before carrying my daughter to her room.

When I laid Poppy in her bed, she mumbled groggily, "Tree done?"

I pulled a blanket over her. "Yeah, sweet pea. You can check it out after your nap."

I thought she'd insist on seeing it right then, but she was so exhausted she fell right back to sleep.

Fallon stepped out of the bathroom at the same time as I was coming out of Poppy's room. Knowing I wouldn't have another chance to get him alone, and Day was around the corner in the living room, I pushed Fallon back inside and closed the door quietly behind us before capturing his lips in a scorching kiss.

"I've wanted to do that all day," I panted when we finally broke apart.

He flashed me a wicked grin. "Too bad we don't have time for more."

"I never thought I would say this, but I can't wait to get back to work."

FALLON AND THE OTHER GUYS HAD LEFT SHORTLY AFTER OUR SNEAKY

kiss in the bathroom, and I started counting down the days until I could see him again.

Later that night, while I lay in bed, I sent Alexis some photos I'd taken during breakfast and then pulled out the prepaid phone to text Fallon.

> I had fun today. Glad we got to spend some time together

I held on to the phone, hoping he'd message back quickly, but minutes passed without a response.

While I waited, I grabbed my other phone and checked my email. One was from Agent Tanner asking me to meet with him the following week to discuss plans for the inauguration in late January. Even though I was technically off work, it wasn't uncommon to get called in. Since I was supposed to be learning more about the detail lead position, it was expected I would be there.

My eyes grew heavy, and I had just drifted off when a notification dinged on the prepaid phone.

> Me too

The short response wasn't quite what I expected, but maybe he was tired too. I sent another message:

> What are you doing?

> Just getting ready to go to sleep

The fact he didn't seem interested in engaging in conversation stung a bit, but I couldn't be mad about him wanting to sleep.

> I'll let you get some rest then. Talk soon?

> Yeah. Good night

> Good night

THE NEXT FEW DAYS PASSED IN MUCH THE SAME WAY. I'D MESSAGE Fallon, and he'd take a while to respond, and our conversations would be brief. Then on Christmas, when I texted him in the morning to wish him a Merry Christmas, I didn't hear from him until almost midnight. I knew he had plans with his family, but I still couldn't help but wonder what I may have done that had him avoiding me.

Two days later, I headed to the command post to meet up with Agent Tanner. Since I had Poppy more, I ended up buying a car so I wouldn't have to rent one each time she stayed with me.

After parking my new vehicle on the street, I made my way into the high-rise. As I walked down the hall, I was tempted to go to Fallon's condo first and talk to him, but with my fellow agents around, it probably wasn't a good idea.

Jones looked up from the camera feeds when I walked inside. "How's it going? Enjoying your time off?"

I shrugged. "It was great while I had Poppy with me. Now, I'm kinda bored."

"Man, you need to get out and live a little." He grinned. "Work isn't everything."

"Says the guy who ditched poker night to volunteer for overtime," I teased.

"I'll catch the next one."

"Davis, thanks for coming in," Tanner said as he stepped out of the hallway. "Let's go to the dining room to discuss plans for the inauguration."

I followed him over to the table where maps of D.C., schedules for the various events happening throughout the day, and blueprints of the hotel where the Inaugural Ball would be held were spread out. While most of the security for the day was being planned out by the agency's leaders, Tanner and I spent hours making plans specific to Fallon's protection. Every agent on his detail would be present that day due to the expected crowds and the logistics of getting him to and from each event he would attend.

By the time we were done, it was almost 2200 hours, and I was ready to go back home and climb into bed.

"Windstorm is ready to leave." I heard the transmission come across the two-way radio on Jones' desk as I passed through the living room.

"Catch you later," I told Jones and headed for the door.

I stepped into the hallway, hoping to see Fallon before he left for wherever he was going. I looked toward his door just in time to see him and a few friends, including Declan, walk out of his condo. Agent Bernard followed closely behind them.

Fallon's eyes immediately locked with mine. "Hey, what are you doing here?" he asked as we all walked to the elevator.

"I had a meeting with Agent Tanner. Where are you off to?" I kept my voice casual because I didn't want him to think I had a problem with him going out.

He shrugged. "We were bored, so we decided to head to Chrome."

He could have texted me if he was bored, but whatever.

13

I HADN'T EXPECTED TO SEE RHETT.

When I asked him what he was doing, he'd said he had a meeting with Agent Tanner. But what was it about? Did he ask to be transferred somewhere else? I knew I was pushing him away, but I couldn't help it. Were we just supposed to date in secret for the next four years? Or was he asking to be relocated so our relationship could be out in the open?

I was quiet on the way to Chrome as I thought about the possibilities. If Rhett asked to be reassigned, would he be moved to my brother's or my sister's team so he could stay in Boston for Poppy? I didn't want him to choose me and then transfer to D.C. or somewhere else just so we could be together. My dad's vice president was from Washington state, which was clear across the country, and Rhett would be so far from Poppy if he were tasked with protecting Vice President Brooks' adult children who still lived in their home state.

"Why are you so quiet?" Declan asked.

I glanced over at him and then back at the road. "Am I?"

"Um, yeah. Usually, you're talking our ears off."

I lifted a shoulder. "Just thinking."

"About what?"

Agent Hottie. "Trying to think of a way I can get laid with all these Secret Service agents around." I looked in the rearview mirror to see Agent Vance tailing me. He was with Agent Bernard and Agent Shea —of course.

"Can't you go to someone's place and have them wait outside?"

I had no clue if I could or not. The agents were so adamant about being inside my condo in case someone came through a window or some shit. The window on the fucking eighth floor. The guy would have to be Spider-Man to get to me. I understood it was protocol, but damn, they had to think it was weird, just like I did.

However, since getting closer to Rhett, I didn't mind it so much. I looked forward to waking up most mornings with him crawling into my bed. How, even when I didn't have school, he was still the agent assigned to work with me. And that was the kicker: I was pushing him away while still wanting my time with him.

Even though I was going to Chrome and my friends thought I was looking for someone to hook up with, I knew I wouldn't. "Maybe. I haven't had the chance, but if I find someone tonight, I can talk to Agent Bernard."

"Can you imagine not getting laid for the next four years?" Marco chuckled in the back seat.

"Hell no," Declan and Luca said in unison.

"There has to be a way," Declan wondered.

There was, but the only one I wanted to be with couldn't be out in the open with me. My friends Tyler and Hayden had dealt with a similar situation when they were messing around while Hayden was our professor. They had almost gotten caught by the school, but they hadn't. They didn't have to wait even a year to be out together, and I had four long years if I kept seeing Rhett.

As I continued to drive and my friends chatted amongst themselves, I realized even though Rhett and I couldn't go out to dinner as a couple or kiss under the trellis in Christopher Columbus Park, we could do other things out in the open that wouldn't get questioned. Or at least I hoped that would be the case.

Could we go to a movie with Rhett sitting next to me while the other agents sat a few rows back? Could we watch a play at the opera house under the same circumstances? Maybe take Poppy to the chocolate factory and say my dad arranged a private tour. We could make our own chocolates and include the other agents, but also share stolen glances and secret touches. We could go ice skating on Frog Pond, and I could accidentally fall on top of him.

So many ideas swirled through my head, and I wasn't sure if any of them would work, but I had to try because the last few days had been torture. I hated it. I felt as though I couldn't text him back right away because I didn't want him to know I was happy he'd texted. I missed him, and while it had scared me before, I had to think something more was possible, given he was the only man I had ever wanted to date.

I suddenly didn't want to go to the club anymore, but since I had my friends in tow, I figured I had to. I didn't even have the prepaid phone with me so I could occupy my time and text Rhett.

Since the Secret Service was following me, they had instructed me to pull my Mustang up to the front and wait while they went inside, then an agent would take my car to park it. I did just that and, like the time I came with Rhett, I walked into the nightclub with Agent Bernard at my side. This time, my friends were following, and we all beelined for the bar.

My friends and I ordered our drinks, I paid, and then we turned to watch the dance floor.

After several minutes, Luca asked Declan, "Anyone catching your eye?"

"Not yet."

"What about you, Fallon?" Luca turned to me.

"Nah. You?"

"There is one hottie out there."

He pointed his finger toward someone on the dance floor, and when I saw who it was, my mouth hit the floor. The guy dancing was a former fraternity brother of mine at Hawkins U: Ford Mahoney. He'd been in the closet and had dated Tyler on the down-low at the beginning of our senior year. Ford had caused a big stink when he caught Tyler and Hayden together and almost had Hayden fired from HU. When I found out what he'd done, I kicked Ford out of our fraternity since I was the president. It didn't matter much. A few weeks later, all of us graduated and went our separate ways, but at the time Tyler was pissed. So was I, because even though Hayden was breaking the rules by dating Tyler, their love was real. So much so the two were getting married.

"Don't do it," I told Luca. "That guy's bad news."

"Really? You know him?" he asked.

I nodded. "We were in the same fraternity. We were friends until he tried to fuck over my friend Tyler. It was a whole thing, and I haven't talked to him since."

"That's a shame," Marco chimed in. "He's cute."

Ford was good-looking, but looks had nothing to do with how much of an asshole he was back then. He hadn't always been that way. Sure, he was a cocky frat guy who banged any chick who wanted to be with him, but he was also fighting with himself about his sexuality. If he hadn't tried to get Hayden fired—because he somehow thought it would make Tyler want to get back together with him—then maybe we would still be friends. Since he was in a gay club, I had to think that things had changed in his life, but I wasn't about to go chat with him— or more.

"He's too young for me," Declan stated. "I'm thinking I want to try someone older. Maybe have them teach me a few things."

"Oh, I wouldn't mind finding a daddy," Marco agreed.

My watch vibrated with a text from an unknown number.

> Come to the bathroom

I glanced across the club to where the restrooms were in the back. Rhett was there, and he nudged his head for me to follow. Since I didn't have the prepaid phone, he'd texted my regular one.

"I need to hit the little boys' room. I'll be back."

"Already breaking the seal?" Declan razzed me.

"Fuck, I know." I chuckled. "Can't help it."

I downed my vodka soda and placed the empty cup on the bar. Agent Bernard followed as I headed toward the restroom. My watch buzzed again.

> Let Bernard do a sweep and then make him stand down the hall

I took out my phone and replied:

> How the hell do I do that?

> Use that sassy mouth of yours and figure it out

Was Rhett teasing me, or was he pissed? I wasn't sure what to make of the sassy mouth comment, but I took a deep breath and continued toward where Rhett had been standing.

"I need to go in first," Bernard stated.

"Of course."

I let him do his thing and searched the hallway for Rhett. I didn't see him, and I wondered how he planned to get inside with me.

Bernard walked out and held the door open. "All clear, sir."

"Great." I tried to keep my cool as I asked, "Can you wait at the end of the hall and not let anyone back? I, ah … need to blow up the toilet, if you know what I mean, and don't want anyone waiting outside the door."

Jesus, help me. I was lying about needing to shit all so I could have a secret conversation with Rhett.

"Sure thing, sir." Bernard switched places with me, and I held the door open as I watched him walk down the hall.

Out of nowhere, I was pushed inside with a hand over my mouth. For a split second, I started to panic, but my eyes locked with Rhett's baby blues and I relaxed. He held a finger over his mouth and then led me into the one stall in the men's room.

"What are you doing here?" I whispered.

"I came to see you."

"Came to see me or spy on me to see if I hooked up with anyone?"

He closed his eyes and shook his head slightly. "I trust you enough for that not to be a concern."

A tinge of sadness hurt my heart. For several days, I had been trying to push him away, and he didn't deserve that.

"I'm sorry." I hung my head.

"For what?"

"I've been trying to push you away."

"What? Why?" He lifted my chin.

I swallowed. "Because as much as I loved spending time with you and Poppy the other day, that could never be us. I'm just the guy you work for, and I figured it was best to end things sooner rather than later."

He took a step back. "You're not just the guy I work for."

"You know what I mean."

"I do, but—"

"But I've had a change of heart."

"Okay?" He arched a brow.

"Maybe there's a way for us to be together and out in the open."

"How?"

"The agency doesn't expect me to sit at home when I'm not in school. Maybe I want to take a walk in Rose Kennedy Greenway Park, or take a drive to World's End and go for a hike when the weather gets warmer. I don't know, but I'm thinking we can make it work."

"I like the sound of those things, but you know we can't touch."

"I know, but at least we can be together outside of my condo."

He took a step toward me and cupped my cheek. "For two guys who haven't been in committed relationships before, we're sure in a crazy situation now, huh?"

"Yeah, but we have to try, right?"

"I want to."

"Me too."

He brushed his lips against mine, and with no hesitation, I deepened the kiss.

"Where were you hiding anyway so Bernard didn't see you?" I questioned once we pulled apart.

"The manager's office across the hall."

"It wasn't locked?"

"Had Perry open it for me."

"Ah. The bartender you've hooked up with." I smirked.

"Be careful what you say, baby boy. You're here with a guy you used to fuck."

"True." I snorted.

Another text vibrated on my watch, and I glanced at it to see it was from Tyler.

> Hayden and I are going skiing in two weeks. Want to come?

"Everything okay?" Rhett asked.

"Do you ski?"

He blinked. "Ski? Yeah, why?"

"Because when you're back on duty, I'm taking you up the mountain and having my way with you."

14

RHETT

I HAD NEVER BEEN AS HAPPY TO RETURN TO WORK AS I WAS WHEN Hawkins Law's winter break was finally over. After the talk with Fallon in the Chrome bathroom, we made an effort to stay connected through texts and nightly phone calls until we could be together again. It wasn't ideal, but we got through it.

Unfortunately, the first week back to school was busier than usual with the start of the new term and rowing practices ramping up. It left little time for us to be alone before and after class. By the time Friday rolled around, neither of us could wait to get on the road for the ski trip.

"Is that everything?" I asked Fallon as I placed his suitcase in the back of one of the SUVs we were taking up the mountain.

Since my colleagues and I would be working three days straight, Tanner was sending two additional agents with us, so we could squeeze in some sleep when possible. Not that I was expecting Fallon and me to sleep much if we could sneak into each other's rooms at the house Hayden and Tyler had rented.

"Yep, and if I forgot anything, we'll hit up a store near the ski resort."

"Let's go," I called out to the other agents standing nearby.

Agents Shea and Vance climbed into one vehicle while Day, Leigh, Fallon, and I got into the other. Sitting together in the back seat with Fallon brought back memories of the first night we went to Chrome. It was then I realized it was going to be nearly impossible to fight my attraction to him.

Day turned toward us. "Are we driving straight to the house or meeting your friends at the lodge?"

"Tyler texted me and said they're done skiing for the day." Fallon replied. "So, we'll meet them at the house."

Hayden and Tyler had made all the arrangements for our weekend away, which wasn't how things were usually done with the Secret Service. But seeing how the trip wasn't official business, certain concessions were made. We'd just have to conduct our sweep of the house when we arrived instead of setting things up in advance. Tyler had sent over the property listing from the rental website of the two-story home, so we'd studied the location and layout. It sat on a secluded part of the lake with few neighbors around to be concerned about, and everyone, including my team, was staying at the house.

The four of us chatted as we began the one-hour drive. With Fallon so close to me, I had to resist the urge to lace my fingers with his or run my hand up his thigh. To distract myself, I stared out the window at the passing mountains dotted with snow-covered trees.

When I glanced back at Fallon, he was typing something on the prepaid phone I'd bought him. A second later, mine buzzed in my pocket.

> You better figure out a way to sneak into my room tonight

I smiled and texted back:

> Only if you promise to be quiet. Who knows how thin the walls are

I'm sure you can think of things to do with my mouth so no one hears me

I groaned and cleared my throat to cover up the sound I'd made. All the while, Fallon sat beside me, grinning and looking quite pleased with himself.

The sun had just started to set when we arrived at our destination. The first thing I noticed when we got out of the car was how quiet it was versus the hustle and bustle in the city.

"Damn, the professor did good," Fallon gushed as he looked toward the house.

The pictures online hadn't done the place justice. The property was stunning, with pine trees surrounding the two-story home and icicles hanging from the roof.

Hayden and Tyler immediately came out to greet us, and after Fallon introduced them to all the agents, Shea and Vance headed inside to conduct their sweep while Leigh and Day walked the outside perimeter.

"Thanks for inviting me up this weekend. I'm sure it wasn't easy to find a place that could accommodate my entourage," Fallon joked with his friends.

"It was no problem at all," Tyler replied. "This lake is where we stayed two years ago, and we just happened to find another rental that was bigger."

Fallon turned to me with humor in his tone. "And two years ago, Tyler thought he was being slick by sneaking away during our fraternity ski trip to spend the weekend with Hayden. But the joke was on them when a storm came through, and they found themselves snowed in. Between Tyler texting me he wouldn't be home until Monday and Hayden canceling class, it wasn't hard to put two and two together and blow their cover."

I found it interesting that Fallon and I were in a similar situation to the one his friends had been in. Maybe that was why he seemed to accept the fact we couldn't go completely public with our relationship.

He understood the risks but had also witnessed how the wait was eventually worth the sacrifices made to be together.

"I'm sure being stuck in a house together for a couple of days wasn't a hardship." I chuckled, throwing a covert wink in Fallon's direction since my team wasn't around.

"I'll admit it was risky, but definitely worth it." Hayden smiled at his fiancé.

Once we got the all-clear, Fallon and I grabbed our luggage from the SUV and walked inside and into an open-concept kitchen that led to a large living room with massive windows overlooking the icy lake.

"Why don't you all get settled upstairs," Hayden suggested. "Dinner should be ready soon."

On the first floor was the primary bedroom, where Tyler and Hayden were staying, and upstairs were four more rooms for the rest of us. Since the other guys were busy retrieving their stuff from the vehicles, Fallon and I headed upstairs to pick our rooms.

He opened the first door and walked inside. I let him check it out because whatever room he chose, I was going to take the one next to it regardless of the amenities.

He stepped out a moment later and waggled his eyebrows. "This bedroom has a bathroom that connects to the room next door."

"I guess I'll take the other one, then." I grinned and went to the other bedroom to unpack.

A few moments later, I spun around as Fallon said, "This is going to be very convenient."

I closed the bedroom door, then walked over to him and wrapped my arms around his neck. "It is, and I plan on taking advantage of it tonight." I placed a gentle kiss on his lips.

"Why wait until tonight?"

"Because your friends are making dinner, and everyone will wonder what we're up to if we don't go down there."

"Fine," he huffed. "But I'm going to call it an early night, and you better not keep me waiting."

"I won't."

HAYDEN MADE A DELICIOUS LASAGNA WITH SALAD AND GARLIC BREAD. While he and Tyler plated tiramisu for us, Tyler turned to Fallon and announced, "We picked a wedding date."

"Oh yeah? When?" Fallon asked.

"Six weeks from tomorrow." Tyler smiled brightly.

"Six weeks?" Fallon echoed. "I still have to plan your bachelor party."

"The bachelor party doesn't have to be a big deal. We can just hit up a bar."

"We aren't going to a bar." Fallon shook his head. "I'll figure something out."

"I'm sure you will. Just don't get my man into trouble." Hayden chuckled.

"What kind of trouble can we get into with all these guys around?" Fallon hooked his thumb in our direction, and we all laughed. I was sure Fallon Donnelley had no problem finding trouble if he wanted to.

After dinner, Tyler turned on the TV and flipped through the channels until he found the Bruins game.

"You're a hockey fan now?" Fallon questioned as he sat on the couch next to his friend.

Tyler shrugged. "Hayden covers their games sometimes, and I've tagged along to a few. Plus, he's friends with Emmett Cooper, remember? They're always talking about hockey when we get together. Figured I should learn more about the sport so I could contribute to the conversation."

"Do any of you guys like hockey?" Hayden asked the rest of us.

"Yeah, but I'm a Flyers fan," I replied.

"But you grew up in Boston," Fallon stated.

"I did, but my dad is from Philadelphia and made me watch all their games as a kid."

"Looks like I need to go to some games when you're on duty so you can watch a real team in person," Fallon mocked.

We all chatted for a little while longer, and then Fallon yawned and stretched his arms over his head. "I'm going to head to bed. The first week back to school kicked my ass."

"Yeah, I think we're going to do the same," Tyler said.

Day, Leigh, and I followed Fallon upstairs. The three of us were going to get some sleep because we were the ones skiing with Fallon in the morning. While we slept, Vance and Shea would cover the night shift.

"Good night," Day said as we walked toward our rooms. "Hope you all sleep well."

Maybe it was the lighting, but I thought I saw a tiny smirk on his face.

"Uh, you too," I mumbled.

Once I was in my room, I pulled out the prepaid phone and sent Fallon a text:

Make sure your door is locked

It is. Now get your ass in here

I double-checked my own door, then walked through the adjoining bathroom and slipped into Fallon's bed. His body was warm as I snuggled against his naked back, and he moaned loudly while pushing his ass against my already hardening dick.

"You need to be quiet, so the others won't hear us." I nibbled his earlobe before I placed a small kiss on his neck.

"I'll be quiet. Just fuck me already."

"Greedy, aren't you?" I chuckled, flinging the covers off us and trailing my hand past his rippled abs to the stiff cock waiting for me.

"For you? Always."

My fingers wrapped around his hard shaft, and he immediately pushed forward, flexing his hips to fuck my hand.

"Please, Rhett, I need more," he whimpered.

"I like it when you beg, baby boy."

I pulled my hand away, reached behind me, and grabbed the bottle of lube sitting next to a condom on the nightstand. Popping the top, I poured a generous amount of the silky substance on my fingers before sliding them down to his ass. I grazed his puckered hole and waited for his body to relax before pressing a finger inside. He immediately squeezed around my digit.

"Fuck, I love how you respond to me," I praised, slipping in another finger.

With the moonlight shining in through the window, I could see his hand fisting his cock as he pumped it slowly.

"I've been waiting for this all day," he rasped, his body writhing against mine.

"You sure this tight hole is ready for me?" I whispered, stretching him a bit more.

"Yes. Fuck me. Please," he groaned.

I withdrew my fingers from him and rolled onto my back. Quickly I unwrapped the foil packet and sheathed my rod before coating it with more lube.

Turning back to him, I lifted Fallon's thigh to give me better access and pushed inside, taking a moment to revel in the warmth surrounding me.

When I began to move, the headboard hit the wall, and we both froze.

"Here." He handed me a pillow. "Put it between the bed and wall."

I did as he asked, and when I moved again, the pillow absorbed the impact. "Good idea." I grasped his chin and angled his face so I could capture his lips in a kiss.

We hungrily devoured each other until I couldn't help but slowly pump into him as we continued to kiss.

Fuck, I could get lost in this man's lips. He was so addicting, and I couldn't get enough.

I knew it wouldn't be long before I came, so I reached around him and gripped his dick and began stroking him.

When he growled into my mouth, I tried to hold back the need to all out fuck him senseless until we both came. Instead, I continued pumping slowly, each thrust bringing me to the brink of ecstasy.

He pulled away from my mouth and pushed his face into the pillow as he moaned.

"Fuck, yeah, baby boy, come all over this bed for me."

It didn't take long before he was gripping the sheets, hot spurts of his cum meeting my hand. I followed right after, filling the condom as I pushed my body fully against his.

We lay there for a few minutes, but I knew I had to get back to my room before we got caught. For a moment, I wanted to pretend we were like any other couple with nothing to hide and could fall asleep with him in my arms.

But I knew that wasn't our reality.

So, with one last kiss I headed back to my bedroom.

AFTER BREAKFAST THE NEXT MORNING, WE ALL HEADED TO THE resort.

The sun shined brightly in the clear blue sky, providing the perfect backdrop for a day on the slopes. We explored a few mid-level runs as a group. The thrill of speeding down a mountain was exhilarating, and I was happy to share the experience with Fallon, as well as have a little bit of fun.

Eventually, Tyler and Hayden decided to take a break and grab a coffee in the lodge. Knowing it might be my only chance to get Fallon alone, I asked him, "Do you want to hit up one of the more advanced trails?"

"Are you trying to show off your stamina again?" He smirked.

I leaned forward and whispered, "Pretty sure I did that last night."

It could have been the cold, but I thought I saw a tinge of red creep up his cheeks.

I walked over to where Day and Leigh stood with their eyes on everyone around us. "Fallon and I are heading up to the top. We'll meet you back down here soon."

Neither of them were expert skiers, so the risk of them wanting to join us was nil, but they also wouldn't stop Fallon from going since I'd be with him.

Day nodded and replied, "Be safe."

"Always," Fallon smirked.

We hopped on the ski lift, and as it began its ascent, I let go of the metal bar and reached for his hand. He squeezed my glove-covered fingers, and a grin spread across his face. It was nice to do something other couples who weren't keeping their relationship a secret did without a second thought.

He placed his head on my shoulder when we were far enough up the mountain that no one could see us, and we continued to hold hands until we reached the top. We hopped off the lift, and instead of going directly to the run, I pulled Fallon in the opposite direction of the other skiers so we could look out over the surrounding snow-covered peaks and valleys sparkling in the sunlight.

"Wow, I've never taken the time to enjoy the view."

Since we were hidden by some trees, I wrapped my arm around his shoulders. "I'm glad we get to enjoy it together."

He turned his head to face me. "Me too."

The chemistry between us was palpable as we stared into each other's eyes. He leaned in closer and captured my mouth with his. We continued to get lost in each other, forgetting about the cold and snow surrounding us.

When we broke apart to take a breath, we stepped behind a group of trees to ensure no one could see us. I ripped the gloves off my hands and tangled my fingers in his hair, pulling him in for another kiss.

"I want you to fuck me so bad," he whispered against my lips.

"Right here?" I asked.

He smiled. "Right here."

15

FALLON

I STARED AT THE NOTECARD IN MY HANDS, BUT ALL I COULD THINK about was the man sitting next to me. Rhett consumed my every thought, and all I wanted to do was take his hand and lead him to my bedroom. Instead, I was studying for a test, and he was trying to help, but my head wasn't in it.

"I need a break." I sighed.

"Okay."

I laid my head on the back of the couch. "I can't wait until the summer when I don't have to study."

"Yeah? What are you going to be doing during your time off from class?" Rhett reached out and grabbed my hand.

He played with my fingers as I responded, "Hopefully interning at a law firm."

"Oh, right. I remember that being mentioned when classes started back up."

School had resumed a few weeks before, and things had been busy since then. In addition to attending classes and our ski trip, I'd also had to fly to D.C. for my father's inauguration. I was officially the son of the president of the United States.

"I don't know where," I said. "We have to apply to law firms; they're not just assigned because we're in law school."

"Right, but it will be exciting to see how law firms function and participate in different interviews."

"For sure. I used to go to my dad's office back in the day before he was a senator, so I'm kinda familiar with some things."

"Did you work there when you were younger?"

I shook my head. "Nah. I would steal snacks from the breakroom, though." We both chuckled. "But I'm not really looking to practice criminal law like he did."

"What do you want to do?"

"Civil rights."

Rhett nodded slowly. "I can see you doing that."

"Are you going to come with me to work too?" I smirked.

He grunted a small laugh. "Pretty much."

"My co-workers and clients are going to love me," I jested.

"They'll feel safe having you as their attorney."

I lifted a shoulder. "I guess."

"Do you think you'll follow in your father's footsteps?"

I arched a brow. "What do you mean?"

"Running for president someday."

"Ahh …" I hesitated. "No, don't think so."

"Why not?"

"As much as politics have been a part of my life, they aren't really my thing."

"Who knows? Maybe that will change. I can see you doing it and fighting for the people."

"Thanks." I smiled warmly. "Guess we'll see what happens, but I'm not sure how the United States would feel about a gay president."

"We won't know until a gay candidate runs, right?"

"Right." I blew out a breath. I wasn't considering running for president, but maybe I'd change my mind in the future. "At least I'll be used to having the Secret Service around by then. I'll make sure you're my lead. You can sneak into the Residence each night."

"By then, I probably won't be working on protective missions."

"Really?"

"Yeah." He nodded. "Agents typically only serve on this kind of detail for about six years before we get burnt out. It's hard working so many hours and not being with family, you know?"

"I do." I frowned. I knew he wasn't able to see his daughter often, but the sadness in his eyes was hitting me hard.

Rhett continued to play with my fingers lazily as he spoke. "I want to help Poppy with her homework, attend her school plays, watch her play sports or dance ballet or whatever she decides she wants to do. I want to spend holidays and birthdays and graduations with her."

I leaned over and wrapped him in my arms. "You will. Even now. Let's make it happen."

"How?"

I pulled back and cupped his cheek. "I guess the easiest is if I had a bond with Poppy and that way, it's not suspicious when I want to join you at those things. I already want to get to know her better, since she's your daughter."

"Oh, yeah?" He arched a brow.

"Of course, I do. She's your kid, and you're my boyfriend."

"Okay, but like when we try to be together, how are you going to do that without the other agents being skeptical?"

I pulled my hand back and thought for a moment as I stared into his eyes. Then my eyes widened as I came up with an idea. "Hold on."

Standing from the couch, I walked to the pile of mail sitting on the dining table I didn't use. I flipped through the junk until I found what I was looking for. It was a flyer to attend a workshop and make a box of chocolates—a Valentine's Day promotion at a local chocolaterie.

I walked back and handed him the flyer. "Let's go make chocolate with her."

Rhett balked slightly. "You want to make chocolate with a three-year-old?"

"Yeah." I lifted a shoulder.

"Do you know how messy that will be?"

"So, we get chocolate on us. I have a washing machine, you know."

"Okay, well, how are we going to pull this off?"

"You're Secret Service, right? You can make anything happen. At least, that's what you told me your first day on my detail."

Rhett snorted. "It's true, but I need a reason for why you want my daughter there."

"Because I like her," I simply responded.

"Do you think that will work?" He grinned.

I shrugged. "I don't know. Just tell them I want to do this and I had the idea that Poppy come along because you'll be there too."

"All right. I'll try to sell this." He stood and wrapped his arms around me, then placed a quick kiss against my lips. "This means a lot to me. Thank you."

***

THE TEAM WAS ABLE TO MAKE THE CHOCOLATE-MAKING WORKSHOP happen. I didn't know many details other than instead of being with a group of people, the chocolatier was letting me and Poppy make chocolates by ourselves. I was almost positive it had to do with me being the president's son and they felt I needed a private lesson. I didn't really enjoy the special treatment, though.

Since Poppy was still in a car seat, Rhett drove her to the chocolaterie, where I was already waiting outside. I beamed brightly as I saw them walking down the street hand in hand. Seeing them smiling and laughing warmed my heart. Damn. I had it bad for the guy.

"Well, hello, Ms. Poppy." I bent to her level. "Are you ready to make some delicious treats?"

"Yeah," she said excitedly. "Can we eat it too?"

"Of course." I held out my hand for her to take and winked at Rhett as I stood. "Let's get inside and fill our bellies with chocolate."

We walked into the building and were instantly hit with the sweet smell of cocoa, and my mouth watered. My detail stayed in the front of the store while Rhett followed me and Poppy.

"Mr. Donnelley, welcome. My name is Elise. I'm a master chocolatier and I'll be your instructor today. Have you ever made chocolate before?"

"No." I shook my head. "First time."

"And what about you, sweetie?" Elise asked Poppy.

Poppy shook her head too.

"Well, in order to do so, you must wear a cool chef's hat and apron," Elise declared.

"Really?" Poppy questioned and peered up at me with her bright blue eyes.

I smiled down at her and then turned to Rhett. He was smiling too.

Elise grabbed two chef hats and aprons from a table that had a giant copper pot on it. "These are for you."

Rhett stepped forward to help Poppy with her hat and child-size apron while I put mine on.

"Poppy, do you want to pick out a shape for the chocolate?" Elise asked.

Poppy nodded enthusiastically and followed Elise to the other side of the room where a table stood with various items on it.

As we watched Rhett's daughter, he leaned over and whispered into my ear, "Bring the apron and hat home so I can fuck you while you wear it."

"Only if I can lick chocolate off of you."

He growled deep in his throat. "Only if I can do the same."

16

RHETT

FALLON AND DECLAN SAT IN THE ROW IN FRONT OF ME IN CLASS. THEY laughed while working on an assignment together, and I couldn't help but think about how the two of them used to hook up regularly. I was no longer jealous of what happened between them, but I was envious they could spend time together in front of others without worrying about the repercussions.

I wanted that. I wanted to date Fallon without feeling as though I needed to look over my shoulder all the time. Without being worried the other agents might think I was standing a little too close or see the desire in my eyes every time I looked at the person who had stolen a piece of my heart already.

Fallon and I took advantage of the time we spent alone in his condo before and after school, but finding opportunities to do things other couples enjoyed was difficult. The trip to the chocolaterie with Poppy a couple weeks ago had been a lot of fun. Watching him interact with my daughter had me falling just a little harder for him, but I also wanted to go on one-on-one dates with him.

When class was over, Fallon and I headed over to The Daily Grind, a coffee shop on campus, for a quick caffeine fix before his last class of the day.

"You want anything?" Fallon asked Day after he completed a quick sweep of the coffeehouse.

"I'm good, but thank you." Day held open the door so Fallon and I could enter but stayed outside.

The smell of coffee brewing and fresh baked pastries filled the small café. We placed our orders at the counter and moved to the side to wait for the barista to prepare our drinks. Fallon had told me earlier he didn't have any plans after school, and an idea struck.

"Do you want to see a movie instead of going back to your condo this afternoon?" I wondered.

He balked slightly. "You'd rather watch a movie than spend the rest of your shift in my bed?"

I shrugged. "I've been wanting to take you on a date for a while, and if we go right after class, we'll probably have time alone at your place before Bernard shows up."

"That sounds tempting. What are you going to tell Day?"

I smiled. "I'm not going to tell him anything. You are."

He glared at me playfully. "So, even though the date was your idea, you're making me do all the work for it to happen?"

I leaned closer to him and whispered, "It's better if he thinks it's a spur-of-the-moment idea on your part. Besides, I'll make it worth your while."

He brushed his hand against my leg and gave it a little squeeze. "You better."

We picked up our drinks when the barista called our names and then made our way outside. Fallon looked at me, and I gave him a subtle nod.

He stepped beside Day and said, "It's been a hell of a week with school. I think I'm going to head to the movies after class to destress."

Day glanced at me, and I gave a curt nod and replied, "Of course, sir. Will anyone be joining you?"

Fallon shook his head. "Nah, I just want to chill."

"Okay," Day said. "I'll let Leigh know about the change in plans while you two are in class."

I escorted Fallon toward the law building with a smile on my face, looking forward to our official first date.

WHEN THE SCHOOL DAY WAS FINALLY OVER, I CLIMBED INTO FALLON'S Mustang while Day got into the SUV with Leigh. Fallon pushed the button to start the car and turned toward me.

"What movie are we seeing?"

"I don't know. I hadn't planned that far." I chuckled and pulled my phone from my pocket so I could search for what was playing.

"We need to work on your dating skills. First you made me talk to Day, and now you don't even know what we're going to watch. You're lucky I'm already into you because if this is the type of first impression you usually make, there may not have been a second date." He winked.

"Hey, it was a last-minute idea. I promise to blow your mind with our next date."

"You can blow something else when we get back to my condo." He smirked and pulled out of the parking spot.

The image of me dropping to my knees in front of him had my dick perking up. It didn't matter that we'd fucked before leaving his place that morning, I couldn't seem to get enough of the man sitting next to me. "I can't wait."

He groaned, and I shot him a grin before scrolling through the movie times on my phone. I didn't care what we watched; I just wanted to be with him. We decided on a random action movie I hadn't heard of that was scheduled to start in thirty minutes.

Finding two open parking spaces close to the theater, Fallon pulled into one while Leigh parked in the other. I'd purchased the tickets on my phone and sent Day his and Leigh's so they could perform their sweep while I directed Fallon to the concession stand.

"Are you a popcorn or candy guy?" I asked when we stepped up to the counter.

"Definitely popcorn."

Once we had our snacks and drinks in hand, Day's voice came through my earpiece. "All clear in here."

"You ready to go in?"

Fallon took a sip of his soda and nodded. "Unless you think we can slip into the bathroom real quick."

Fuck. It didn't take much for me to consider throwing all caution to the wind and taking him up on his offer, but being out in public together was already a risk. I didn't need anyone complaining to management that people were getting it on in a public restroom. Still, I couldn't stop myself from peering around the nearly empty lobby and pressing my body against his. "Let's leave something for the end of the date, yeah?" I placed a brief kiss on his neck.

I felt him shudder, and when I pulled away, he stared at me with heat burning bright in his gorgeous greenish-blue eyes.

We entered the theater, and I took note of the handful of people waiting to watch the movie. Leigh sat toward the front near the emergency exit while Day sat in the back. I took a step toward Day pretending I planned to sit in the same row.

"You're not going to make me sit by myself, are you?" Fallon grumbled.

On the drive to the theater, we came up with the idea for Fallon to say something so it wouldn't raise suspicion about why I was sitting with him, and he played his role perfectly.

"Uh, I guess not." I looked at Day and shrugged.

It was possible the concern I had about someone figuring out Fallon and I were dating was getting the better of me, but I could have sworn I saw Day smirk like he had at the lake house when Fallon and I had gone to bed.

Thankfully, no one else was sitting nearby. We both took off our jackets, and I went to place mine on the empty spot next to me, but Fallon stopped me by clearing his throat.

"Put it on your lap."

I cocked an eyebrow but did as he instructed.

The lights dimmed, and I sank further into my seat, causing my knee to bump into his. The trailers began to play, and he slipped his hand under my jacket and rubbed my thigh. My breath caught as he slowly inched his fingers up to where I wanted his touch.

With my eyes focused on the screen, I helped him unbutton my jeans and I spread my legs to give him better access. Day sat several rows behind us, and I knew he couldn't see as long as Fallon and I faced forward and pretended we were only watching the screen. I felt like a teenager again, but I'd be damned if I was going to stop my boyfriend from touching me, because I was aching for him.

Without hesitation, he reached into my boxer briefs and wrapped his fingers around my hardening dick. When he began to move his hand up and down, my nails dug into the armrest as I tried to maintain my composure. Between him touching me and the danger of getting caught, I knew it wouldn't take long for me to come.

He rubbed his thumb across the crown of my cock, making me shiver and groan slightly.

"You need to be quiet, or I'll have to stop."

I wrapped my hand around his, making him jerk me faster. "You better not. I'm already close."

Pleasure overwhelmed me, and my pulse quickened as he continued to work my shaft with just the right amount of pressure and speed. I tried to focus on the movie trailers playing on the screen but found myself thrusting my hips to match his strokes instead. My entire body shivered when I felt my balls tingle with my impending release.

"That's it, baby. Let me feel you come." Fallon's voice was so low, I could barely hear him over the sounds coming from the speakers.

With a few more pumps, I shot my load all over his hand. From the corner of my eye, I could see the glow from the screen lighting up his face as he smiled brightly, clearly pleased with himself.

Grabbing the pile of napkins I'd gotten from the concession stand, I handed him a few while I used the rest to wipe up. Instead of cleaning his hands right away, he stuck a finger into his mouth and made a show of licking all traces of my cum away.

Damn. So fucking hot.

"I can't wait to get back to your place, where I can have my way with you," I said quietly enough so only he could hear me.

"Looking forward to it."

17

FALLON

WHEN I'D TURNED TWENTY-ONE, A FEW COLLEGE BUDDIES, INCLUDING Tyler, and I had spent the weekend getting shitfaced and gambling in Atlantic City. We partied at the pool during the day, and at night we hit up every club and casino we could. We got little sleep, and it was one of the best times I'd had in my life. I knew I had to take Tyler back for his bachelor party.

While we waited on the tarmac, I pulled out the prepaid phone and sent Rhett a text:

> Think the others will notice if we both slip into the bathroom when we're in the air?

> Want to join the Mile High Club?

> Join? What if I'm already a member?

Rhett's gaze quickly cut to me from where he sat at the front of the private jet across the aisle from Agent Shea. Their seats faced the back of the plane with two empty seats turned forward in front of them. I was on one of the couches, and Tyler was on the other across from me. When my eyes turned to my friend briefly, he cocked his head slightly. My breath hitched. *Shit.*

> Are you?

> No, but it would be fun

> It would, but yes they would notice given there's only four of us on board right now

So far, Tyler thought we were waiting for the pilot and crew to get us going, but little did he know, his brothers were flying into Boston and meeting us at the small regional airport. They had flown in from LA, and I'd had a car service pick them up at Logan International to meet us on the tarmac. I eyed my friend again, and he gave me a look with a raised brow that I took to mean he knew Rhett and I were messing around. His text on my regular cell confirmed it when I slid it from my pocket.

> You either have it bad for your bodyguard or you two are doing more than keeping it professional

I typed out a quick reply:

> What makes you say that?

> You're texting and keep looking at him. Doesn't take a genius to figure it out

> Don't say anything. He could get fired

> I'm not going to say anything but you're messing around with him?

> We're dating

Tyler snorted a laugh, and I glanced to the front to see both Rhett and Agent Shea looking at us. Tyler texted:

> Fallon Donnelley is dating?

> Shut up! But seriously don't say anything

> I won't. You kept my secret about Hayden

> Thank you

A text from Rhett came through on the prepaid phone:

> What's that all about?

> He figured us out

I looked to where Rhett was sitting to watch his face as the text came through. His eyes widened, and he peeked up from the phone.

I sent another text:

> He won't say anything. I knew he was dating our professor and that could have caused a lot of problems. We can trust him

> Hope so or shit will hit the fan

Before I could text either man back, both Rhett and Agent Shea stood. I peered out the small window to see a black town car pull to a stop outside of the plane where Agent Vance was waiting by the steps. Tyler was so engrossed in his phone that he didn't know anything was happening. I didn't make a move, and when his brothers, Dylan and Jase, stepped aboard, the bachelor party officially started.

"Surprise!" they both shouted.

"What are you two doing here?" Tyler stood and rushed toward his brothers. He hugged Dylan.

"Heard there's some guy getting married, and we came to party with him," Dylan stated.

Tyler hugged Jase. "Yeah, but I didn't know you two were coming."

"Fallon called, and we couldn't pass up a trip to Atlantic City," Jase stated.

I stood and shook both of their hands. "It's good to see you two again. Hope the flight from LAX was all right."

"Not as sick as this one," Dylan observed as he checked out the private jet with beige leather seats, white sofas, and all the leg room anyone would need.

"I know," Jase agreed. "Too bad we couldn't take this plane all the way from LA."

The two guys plopped onto the couch where I had been sitting, and Rhett cleared his throat. Tyler eyed me curiously, and I lifted a shoulder and then sat on the sofa next to him.

"Gentlemen, I'm Agent Davis, and I'll be the lead agent on this trip. These are Agents Shea and Vance. Let's go over how this weekend will play out while we get in the air."

TWO AGENCY VEHICLES WERE WAITING FOR US WHEN WE LANDED IN Atlantic City about an hour and a half later. Tyler and his brothers slid into one with Agent Vance, and Rhett, Agent Shea, and I went in the other. I didn't know the agent driving, but I had to guess he was from the New Jersey field office.

When we arrived at the oceanfront hotel and casino, Agent Shea stayed in the SUV with me while Rhett checked in. Once he was done, he came back and opened the back passenger door, where I was sitting.

"Your room is ready, sir."

I slid out and followed him to the elevators. Agent Shea had my bag, and even though Agent Vance was part of my detail, he stayed to help Tyler and his brothers get their things and take them up to their rooms.

People watched us curiously as I slipped into a vacant elevator. When a man tried to join us, he noticed the two men in black, and he slowly backed up. No matter how comfortable I'd become with having a detail, it was still weird to be out in public with them.

We rode up to the forty-third floor, and I followed Rhett as he led us to my room.

"Go ahead and get settled into your room." He handed Agent Shea a keycard and nudged his head down the hall. "Pick your bed or whatever before Vance does, and I'll get Windstorm square with his room."

"Are you going to help me unpack?" I teased.

"You know the rules, sir." Rhett glared.

"Whatever. Just hurry and sweep the room so I can piss."

Agent Shea set my bag down. "Are you sure you don't need my help?"

"I got it," Rhett replied and took the keycard for my room and unlocked the door.

I waited a few seconds while he went inside and Agent Shea walked a few doors down. He watched me until Rhett called, "All clear, sir."

I picked up my bag and stepped into the spacious room. As soon as the door clicked shut, Rhett grabbed a fistful of my sweater and pulled me against his solid body.

"What am I going to do with that smart mouth of yours?" he growled, then kissed me hard.

I moaned into his mouth, my dick hardening, and all I wanted to do was strip my clothes off and let him have his way with me.

Rhett pulled back. "We don't have time for that."

"Oh, come on. We can be fast." I reached for the hem of my sweater and pulled it over my head.

"I thought you guys wanted to play blackjack?"

"Tyler knows about us. I can text him and tell him to stall."

"Fuck." He breathed. "Are you sure he won't say anything?"

"Yes." Since I kept Tyler's secret back at Hawkins University, I had no doubt he would keep mine. "What would be his reason for telling anyone?"

"I don't know." Rhett ran his middle finger down my bare chest to my stomach. "But you know I worry about the agency finding out."

"Agent Shea thinks you're helping me unpack," I joked. "Agent Vance is with Tyler. I think we can make this work."

Rhett grabbed a hold of my belt buckle. "You have a way of breaking down my resolve."

"But giving in to temptation never felt so good."

"Yeah. Now, get naked, baby boy."

RHETT LEFT AFTER OUR QUICK TRYST AND HAD AGENT SHEA STAND watch outside my door while I got ready to head out for the night. I didn't have to text Tyler to cover for us because the thought of someone knocking on the door at any second made me and Rhett race to the finish. I finally understood the appeal of a quickie.

After one last look in the mirror, there was a knock on my door, followed by, "Let's go!"

I swung the door open to see everyone standing there: Rhett, Agents Shea and Vance, Tyler, Jase, and Dylan. "Fuck, I'm coming."

Rhett choked slightly at my choice of words, and I knew instantly he was thinking about our quickie.

"That's it, baby boy. Let me watch you come."

We shared a look, and then he pulled it together and led us to the elevators. Everyone in the group was dressed in various colored long-sleeved button-down shirts, including the agents so they could blend in. The only difference was they had on jackets to cover the bulges on their sides where they were carrying their guns.

"So, what's the protocol if one of us wants to bring a chick back?" Jase asked.

"You're not hooking up in our room," Tyler scoffed.

"You go to theirs." I winked.

Rhett pushed the down button. "Our main priority is to keep everyone safe. The three of you are free to do as you please, but under no circumstance are you to tell anyone his room number."

"Gotcha," Dylan said.

"Or you two can keep it in your pants and have fun with us," Tyler suggested. "You flew here for me."

Jase slung an arm across Tyler's shoulders as the elevator doors opened. "We're just teasing, big bro. But we *are* ready to get drunk as fuck."

"Were we like that?" I asked Tyler.

"Were?" He snorted, and we piled into the lift. "Don't you go to Chrome, like, every weekend?"

"What? No." I scoffed. "I'm busy with law school, thank you very much."

"I'm teasing." Tyler winked.

Tyler was right, though. Before Rhett, I did frequent Chrome looking for someone to hook up with on the weekends if I wasn't too busy with school work.

The doors closed with me between Rhett and Tyler in the back of the elevator. Dylan and Jase were in the middle, and Agents Shea and Vance stood in the front. Slowly, I reached my hand toward Rhett's and linked our pinkies. It was the only subtle thing to do, and he used another finger to rub my palm.

A part of me wanted to fake stomach issues again and have Rhett tend to me in my room while giving the other guys the night off, but I knew that wouldn't work. It would also be unfair to Tyler.

Once the elevator made it to the ground floor, we all piled out, and they followed me to the blackjack tables. All of them were full, except one had four spots open. Tyler, his brothers, and I each placed a hundred-dollar bill in front of us and waited for the dealer to exchange our cash for chips.

Agent Vance walked one way while Agent Shea went the other, and each of them circled the card area. Rhett hung back a few feet and gave me and my friends some space, but I felt his eyes on me.

It didn't take long for a cocktail waitress to appear, and we all ordered drinks. Somehow, the dealer was dealing me shit cards, and my pile of chips was slowly dwindling while Tyler was raking them in.

"Switch spots with me," I said to him.

"What? No." He laughed. "It's not my fault you're bad at this."

"I'm not bad. I'm just getting shit cards."

A man appeared at my side, and I glanced at him to see him leaning on the card table. "Well, lookie who it is."

I arched a brow. "Do I know you?"

"Ah, come on, Mr. Donnelley. I know it's been a few years, but I'd expect you to remember an old friend."

Out of the corner of my eye, I saw Rhett take a step forward. I shook my head slightly and responded to the guy, "And how do you think I know you?"

"Do you forget everyone who lends you money?"

"Ohhhh." I nodded my head. "I get it. Look, dude, I'm just here to celebrate my friend getting married in a few weeks. You need to find my brother."

The guy snorted. "Don't play games with me. Give me the fucking money you owe me."

Before I could utter another word, Rhett moved in and stood between me and the man. "I suggest you walk away," he seethed.

"Or what?" the guy challenged.

Rhett moved his jacket slightly and revealed his gun. "Or we're going to have a problem, and my friends and I"—he nudged his head toward Shea and Vance, who were quickly making their way to us— "don't like problems."

"You can't bring guns in here." The man scanned the casino as though he was looking for security or someone to help.

"The federal government says otherwise. Now, fuck off." Rhett flashed his badge. Seeing him in action was doing all sorts of things to me. All sorts of delicious things.

"This isn't over," the guy bellowed. "I want my money, Donnelley."

Agents Vance and Shea moved in and walked the guy backward and away from us. My gaze met Rhett's as he turned toward me, and I smiled.

"You're my hero," I gushed.

"This is a problem, Fallon," Rhett clipped. "It sounds like your brother is in deep with some people. You need to take this seriously."

"I am taking it seriously, but what do you want me to do?"

"Don't joke about it, okay?"

"Okay." I nodded.

"I'm going to talk to Finnegan's agents, but you should also speak with your brother. If he really does owe that guy money, he needs to pay his debts before this gets out of hand," Rhett stated.

I didn't think Finn would pay, given my brother had asked me for money. Instead, I said, "Yeah, I'll tell him."

"Good." Rhett pulled out his cell.

I turned back to the table and placed my bet as I said to Tyler, "Sorry about that."

"Don't be." He clapped my shoulder. "I can't wait to tell Hayden I saw the Secret Service in action."

I snorted a laugh. "It was hot, huh?"

"Hell, yeah."

Rhett looked up from his phone, clearly listening to our conversation, and gave me a flirtatious smile. My heart skipped a beat.

I don't know when it happened, but I realized I'd fallen in love with Agent Rhett Davis.

18

RHETT

THE MONDAY AFTER TYLER'S BACHELOR PARTY, WE FLEW TO Washington, D.C., because President Donnelley was hosting the first state dinner of his presidency, and he wanted his family in attendance.

Walking the halls of the White House was surreal. Only a few months prior, I had believed I would be working there while protecting the president. I hadn't expected to be reassigned to Fallon, nor did I ever imagine falling for him. Any disappointment I'd felt when I was informed I'd be staying in Boston was long gone, and I was starting to believe fate had intervened and brought us together.

I received a text from Fallon:

> Can you come to my room?

> On my way

I headed in his direction, passing a couple of agents on duty along the way, and knocked on the door of the guestroom in the Residence where Fallon was staying.

"Come in," he called out.

"Everything okay?" I asked as I stepped into the room and shut the door behind me.

Fallon stood in the middle of the room looking hotter than sin in his black tuxedo, which highlighted his well-developed arms and chest. I couldn't help but stare.

As he walked closer to me, my eyes flicked up, and I saw the intensity in his gaze. He stopped when we were toe-to-toe, wrapped a hand around the back of my neck, and crushed his lips to mine. The kiss sent sparks of electricity through my entire body.

When we pulled away to catch our breaths, he leaned his forehead against mine. "I wanted to do that now because I don't think we'll get another chance the rest of the night."

"I'm not sure that was a good idea."

He took a step back. "Why not?"

"Because it was already going to be nearly impossible to keep my hands off you, looking as gorgeous as you do." I ran my hands down his chest. "But now I'll be spending the rest of the night thinking about your mouth and all the other things you can use it for besides kissing."

"I really wish we had more time to explore that, but I'm supposed to meet the president of France in about five minutes." He winked.

"I know, baby boy." I straightened his bowtie. "Let's go join your family."

Fallon reached for his phone, and I shook my head.

"Shit. Of course, my dad would have a fucking no electronic devices rule. I'm already not wearing my watch. Can't I keep my phone in my pocket?" he all but whined.

"I doubt your father will be thrilled if your phone goes off while you're sitting with President Durand."

"I'll put it on silent."

"And if you get a call or text, what will you do?"

"I can be discreet and check it under the table or something." He stuck out his tongue, and I resisted silencing him with my mouth.

"I think you can manage a few hours without it."

"Fine," he groaned. "Stupid rules."

I chuckled. "Some rules are made to be broken, but I think this one you can handle."

"Says the man who doesn't have to spend all night listening to political talk."

I reached for the doorknob. "I'm sure you'll find some way to entertain yourself."

"I know exactly the kind of *entertainment* I'd rather have."

I opened the door instead of responding. If we continued flirting, we would both be naked in seconds, and we couldn't do that for a number of reasons.

At the entrance of the State Dining Room, President Donnelley and his wife waited with Finnegan and Faye for Fallon to join them. The second I caught sight of Finnegan, my fists clenched as I remembered the danger he'd put my boyfriend in during our trip to Atlantic City. I hated to think what would happen if Fallon hadn't had his security detail with him. That was probably why Finnegan was still hitting the card tables hard. Maybe he assumed he was untouchable since he had the Secret Service watching his back.

After the asshole approached Fallon at the blackjack table, I reported the incident to Agent Tanner. Within a short time, the team had managed to get an ID on the guy. He had a few misdemeanors, but nothing that caused concern. And since no actual threat was made, we couldn't go after him. Still, I made it clear to Fallon he needed to confront his brother about the incident. He promised me he would handle it, and while I trusted him to keep his word, I was going to use my time during the dinner to do a little investigative work of my own.

Before I could say anything to Fallon about my plan, he was called for by the press so they could capture a few photos of the entire Donnelley family together. I stepped back, making sure I didn't appear in any of the pictures.

"Agent Davis, how's it going?"

I glanced to the side and found Agent Ramos from Finnegan's protective detail making his way toward me.

Perfect.

"Just the man I wanted to see." I stuck out a hand for him to shake.

His brow furrowed, but he clasped my hand anyway. "Really? Why's that?"

"Let's move away from all these cameras," I suggested.

President Donnelley's agents were covering the inside of the dining room while the rest of us were expected to monitor other locations throughout the White House, and that provided the perfect opportunity for us to slip away undetected.

I led Ramos into the Red Room to give us some privacy and closed the only open door.

He crossed his arms over his chest. "What's up?"

"I need to ask you a few questions about Finnegan."

"What about him?"

"Back at Thanksgiving, you mentioned he plays poker at some sketchy places." He nodded, and I continued, "Do you know if he owes anyone money?"

Ramos shook his head "Not that I know of."

"No one has approached him while he's been playing?" I pressed.

"I haven't seen anybody. Why?"

"A guy named Joseph Hughes came up to Fallon while he was playing blackjack in Atlantic City. Hughes demanded "Mr. Donnelley" repay him the money he borrowed, but Fallon doesn't owe anyone money. Since Hughes used their last name, we're assuming it's Finnegan he's looking for."

"Could be. Did you bring in the FBI?"

"No. No crime was committed, and when I reported it to my team lead, he said it needed to be handled as a family matter, so the press didn't get a hold of the story." I crossed my arms over my chest. "We did, however, get access to the cameras from the casino so we could identify the guy."

"Shit," Ramos muttered. "This could get messy."

I nodded. "I know, and I agreed to give Fallon time to handle it with Finnegan because he doesn't plan on going back to Atlantic City any time soon. Our investigation into this guy didn't raise any red flags, and I'm assuming he just wants his money back and then will go away quietly. But I'd still like to gather as much information as possible."

Ramos ran a hand down his face. "A few weeks ago, I overheard Finn talking to someone on speakerphone, and they called him Fallon. I thought it was weird, but I didn't think about it any further. It's possible Finn has been using his brother's identity when borrowing money."

I sighed. It was likely that was what was happening, but it was all speculation. I needed more than assumptions. "Do you think you could try to find me proof?"

"That's probably not a great idea."

"Why not?"

He rubbed the back of his neck. "C'mon. Would you let someone search through Fallon's things."

"I would, if it was a matter of keeping another member of the president's family safe," I lied. Once I'd reported the situation, Tanner became responsible for deciding how it was handled, but I couldn't seem to drop it.

Ramos considered it for a moment, and then said, "Finn left his phone and wallet in the guestroom he's staying in. We can start there."

While Fallon had bitched about the no electronic rule, I was instantly grateful for it. Searching the room of the son of the president of the United States definitely crossed some lines, but there wasn't anything I wouldn't do to keep Fallon safe.

"Let's go."

I followed Ramos toward the stairs to the Residence, and we both nodded at the various agents we passed along the way. Luckily, once we reached Finnegan's door, no one was there, and we were able to sneak inside without anyone noticing us.

On top of the dresser on the far wall, I saw Finnegan's cell and wallet Ramos had mentioned. The phone was password protected, and it was highly unlikely we'd be able to bypass the security feature without the help of one of our tech guys. Knowing that was a dead end for now, I grabbed the black leather wallet and flipped it open.

Jackpot.

"Did you find something?" Ramos asked.

"Yeah." I slipped the evidence out of the wallet and headed to the door.

"Wait, you can't take Finn's stuff. He's gonna notice."

"Technically, it's not Finnegan's."

"What do you mean?" He walked over to me.

I flipped over the card in my hand, so he could see it. "It has Fallon's name on it."

"Shit." He sighed.

"I have to take this to him."

Ramos nodded. "All right, but keep me posted. If shit is going down, I need to prepare my team."

I had no idea how things would play out after I talked to Fallon, but I understood the need for my fellow agent to be kept in the loop. "Will do."

The wait staff was serving the main course when I stepped inside the large dining room. I searched for Fallon near the head table, and when our gazes met, I nudged my head for him to join me, hoping he understood I needed to speak to him.

He took a sip of water and then whispered something to his mother before he walked in my direction. I led him to the same room where I'd talked to Ramos and closed the door behind us.

"What's up?" Fallon asked.

"Take a look at this." I handed him the plastic card and waited as he flipped it over.

His forehead creased in confusion. "What are you doing with my credit card?"

"Good question. But you might want to ask your brother since I found it in his wallet."

19

FALLON

I STARED AT THE CREDIT CARD IN MY HAND. HAD FINN STOLEN IT FROM me? How did he get it, and why did he have it? I had no clue because we didn't pay our credit card bills. My parents' money manager took care of everything.

"You need to speak with Finnegan sooner rather than later," Rhett urged. "Agent Ramos heard him use your name when he was on the phone with someone. I don't like that."

My head shot up to look back at Rhett. "My name?"

He reached out his hand but pulled it back quickly. "Something isn't right, Fallon. That guy in Atlantic City, Finnegan using your name, and now finding your credit card. Your brother is involved in some shady shit, and you need to find out what it is."

I continued to study the card in my hand, my mind spinning. Was it a new one from my parents or one Finn had opened using my name? And why? "He asked me for money, you know?"

"He did? When?"

I nodded and met Rhett's stare. "Yeah, at the Breakfast with Santa."

"Why didn't you tell me?"

I lifted a shoulder. "Didn't think it was anything serious. I know he has a gambling problem and thought he just blew through his allowance for the month."

"Did you give him any?"

"No." I shook my head. "Of course not. And I don't think this is one of my credit cards."

"I figured that."

"Fuck." I ran my hand down my face. "What do I do?"

"Talk to him."

"Now?"

Rhett looked toward the door. "Yeah. Never mind he's fucking up your credit by getting cards in your name, he's also putting you in harm's way, and you know this because of Atlantic City. You need to deal with it now."

"But what about the dinner?" I knew Rhett was right, but having a confrontation with my brother at the White House during a state dinner wasn't something I wanted to do. I didn't want word to get out to anyone in attendance, especially my parents and the president of France. That was all my father needed.

"I know right now isn't ideal, but we need to get ahead of this. You were already approached by someone wanting their money back. What would have happened if my team and I weren't there?"

"I would have kicked that guy's ass." Rhett tilted his head and stared at me without a smile. I grimaced. Clearly, he wasn't in the mood for my jokes. "I'm kidding. I don't know what would have happened."

"Let me get Ramos to bring Finnegan in and put a stop to this shit so nothing else happens."

"Okay." I blew out a breath. "Bring me a shot of vodka too."

Rhett turned and left the room. A few minutes later, Finn walked in with Rhett and Ramos on his heels. Rhett *didn't* have my shot of vodka.

"What the hell, Fallon?" Finn questioned as he walked closer.

Rhett closed the door they passed through.

"You tell me." I flung the credit card at my brother.

He picked it up. "Going through my things?"

I crossed my arms over my chest. "That's not the issue here. Why the fuck do you have a credit card in my name *in* your things?"

"Don't worry about it," he scoffed. "It's not like you pay the bill."

"That's not the point. You're committing fraud and can go to jail."

Finn chuckled. "Are you going to call the cops?"

"Do you think this is a fucking joke?" I bellowed. My body temperature was rising, and I could no longer keep my cool. I didn't expect my brother to be so nonchalant about the situation.

He glanced toward where Rhett and Agent Ramos stood by the door and then back at me. "Look, I needed money, so I took an advance out on the credit card. I have it under control."

"You have your own cards. Why the fuck did you need one in my name?"

"Mine are maxed out." He shrugged.

"Then open another one in your own name!" I roared.

Rhett took a step forward, and I cut my eyes to him. He got the hint and stepped back again.

"I did, but the last time I tried, I was denied," Finn responded.

I balked. "What? You've opened up cards on your own and not paid them or something?"

"I will pay them. I just need to win—"

"*Will* pay them?" I threw my hands in the air and looked up at the white ceiling. "Jesus Christ, Finn. Are you paying the one in my name? Are there more?"

"I have it under control."

"And what about Joseph Hughes?"

He blinked. "Joseph Hughes?"

"Yes!" I paced in a circle. "He came up to me in Atlantic City asking for his money."

"Oh. Don't worry about him." Finn waved his hand in front of him as though it was no big deal. "I don't go there anymore."

"But I do, and we fucking look identical, you asshole."

"I said I have it under control, okay?"

"You fucking better." I snatched the credit card from his hand. "If I find out that you opened another card in my name—"

"What? You'll tell mommy and daddy?" Finn mocked.

I was two seconds away from punching my brother in the face. Instead, Rhett strode across the room and got in the middle of us.

"We're done here," Rhett stated and grabbed my elbow. "Let's go."

I didn't hesitate as he escorted me out of the room and toward the stairs leading up to the Residence. "Where are we going?"

"To cool off before you go back to dinner and cause a scene."

"This was your idea," I reminded him.

"I know." He released my arm as Agent Day came into view.

"Everything okay?" Day asked.

"Yeah," Rhett replied as we started up the stairs. "I'll fill you in later. Fallon needs to cool off for a bit. We found out some info about the guy in Atlantic City and his tie to Finnegan."

"Shit. Okay. Let me know."

Once we got to the top of the stairs, Rhett said to me, "You need to have whoever manages your money do a credit check to make sure there aren't other accounts."

"Right." I blew out a breath. "What the fuck is Finn thinking?"

"Addictions are real. He needs help."

"Yeah."

We walked into my room, and Rhett closed and locked the door. I tilted my head slightly as I wondered why he had locked it.

"Pull your pants down," he ordered.

"Wha … what?"

Rhett licked his lips. "Seeing you stand up for yourself was fucking hot, baby boy. Now, pull your pants down and let me make you come so we both feel better."

I gulped. He couldn't be serious, could he? We were in the White House.

My heart was still pounding after my confrontation with my brother, and seeing the look in Rhett's heated gaze, another part of me was definitely pumping.

He kept his eyes locked on mine as he slowly took a step forward and dropped to his knees. "I said take off your pants," he growled, and unhooked my belt.

Looking deep into Rhett's ocean-blue eyes, I held his stare while helping him pull my dress pants down and free my dick.

He licked his lips again and leaned forward before barely grazing his mouth against my tip.

"Fuck," I moaned, raking my fingers through his hair.

"That's just the beginning tease, baby boy," he murmured, one hand going to my hardening shaft as the other cradled my aching balls.

His rough hands were like heaven against my body, and my hips met the rhythm of his hand pumping my cock.

"Yeah, that's it, show me how much you want this. How much you *need* this," he rumbled before trailing his tongue down the thick vein of my length.

"I do need this," I managed to breathe as he wrapped his plump lips around the head of my dick.

His tongue moved with the bobbing of his head, taking me almost to the hilt. All the while his stare stayed locked on mine. Fuck, there was nothing hotter than seeing him engulf me before pulling back and jerking my cock coated with his spit.

He dove back in and sucked me harder.

"Your mouth feels so good," I murmured, and guided him in the same tempo as my hips. "Will you let me come down your throat?"

His strangled response reverberated around my shaft as he nodded.

"Fuck, Rhett. Fuck," I moaned, my eyes rolling to the back of my head as his tongue did wicked things to me.

I was so close.

As if he knew how near I was to erupting, he lifted his free hand between my legs. His fingers worked quickly, trailing the sensitive skin leading up to my puckered hole. I braced myself against the wall as my knees started to shake.

"I'm going to come," I moaned, and a few seconds later, my body jerked as I unloaded into his sinful mouth.

Rhett closed his eyes briefly as he swallowed, taking every last drop, then he stood and wiped his mouth with the back of his hand before grabbing the back of my neck. He tugged me to him, and our lips met, tongues intertwined as I tasted my own saltiness as we kissed.

I reached for the bulge in his pants, but he stopped me by stepping back.

"There will be more time for that later, baby boy. We should get back before anyone starts questioning our absence."

"Promise?"

He pulled my hand to his lips, placing a light kiss against my knuckles. "Promise."

THE FOLLOWING MORNING, WE WERE SUMMONED TO THE OVAL OFFICE, and I felt like I was back in high school and being called into the principal's office. I wasn't sure how my father found out, but when Rhett knocked on my door and told me my dad wanted to speak with me and Finn about the incident in the Red Room, I figured that my dad knew shit was going down.

"You should know I was the one to tell your father," Rhett stated.

I glanced over at him as we neared the West Wing. "How?"

"I went to his lead agent and told him what was going on and that I needed to speak with your dad."

"Oh," I breathed. It didn't bother me that Rhett had gone to my father without me knowing because it was likely part of his job, and he could get in trouble for not reporting the situation. Plus, it also showed me he would go above and beyond to keep me safe.

"You're going to lay it all out there, right?" he asked.

"Absolutely. Finn pulling this shit isn't cool."

"And it's dangerous."

I stopped and faced Rhett. "I know, but lucky for me, I have you to keep me safe."

"Oh, now you like having a detail on you." He smirked.

I stepped closer and lowered my voice. "On me. *In* me. I love it all now."

Finn walked around the corner, and I stepped away from Rhett. My brother didn't say anything as he passed us and entered my father's office.

"Go put an end to this so we can head home," Rhett ordered.

"Or"—I grinned—"we can wait for my dad to leave his office, and then we can role play. I'll be Monica and you can be Bill."

Rhett shook his head and chuckled. "I'm going down to work out in the gym so I can continue to build up my stamina up for you."

"So, Mile High Club, then?"

Rhett was still shaking his head and laughing as he walked away without responding. One day, we would join that club.

Taking a deep breath, I made my way to my father's office door. It was open, and I stepped inside.

"Close the door and have a seat," my dad instructed and motioned to the empty chair on the left side of his desk. Finn was seated in the chair on the right, and I knew the conversation was serious because instead of sitting on the couches in the center of the room, it was as though we were being separated like children fighting.

My father sat in his black leather chair behind the desk and took a deep breath. "I had a nice chat with Agent Davis this morning. Imagine my surprise when he told me my son was committing fraud."

My gaze shot to Finn's, and he glared at me. "Your guy ratted me out?"

My guy ...

"You're the one who's a criminal," I spat.

"Enough!" Dad bellowed and slapped the top of his desk. "Agent Davis came to me personally to avoid word getting out about my son opening credit cards in someone else's name."

"I don't see the big deal," Finn scoffed. "I'm going to pay the bills."

I snorted. "Do you even know how? You've never paid a bill in your life."

Dad stood abruptly, the chair hitting the table behind him. "Both of you knock it off. I didn't call you two in here to fight. I heard you did that in the Red Room last night. If anyone heard you two and reported it to the media, do you know how bad that would look for our family?"

"Why am I even here?" I questioned. "Finn's the one who's stealing my identity and opening credit cards in my name, as well as borrowing from loan sharks. I've done nothing wrong."

"You never do anything wrong. You're the golden child," Finn mocked and rolled his eyes.

I opened my mouth to respond, but my father spoke instead. "You're here so you can be assured the situation is being handled."

"I'm, like, one win away from paying everything off," Finn huffed. "Calm down."

I rolled my eyes but kept my mouth shut, waiting for my father to lay out his plan.

"You're not gambling anymore. We're going to pay off your debt, and you're getting treatment for your addiction."

"I don't need help!" Finn stood.

"You will, and that's an order."

"From my father or the president?" Finn snorted as he paced in a circle.

"Do you think this is all a joke?" Dad asked. "Do you know what could've happened to Fallon in Atlantic City if his detail hadn't been there?"

"He would have just been roughed up a little."

"Roughed up?" I scoffed. "You really are delusional."

"All right. We're done here," my father stated. "If I get wind of any more wrongdoing, the consequences will be worse."

Finn wasn't really facing any consequences, considering he got his debt paid off, but whatever.

At least my name wouldn't be involved in his schemes anymore.

20

RHETT

> Be ready to haul ass as soon as class is over

A SMALL CHUCKLE ESCAPED MY LIPS AS I HELD THE PREPAID PHONE under the table and typed out a reply to Fallon:

> You expecting some action before you take off for the wedding?

> Hell yeah I am

Fallon was leaving in a couple of hours to attend Tyler and Hayden's wedding, and I wasn't going with him. Once he left, I was heading to Alexis' house to pick up Poppy. She was turning four and it was the first time since she was born that I would be spending her birthday with her.

The moment Professor Holmes dismissed the class, Fallon jumped out of his seat and headed for the door. When we entered the hallway, Day met us and followed us outside.

"What's the rush?" Day asked as Fallon practically ran down the steps outside.

"I forgot to wrap Tyler and Hayden's present," he lied. I'd seen the gift on his coffee table before we'd left for school. "I suck at wrapping, so it'll probably take me a while, and I want to make sure we leave on time."

Day glanced at me, and I shrugged, hoping he bought the excuse.

Fallon unlocked his Mustang, and I slid onto the leather passenger seat. Before I had a chance to buckle my seat belt, he shifted the car into reverse and pulled out of his spot.

"You need to wrap Tyler and Hayden's gift?" I gave him a teasing look.

He barked out a laugh. "It was all I could think of. I couldn't exactly tell him I was in a hurry for you to fuck me before I left, now, could I?"

"Good point." I placed my hand on his thigh. "But maybe you should slow down a little so we make it back to your place in one piece."

"Fine." He slowed down. "That just means you're going to have less time to rock my world. Hope you're up for the challenge." He waggled his eyebrows.

"What's up with you doubting my abilities?" I grinned. "If we weren't so close to your place, I'd show you how quick I could make you come right here in your car."

"Sounds like something we need to test out the next time we go for a drive." He winked.

A few minutes later, Fallon turned into the parking garage and pulled into his space. We climbed out of the car and walked toward the elevator, where Day joined us while Leigh went to the front of the building to sweep the perimeter. We rode up to the eighth floor and walked toward Fallon's condo.

"Do you still want to leave in an hour?" Day asked as Fallon unlocked his door.

"Yeah. I think an hour should be enough time for me to do everything I need to." Fallon glanced at me and smirked.

Day nodded. "Okay. I'll make sure the team will be ready to go."

Along with Day, agents Vance and Bernard were going with Fallon to the wedding while Leigh and I took the afternoon off. As much as I was looking forward to spending the evening with my daughter, I also wished I could go with Fallon. If we were careful, we could have treated the wedding like another date. Plus, I could have stared at my hot boyfriend in formal wear all night. Flashes of me on my knees sucking him off while he wore his tux at the White House crossed my mind. Damn, I was already hard.

"Thanks." Fallon opened the door. "I better go wrap that present."

I choked back a laugh and followed him inside. The second the door clicked shut behind me, Fallon pushed me against the wall and captured my lips with his.

I wished we had time to take things slow, to savor every last minute we had together. But as soon as I ripped Fallon's shirt over his head, my cock had other ideas.

We fumbled across his condo before finally entering his bedroom. The rest of our clothes were shed and left in a pile on his floor. We collapsed on the bed together, and Fallon twisted around to open his bedside drawer. In no time, a bottle of lube and a condom were shoved into my hand.

"If you're that eager, why don't you take charge?" I smirked.

"You mean …?" he whispered.

I propped myself up against the headboard and pulled him onto my lap. "Wrap me up and then ride me," I growled, handing him the foil packet.

A wicked gleam caught his eye as he ripped open the condom and slid it down my aching cock. Fallon's hard dick grazed mine, causing him to moan as he snatched the lube and let the liquid flow down my shaft.

Grabbing the back of his neck, I brought his lips to mine. Our tongues tangled as we rubbed our bodies together, the friction alone making me groan.

"I've been wanting you to fuck me all day," he whispered into my ear.

"Then take what you want, baby boy."

He squirted more lube onto his fingers and reached behind him as he rose onto his knees. His eyes closed as he prepared himself for me.

Once he was ready, he grabbed the base of my dick and then slowly inched his ass down onto me.

"Oh, I think I like this angle," he breathed, running his tongue over my bottom lip.

"Me too," I gasped, lifting my hips to push into him, and relished the feeling of his tight little hole.

"Stroke my cock while I ride you," Fallon ordered and then gripped my shoulders to use them as leverage while he rode me.

"Yeah, just like that." I slipped my hand between us and pumped his swollen cock.

He picked up the pace, and my balls started tightening. I stroked him faster, my heart rate picking up as I felt my release building, but I refused to fall over the edge without him.

"Come for me. Let me see you," I breathed.

"Fuck," he cried, warm spurts coating our chests.

"Yes," I grunted, filling the condom.

He collapsed onto my chest, both of us sweaty and sticky.

Once our breathing returned to normal, Fallon stood and reached out his hand for me. "Come shower with me."

I checked the time on my phone. "You've only got a few minutes before you're supposed to leave."

He smiled. "We'll be quick."

I followed him to the bathroom and took care of the condom while he turned on the tap. We stepped inside, and despite knowing he needed to hurry, the rivulets of water running down his body highlighted his powerful muscles and had me dropping to my knees.

"Fuck, Rhett," he moaned as I took him to the back of my throat.

Between my hand playing with his balls and my mouth working him over, it only took a few minutes for him to say, "I'm going to come," and then spill his seed across my tongue.

"Looks like I had enough time to make you come twice." I beamed as I stood.

"Fine. I won't question your abilities next time." He rolled his eyes playfully. "But now, I'm late."

We stepped out of the shower and began drying off. "I'm going to grab us a couple bottles of water, and I'll let Day know you'll be down in a few minutes."

He placed a soft kiss on my lips. "Thanks."

I slipped on my jeans and grabbed the rest of my clothes and two-way radio from the floor. Walking into the living room, I tugged my shirt over my head. When the fabric cleared my face, I stopped dead in my tracks.

Day stood in the middle of the room. When our eyes met, he lifted a brow in question.

"Uh …" I tried to think of any plausible excuse as to why I walked out of Fallon's bedroom half naked. I came up blank.

Day's face was red as though *he* was the one who had been caught in a compromising position. "Team is ready to go. Wanted to see how much longer Fallon would be."

Panic started to set in. "He's almost ready. Did you try to call me on the radio?" If he had, that meant the other agents on duty would know we were unresponsive.

He shook his head. "I knocked, but when you didn't answer, I let myself in. I heard the water running and both your voices coming from the bathroom."

"I can explain," I grimaced.

He let out a breath. "You don't need to explain anything. To be honest, I've suspected something was up for a couple months now."

"You have?"

He chuckled. "I noticed how close you and Fallon had become, and after you told me you were seeing someone, it wasn't hard to put two and two together. Besides, you two aren't nearly as sly as you probably thought you were."

I sat on the couch and rubbed a hand over my face. "Do you think anyone else has noticed?"

"Probably, but no one has said anything to me."

"Look, I know I need to tell Tanner. Just give me some time."

He held up his hand. "Hey, I'm not going to tell our boss. It's no one's business."

"The agency probably disagrees with that."

"Yeah, probably. But I also know how hard it is to juggle a relationship and this job. If you found someone you want to be with, I won't judge you for it. If anything, you're smarter than the rest of us. At least when you have to travel for work, you still get to be with your person."

A smile spread across my face. I shouldn't have expected anything different from my fellow agent, who was also one of my best friends. I knew I could trust him to keep our secret until it was time to come clean.

"Hey, handsome, did you let—" Fallon rounded the corner and then came to an abrupt halt. His gaze flicked between me and Day.

I stood and walked over to him. "He knows. In fact, he's suspected for a while."

Fallon rubbed the back of his neck. "Is … ah, is that going to be a problem for us?"

"No." Day shook his head. "Your secret is safe with me."

"Thank you," he breathed and then turned to me. "I guess I should hit the road. I don't want Tyler panicking because I'm not there."

"I'll be waiting in the hall," Day advised and opened the front door.

Once the door was closed, I cupped Fallon's face and captured his mouth in a passionate kiss.

Fallon squeezed my hand. "Tell Poppy happy birthday for me."

"I will." I grabbed my shoes and put them on while Fallon made sure he had everything he needed.

We walked as a group to the parking garage, and with one last glance, we went our separate ways.

21

FALLON

TYLER AND HAYDEN WERE GETTING MARRIED ABOUT THIRTY MILES south of Boston on Lake Massapoag. It had snowed the night before, and as Agent Vance pulled up to the charming two-story manor house, staff members of the estate were plowing paths and sprinkling salt on the walkways. While I was excited for my friends, I couldn't help but feel a little bit of sadness since Rhett wasn't with me.

Agents Day and Bernard stepped out of the SUV, and Agent Day turned back to me. "We'll be back, sir."

I took the prepaid phone out of my jacket and sent a text to Rhett:

> I miss you already

He quickly replied:

> Me too, baby boy. Are you there yet?

> Yeah. Just got here. D and B are doing their sweep

Have fun tonight and video call me when you're home, okay?

Will you be naked?

Probably

Think we can convince D to take me to your place afterward?

While I would love nothing more, we can't get him involved more than he already is

I sighed as I read Rhett's text. He was right. Day was cool with me and Rhett being together, but that didn't mean we should ask him to help us sneak around. I hated that my relationship with Rhett would be frowned upon if others found out. Falling for someone whose job it was to protect me might be seen by some as a conflict of interest. But wouldn't Rhett, the one who saw me as more than a job, do everything in his power to protect me?

Rules fucking sucked.

I texted:

I know. Don't forget to tell P happy birthday for me

Already done

Before I could send another text, Day walked back to the SUV and opened the door. "Ready?"

"Yep." I slid out of the vehicle and grabbed Tyler and Hayden's gift.

"Tyler is in the house next to this one," Day advised.

"Awesome. Thanks."

I walked up the front steps and into the home that had been renovated to hold various events. Rows of white chairs flanked a white runner leading to a grand fireplace, the mantle adorned by white roses. I expected nothing less than how elegant everything looked.

Walking into an adjacent room, I spotted a stage at the front for a band and round tables with place settings set up for the reception. After leaving the present on the gift table, I made my way through the manor with Agent Day, and noticed a few bars being stocked. I walked to the nearest one.

"Hey, man. Sorry, I know you're getting set up. Any chance I can get a few shots of vodka for one of the grooms?"

"Sure. How many do you need?" he asked.

I counted in my head who I thought would be with Tyler while he got ready. "Six."

The bartender grabbed the shot glasses, placed them on a tray, and then began pouring the shots. "You're Fallon Donnelley, right?"

"I am." I nodded.

"Cool. I voted for your father."

"Thanks, bro. I appreciate that." I pulled out a twenty and put it into his tip jar.

"Thanks."

I picked up the tray, then Day and I walked out the door and across a small walkway to another house next to the manor. It was much smaller but also two stories. Knocking, I let myself in. Agent Day retreated and left me to be with my friends.

"Who's ready for some shots?" I bellowed.

Tyler, Dylan, Jase, and their fathers, Gage and Chase, turned.

"Hell, yeah!" Dylan yelled and stood to grab a shot.

I turned the tray so he couldn't take one. "Your brother's first. It's his big day."

Tyler smiled, and I passed him a shot of the clear liquid.

"I think you need to give a toast," Chase said to me.

"I have to give one later," I reminded them.

"Well, don't be coming in here with shots if you aren't going to back them up." He squeezed my shoulder.

"All right. I'll give a toast." Everyone grabbed a glass, and I shrugged out of my jacket. We lifted our shots, and I said, "Here's to the nights we'll never remember with friends we'll never forget."

"Aw. You're getting all sappy on us." Tyler winked and then threw back the shot.

We all followed and downed the vodka.

"Just happy for you." I hugged him.

"Thanks."

"We all are." Gage stood and hugged his son.

"Okay. We don't need everyone getting emotional," Tyler chuckled.

"No." Jase shook his head. "We need more shots."

"No," Chase clipped. "Tyler isn't going to get drunk before his wedding."

"But we can." Jase and Dylan bumped fists.

"No one is getting drunk until after the ceremony." Tyler rolled his eyes and then grabbed his black tux jacket. "Plus, we don't have much time."

We had about a half hour before guests would arrive, but I didn't say anything. I could tell my friend was antsy. I would be too, if I were about to marry the love of my life. Would that ever happen for me?

Before Rhett, I never thought about marriage or long-term commitments. Never wanted them. But with him, I wanted it all. Of course, I hadn't told him any of that or that I loved him, but I *did* love Rhett, and a sense of urgency washed over me that I needed to tell him.

I stood to grab my jacket so I could step outside and call him, but there was a knock on the door. Gage opened it, and the photographer peeked his head in.

"I'm here to take pictures of you guys getting ready before the wedding."

Gage waved the man inside, and instead of leaving to confess my love over the phone to Rhett, which was probably a shitty idea anyway, I posed for photos with everyone to capture Tyler's big day.

THE SOFT CRACKLING OF THE FIRE BEHIND ME MIXED WITH THE officiant's voice as he spoke about the love Tyler and Hayden shared.

They faced one another, their hands clasped together, and the sight of them in their perfectly tailored tuxedos was nothing short of breathtaking. I was truly happy for my friends.

They spoke their vows, exchanged rings, and then shared their first kiss as husband and husband. I got a little choked up, but that quickly changed when everyone clapped and the happy couple made their way back down the aisle.

I took the prepaid phone out of my pocket and sent a text to Rhett:

> Do you ever want to get married?

It didn't take him long to reply:

> Are you proposing via text?

I snorted a laugh and sent back:

> Not proposing but watching my two friends get married is doing something to me

> What kind of things?

> IDK but I feel all emotional

> I heard that happens at weddings. Go get a drink and all will be good

I headed toward the bar in the other room as I texted:

> Okay but do you want to get married one day?

No reply came by the time I ordered a vodka soda, and I wondered if my question was too much for Rhett. Maybe it sounded like I *was* proposing, and maybe a part of me had hoped he would say yes and we would one day take that next step.

With my drink in hand, I made my way to the porch, where people had gathered to watch Tyler and Hayden take their photos.

They posed with their families, and then I was being waved over to join in.

Once we were done, I went back inside and saw Rhett had replied.

> Yes

It was a simple answer, but one that made me hopeful.

DINNER HAD COME AND GONE, AND IT WAS TIME FOR ME TO GIVE MY speech. I grabbed the drink I was sipping on and walked to the stage. I snatched the mic, tapped it a few times to make sure it was on, and then smiled at the crowd.

"Good evening, everyone. For those of you who don't know me, I'm Fallon, and after all these years, Tyler has admitted I'm the best man. Well, at least one of them. Not sure I can compete with *the* Emmett Cooper." I smiled at Hayden's friend, who was the captain for the Boston Bruins and the other best man. "As part of my duties today, I get the honor of sharing a few words about these incredible love birds, but first, can we take a moment to appreciate the impeccable taste of these two? I mean, they've not only found each other in this crazy world, but they've pulled off a wedding that's giving Pinterest a serious run for its money."

The crowd laughed, and I continued. "Now, some of you are probably wondering what I know about Tyler and Hayden that no one else does, and let's just say these two could never keep a secret from me. I saw them fall in love back when no one knew they were a couple, and I have to say, that was a shame. Who cares if Hayden was our professor and gave Tyler after-hours lectures? We all know I was Professor Foster's favorite student." I winked at the couple. "But in all seriousness, you both are an inspiration to us all. You've shown us that true love knows no bounds, and your journey is one I'm happy to be a part of.

"So, let's raise our glasses high and toast to these two remarkable men. May your marriage be filled with more laughter than a stand-up comedy show, more love than all the rom-coms combined, and more adventures than a trip to an unlimited mimosa brunch. Cheers!"

I drank the rest of the drink I was holding and then returned to my chair while Coop gave his speech. Chase and Gage said some words too, and then the party really started.

Tyler and Hayden shared their first dance and afterward invited everyone else to join in. I wasn't one to shy away from the dance floor, and danced my ass off. Maybe there was something to be said about weddings that gave people some sort of lovestruck fever because I was eager to see Rhett and tell him I loved him.

THE NIGHT WAS WINDING DOWN, AND I WAS BEAT. I COULDN'T IMAGINE how Tyler and Hayden were feeling. Not only did they dance the night away, but they mingled with all of their guests too. It was an epic wedding, but I felt it was my duty to give the lovebirds a good send-off.

"You two heading out soon?" I asked over the loud music.

"Why? You want to go home to your man?" Tyler teased.

I did but couldn't. "He's at his place with his daughter. I'll see him tomorrow."

"Then video sex tonight?" Tyler continued to jest.

"All right. Fine. You caught me. But at least you two are doing the real deal tonight." I waggled my eyebrows.

"Yeah, we will." Hayden pulled Tyler close and seized his lips, and a pang of jealousy hit me.

"Go say your goodbyes." I shooed them.

The happy couple made their rounds, and I pulled the prepaid phone from my pocket and sent a text to Rhett.

> Wedding is coming to an end. I should be home in about an hour. You better be naked and hard when I call

Rhett didn't reply, and I had to think he was putting Poppy to bed or something.

After Tyler and Hayden rode away in their limo, people were gathering their stuff to leave too. I headed to the bar for one last drink as Agents Day and Bernard stayed near the front door and waited for me.

"One more for the road," I said to the bartender, the same one who had given me the shots when I'd first arrived. He had been on his feet the entire night.

My phone finally buzzed with a text, and I pulled it out of my pocket.

Hurry

The bartender placed a fresh vodka soda in front of me, and as I reached for it, someone came up and stood to my right. Instantly, I felt a jabbing pain in my side.

"Mr. Hughes wants his money," a gravelly voice hissed.

I looked beside me to see a man I didn't recognize, his eyes cold and calculating. "This shit again? You want my brother," I shot back, my voice dripping with defiance.

"He thought you'd say that," he sneered, pressing whatever object he had harder against my side.

I clenched my teeth and groaned in pain. I lifted my gaze. The bartender's eyes were wide, and a look of terror laced his face. My heart raced as I scanned the dimly lit room for Day and Bernard.

The moment my eyes locked with Agent Day's, I saw him rush toward me.

Summoning all the strength I could muster, I shoved my elbow into my attacker's gut, causing him to stagger back.

I saw the glint of a gun in the man's hand as he pointed the weapon at me. In the blink of an eye, a gunshot rang out, the sound deafening since it was so close to me.

The impact hit me like a freight train, sending searing pain through my chest. I stumbled and fell to the ground, the taste of blood filling my mouth.

Madness erupted around me as wedding guests screamed and scrambled. Another shot was fired, and through the haze of pain and confusion, I saw the stranger collapse to the ground near the door by the bar.

Before I could fully comprehend everything, Agent Day was by my side. "Stay with me, Fallon," he urged.

As I stared up at him, it became harder to breathe.

The room faded around me, and the pain in my chest became a distant ache.

My vision blurred, and then everything went dark.

22

AGENT DAY

THE MOMENT MY EYES CONNECTED WITH FALLON'S, I KNEW something was wrong. I moved toward him, and when he elbowed the guy, my gaze dropped to the weapon in the man's hand.

"Gun!" I screamed to Bernard as I pulled mine.

Before I could move closer to Fallon, his attacker fired.

Chaos ensued behind me as I squeezed the trigger, a single shot ripping through the air. The round found its mark, slamming into the stranger's back as he rushed for the side exit to escape. Bernard closed in on the assailant, and I bolted to Fallon's side.

"Stay with me, Fallon," I begged.

Blood saturated his pristine white tuxedo shirt. His eyes closed, and my heart raced. *Fuck.* I tore open his shirt, the buttons clattering across the wood floor, exposing the bullet wound to his chest.

"Talk to me," Vance said in my earpiece.

I lifted my arm and spoke into the concealed mic in the sleeve of my jacket. "Windstorm's been shot. Call 9-1-1 and report it to Tanner."

Reaching into the breast pocket of my jacket, I pulled out a chest seal and ripped it open with my teeth. My combat medic training kicked into gear, knowing in mere minutes, Fallon could bleed out and any air entering his bloodstream could be fatal.

I couldn't let that happen.

I applied the transparent seal over the oozing wound. It wouldn't stop the bleeding entirely, but it might save his life. Did the bullet sever an artery, puncture a lung, disrupt a vital organ, or simply pass through? I rolled Fallon onto his side, moving his shirt so I could check his back. I found no exit wound.

Shit!

Bernard was securing the immediate area, and I glanced over to see the attacker was down and not moving. Were there others nearby? Who was that guy, and why did he shoot Fallon? As far as we knew, everything with Finnegan had been taken care of, and that had been the only issue we'd been aware of. The gunman didn't look like the guy from Atlantic City, but could he be part of Hughes' crew? Maybe it was another person Finnegan owed money to? Or was it a new threat entirely?

Every passing second weighed heavily on me as I stared down at Fallon. His breathing had slowed tremendously, but a pulse still throbbed faintly beneath my fingertips on his neck. I felt utterly powerless. Even with all my training, there was nothing more I could do except wait for help to arrive.

"Where the fuck is the ambulance?" I barked into my comm.

"I hear them. They're close," Vance responded.

"Hang on, Fallon," I implored. His life hung in the balance, and the weight of that responsibility pressed down like a vise. If he died, I wouldn't forgive myself.

And what about Rhett? He was one of my best friends. What would he do when he found out something happened to his boyfriend? Any minute, Tanner would send out a message to all agents, and Rhett would want answers.

Answers I prayed wouldn't be his worst nightmare.

Fuck.

Before I could beat myself up more, I heard the sirens. They were getting closer with each second.

"Help is here, Fallon." I didn't know what else to do except talk to him.

Moments later, the paramedics burst into the room like a whirlwind of urgency, their equipment clattering as they rushed toward Fallon. Bernard and Vance exchanged anxious glances with me, and the three of us stepped back to let the experts work.

"What happened?" one of them asked.

I took a step forward and spoke. "GSW to the chest. No exit wound that I could see. Pulse is faint."

Swiftly, the paramedics secured Fallon onto a gurney, and before I knew it, we were racing through the corridors of the manor and into the waiting ambulance.

"I'm going with them. Wait for the local PD and the FBI then meet me at the hospital. Tanner will want you both there," I told Bernard and Vance.

They both nodded as the ambulance doors slammed shut. The paramedic inside moved with practiced precision, wasting no time as he plunged needles into Fallon's veins, establishing vital IV lines, and hooked him up to a cardiac monitor.

Fallon lay there, pale and still, his life hanging by the thinnest of threads. The ambulance sped through the snow-covered streets, bouncing over potholes and sharp turns.

Come on, Fallon. Hang in there.

As minutes stretched into an agonizing eternity, I couldn't help but replay the event in my mind. The guy was dressed like the catering staff. Could we have prevented Fallon from getting shot? My thoughts were a whirl of questions.

My phone in my jacket pocket rang, but I didn't answer it. I knew who was calling, and I wasn't ready to tell *him* anything until I knew Fallon's fate.

Then it happened ...

The beeping on the monitor became erratic, a piercing alarm that penetrated my ears. I locked eyes with the paramedic.

Fallon was coding.

The paramedic grabbed the defibrillator pads and yelled, "Clear!"

He shocked Fallon, and his body twitched in response.

No immediate sign of life returned to him.

"Again!" the paramedic barked, and he shocked Fallon once more.

Each excruciating second felt like forever as he desperately fought to bring Fallon back.

23

RHETT

POPPY WAS SNUGGLED INTO MY SIDE AS SHE SLEPT PEACEFULLY. IT WAS a perfect way to end her birthday celebration, which included pizza, cake, ice cream, and her favorite movie. My time with her was exactly the sort of life I wanted, but the only thing missing was Fallon.

Trying not to wake Poppy, I slowly scooted off the couch and then scooped her into my arms and carried her to her room. After laying her in her bed, I tucked her in, placed a kiss on her head, and then made sure she had her purple stuffed unicorn before tiptoeing out of the room and closing the door behind me.

With her asleep and the apartment cleaned up, nothing was left for me to do except think about the text Fallon sent me earlier. The one where he asked if I wanted to get married someday. The question had thrown me for a loop because I hadn't expected him to admit that watching his friends get married had any sort of effect on him.

When he pushed for me to answer, I had to tell him the truth. I absolutely wanted to get married one day, and my mind filled with all the possibilities of a life spent with him. Maybe we could move in together one day. We would stay up late talking about our hopes and dreams. We could have family movie nights with my daughter, who he'd already formed a bond with. Go on family vacations and eventually stand in the driveway together as we watched Poppy drive off to college.

My chest filled with happiness as I realized, despite the obstacles in our way, Fallon was the one I wanted to build a future with because I was hopelessly in love with him.

I knew what I needed to do next, and that was to tell him how I felt. I expected him to call me once he got home, but as I looked at the time, I knew it was likely I wouldn't hear from him for a couple more hours.

I flipped through the channels on the TV, searching for something to distract me while I waited. I settled on a Marvel movie and lay across the couch. The colors on the screen blended together as I relaxed into the cushions, and my eyes became heavy. Despite my best efforts to stay awake, I felt myself start to drift off.

I had no idea how long I'd been asleep when a text notification on the prepaid phone startled me awake. Rubbing my eyes, I read the message:

> Wedding is coming to an end. I should be home in about an hour. You better be naked and hard when I call

I grabbed both my phones and hauled myself off the couch to head toward the bathroom for a quick shower. I would definitely be ready when he called.

While I stood under the hot water a few minutes later, I heard another message come through on my primary phone. I stepped out of the shower and dried off.

When I picked up my regular cell, my heart sank. The message from our command center was one no agent ever wanted to read:

> Critical situation. Report to the command post immediately.

A cold sweat ran down my spine.

Critical situation.

That could only mean one thing: something had happened to Fallon.

My hands shook as I scrolled through my contacts and called Alexis.

"Hey, I need you to come over and stay with Poppy," I said frantically when she answered the phone.

"What's going on? Is everything all right?" Panic laced her tone.

"Work emergency," I replied and wondered if she heard the tremble in my voice.

"I'll be right there."

I hung up and rushed into my bedroom to get dressed. While tying my shoes, there was a knock on the door. I flung it open, and Alexis raced in.

"Thank god you're here. Poppy's in bed. You're welcome to stay here or take her back to your place." I let out a sigh of relief that she lived close by and was able to get to my apartment quickly.

I ran back to my room and grabbed my gun from the locked case. With one hand, I shoved the weapon into my holster while I used the other hand to snatch my keys off the dresser.

"I'll text you later," I said to Alexis as I hurried out the door.

Since Poppy was staying with me for her birthday, I'd opted to drive my car to and from work early in the day, but at that moment, I wished I had an agency vehicle with emergency lights so I could get to the command post faster.

The second I climbed into my car, I tried to call Day. My fingers tapped against the steering wheel as I listened to the phone ring. His voicemail picked up, and I stabbed at the End Call button. I tried to reach Bernard and Vance with the same result.

Why the fuck wasn't anyone answering their phone?

When I reached Fallon's building, I didn't bother pulling into the parking garage. Instead, I double parked alongside one of the black SUVs. I didn't give a shit if someone towed my car; my only concern was getting inside as soon as possible.

I ran toward the elevator and pressed the button repeatedly until the damn doors opened. It seemed to take forever as it traveled up to the eighth floor. Once on Fallon's floor, I raced down the hall.

The command post was buzzing with activity as I stepped inside. Tanner was on the phone shouting out orders while others huddled together.

Agent Jones was at the computer, so I walked over to him. "What the hell is going on?"

"Fallon's been shot," he replied without looking in my direction.

The room began to spin, everything blurring around me. Day was an excellent agent. No one would have been able to get close enough to Fallon. It all had to be a misunderstanding.

Before I could question Jones further, Tanner's booming voice filled the room. "At approximately 2200 hours, Fallon was shot at the wedding reception he was attending. An ambulance took him to the local hospital, but he's being airlifted to St. Thomas. The president is en route, and I'll send most of you to the hospital to keep guard. Be aware that the FBI is taking point on the investigation, and they may pull some of you aside for interviews."

St. Thomas was a level one trauma center in Boston, which only ramped up my anxiety. Without another thought, I headed for the door.

"Agent Davis, where are you going?" Tanner called out.

"St. Thomas," I answered without stopping.

"I haven't given out assignments yet."

Fuck the assignments. There was no way I was going to stand around and wait for Tanner to decide who he was sending to the hospital and who was staying behind.

I needed to get to Fallon.

Instead of waiting for the slow-ass elevator, I raced down the eight flights of stairs and jumped into my car. I threw my phone onto the passenger seat and took off.

The world blurred around me as I gripped the steering wheel, my knuckles white with tension. Although traffic was light since it was late at night, I cursed every red light for creating an infuriating delay that kept me from the man I loved.

Images of Fallon flashed in my mind—him concentrating on his schoolwork, him dancing at Chrome, his eyes lighting up whenever he flirted with me. Anxiety consumed me as I wanted nothing more than to see those greenish-blue eyes shining brightly at me.

I glanced at my phone. I wanted it to light up with his name and hear his voice telling me everything was okay, that it wasn't him but someone else who had been shot. Or that it wasn't true at all. But the screen remained dark, just like the unwanted thoughts in my head. I called Day a few more times, each attempt ending with his voicemail answering.

It only took me twenty minutes to arrive at the hospital, but it seemed like an eternity before I finally turned into the parking lot. I pulled into the first open space and raced toward the emergency department doors. I approached the desk, and before the receptionist could speak, I flashed my badge.

"I need to see Fallon Donnelley immediately," I said, keeping my voice low to avoid others from overhearing me.

She nodded. "Right this way, sir."

I followed her through a few doors until we reached a checkpoint, where a security officer stopped us.

"He's with the Secret Service," the receptionist explained to the guard.

"Come with me," he said and led me to the elevator. "Your team is on the third floor."

When the doors opened on the third floor, Day was in the hall, his hands pulling at his hair as he paced.

I raced to his side. "Where is he?"

Day's head snapped up, and he grabbed my arm, pulling me into an empty room. He closed the door behind us. "He's in surgery."

"But he's going to be okay, right?"

Day's eyes turned glassy. "I don't know. He coded in the ambulance, and as soon as we got here, they rushed him into the OR. We haven't received an update yet."

My knees buckled, and I crumpled to the ground. Tears streamed down my cheeks, and I buried my face in my hands. Only a couple hours earlier, I had been dreaming about our future together, but at that moment, I wasn't sure if I'd ever get the chance to tell him how much I loved him.

Sobs wracked through me as a sharp pain like nothing I'd ever felt before stabbed me in the heart.

I couldn't lose Fallon.

Not like this.

24

RHETT

The fluorescent lights buzzed above me, and the smell of antiseptic filled the air. My world was collapsing around me as I sat on the floor of the hospital, my forehead resting on my folded arms across my bent legs. My body shook as I wept thinking about Fallon clinging to life somewhere in the building. Whether or not he survived was out of my hands, and suddenly, I couldn't breathe. He might be dying, and I couldn't do a damn thing about it.

Day wrapped his arm around me as he slid down the wall beside me, and we sat together for a few minutes. "Just got word that Tanner's on his way up here." He pointed at his earpiece.

I nodded and pushed myself off the floor, needing to regain my composure before our boss saw me. I knew it was likely I'd face disciplinary action for leaving the command post before any official orders had been given, but in that moment, all I had cared about was getting to Fallon.

I wiped away the tears because I didn't need to give Tanner any reason to think I wasn't fit to be on duty, and pulled the door open.

Shoving my hands into my pockets so no one could see them shake, I called upon years of training to push my emotions down deep while I watched Tanner step out of the elevator with a few other agents in tow.

"Agent Day, has there been any update on Windstorm's condition?" Tanner asked before briefly glancing in my direction.

"Not yet, sir," Day replied.

"Leigh, see if you can gather any information at the nurse's station. Shea and Brown, work with security to clear out a space for the family to wait once they get here. Warrior's team has advised me they're en route." Tanner barked out orders about the president's arrival with precision, and under any other circumstance, I'd try to learn as much from the situation as possible. Instead, his words were an unwelcome interruption to my internal pleading to a higher power for Fallon to pull through.

After the other agents walked away to handle their tasks, Tanner looked at Day. "FBI agents are downstairs and need to speak to you."

Day gave Tanner a curt nod. "Yes, sir." Then he turned to me, and I could see the unspoken question in his eyes: *Will you be okay?*

I needed to offer my friend some reassurance, but my mind was still filled with uncertainty. I wasn't positive I could keep it together much longer. And despite the conflict warring within me, I attempted to give Day a small smile and mouthed, "I'm good."

Once he entered the elevator, I was left standing alone with Tanner. He cleared his throat, and I braced myself for whatever he was about to say. He motioned for me to follow him into the room I'd been in with Day. The door clicked behind us.

"Agent Davis, you know the rules. You should have stayed at the command post until you received orders."

"I'm sorry, sir. I—"

"I understand in our line of work friendships often develop between agents and protectees."

That's one way of putting it.

He continued, "However, we still have protocols to follow. I had planned to send you back to the command post, but we need the extra hands here while the FBI interviews your colleagues. Therefore, you're staying, but I will send you back to the condo if need be. Am I clear?"

"Yes, sir." I'd expected to be reprimanded by him but was grateful he was allowing me to stay in an official capacity because the truth was, I would refuse to leave if he tried to send me away.

A SHORT TIME AFTER MY CONVERSATION WITH TANNER, AGENT JONES showed up with equipment for those of us who hadn't grabbed our earpieces or other items from the command post. Once I had everything I needed, Tanner assigned me to stand guard in the hallway near the elevator.

Even though I had a task to perform, I couldn't stop thinking about Fallon and felt myself sinking further into the darkness threatening to consume me.

We'd received an update stating he was still in surgery, which at least meant he was continuing to hang on. I had no choice but to cling to the hope he would recover.

As we waited for more information, I spoke to a couple of agents who passed my way. It sounded as though the FBI had identified the asshole who had shot Fallon.

Since Day's bullet had taken the suspect out, law enforcement was going to have a harder time figuring out his motive, however, I heard his driver's license had been issued in New Jersey, which led me to believe he was connected to Hughes and meant the whole shitshow could be tied to Finnegan.

I had no idea how much time had passed as I paced the corridor. Eventually, we received word that Fallon's family was in the building. I didn't understand why Finnegan and Faye waited for their parents to travel from D.C. before coming to the hospital, but it sounded as though all four of them had finally arrived.

I saw Tanner head in my direction, and then the elevator dinged and opened.

Suddenly, the hallway was filled with the First Family as well as several agents. The president's face was lined with concern, and his wife's eyes were puffy and red. No doubt she'd spent the entire flight to Boston fearful for her son's life. My heart broke for them because I understood the devastation they were feeling.

However, when my eyes locked on Finnegan, an overpowering rage consumed me. While the circumstances surrounding the shooting weren't clear yet, I knew deep down Fallon wouldn't be clinging to life if it weren't for his brother's stupidity.

I took a deep breath and tried to gain control of my anger. My job required me to not let my personal feelings get involved, but I couldn't stop myself. I grabbed a hold of Finnegan's arm and pulled him off to the side.

"You were supposed to take care of your shit," I yelled in his face.

Ramos pulled me back. "Let him go, Davis."

I shrugged Ramos' hand off and met Finnegan's gaze head-on. "If your brother dies, the blame lies solely with you."

It didn't matter that the shooting was under investigation; I knew in my gut it all came back to his gambling addiction, and I'd never forgive him for putting Fallon in danger.

Everyone stared at me with wide eyes, and Tanner demanded, "Davis, come with me. Now!"

Fuck. I may have just ended my career, but at that moment, I couldn't find it within myself to give a damn.

I followed my team leader to the same room as before. He closed the door behind us and growled, "What the hell was that all about?"

I hung my head and sighed. "I lost my temper, sir."

"That's a fucking understatement. You just attacked the son of the president of the United States!"

"I was out of line—"

"Out of line doesn't even begin to cover it." He ran a hand down his face. "What's gotten into you? I've never known you to be anything except professional until today."

I could either lie and try to make excuses, or I could come clean about my relationship with Fallon. Neither option was ideal, but the repercussions would likely be worse if it came out later.

I stared at the floor for a few moments before meeting Tanner's scrutinizing gaze. "Fallon and I are together ..."

"Together?" His forehead creased in confusion. "Do you mean romantically?"

I nodded.

"How long?"

"Since December." I swallowed.

"December?" he shouted.

Before he could question me further, a transmission came through our earpieces. "Windstorm is out of surgery and is being moved to a room on the VIP floor."

My entire body sagged in relief, and I had to brace myself against the wall to remain standing.

Fallon was alive.

Tears of joy pricked at my eyes, while the need to see that he was okay for myself had me turning to leave, but Tanner stopped me as I reached for the door handle.

"I need your gun and badge."

My brow furrowed. "What?"

"You heard me." He reached his hand out.

I grabbed both items and reluctantly handed them over.

"I'm relieving you of duty until further notice."

"Sir, you can't do that," I pleaded. "I need to be here. With Fallon."

"You've left me no choice. Your actions with Finnegan show you're not able to perform your job duties in a professional manner. Monroe will decide what disciplinary action to take, but I can't have you causing more problems."

Steeling my spine, I looked Tanner in the eye and announced, "I'm not leaving this hospital."

He sighed. "Whatever you decide to do as a private citizen is your choice. But you'll be doing it in the waiting room away from his family and the Secret Service."

With that, Tanner walked out of the room.

As I watched him leave, a wave of emotions washed over me. I was filled with relief that Fallon had made it through surgery, but I was upset Tanner felt it necessary to take my gun and badge.

Still, if I had to choose between my job and Fallon, it would always be him.

25

FALLON

I COULD SEE RHETT STANDING IN THE DISTANCE. HE WAS BATHED IN A warm, soft light, and I ran toward him. His smile, brighter than the sun, melted my heart. He reached out his hand, and I took it without hesitation. Our fingers interlaced, a perfect fit, as if we were made for each other.

"I missed you," he whispered.

"I missed you too."

We began walking. The grass beneath my feet was soft and cool. The sky above us was painted in hues of pink and orange and cast everything in a gentle glow.

"Where are we?" I asked.

"Here," he answered.

Where is here?

Rhett's eyes met mine, and I was lost in their depths. They were like an ocean of love, and I never wanted to look away.

He pulled me closer, and we danced together, our movements

effortless and graceful. Every step was in perfect harmony, as if we'd been practicing our whole lives.

"I love this song," I admitted as I heard the soft melody.

"And I love you." Rhett kissed me.

We stopped by a serene pond; its surface reflected the colors of the rainbow sky above us. Rhett leaned in, his lips meeting mine in a tender kiss again. It was a kiss filled with all the love in the universe, a kiss that made time stand still.

"I want to do that forever," he said against my mouth.

"Please," I begged and held him close. The beat of his heart matched mine. "I never want you to stop."

We lay down on the soft grass, our fingers still intertwined. I rested my head on Rhett's chest, and I could hear the steady rhythm of his heart again. It was a comforting sound.

"I never want to leave." I ran circles on his hard chest.

"But you have to, baby boy."

"Why?" I rose onto an elbow and peered into his sad eyes.

"Because I need you to."

Slowly, the surrounding colors faded. I felt a growing sense of unease, a distant awareness that something wasn't right.

"Wake up for me," he pleaded.

"Wake up?" I echoed.

Rhett's voice became fainter, his touch less real. I reached out to him, but he slipped away, and a feeling of intense loss washed over me.

My eyes fluttered open, and I stared up at an unfamiliar ceiling.

The slow beeping of a machine filled my ears, and I turned my head to find IV bags and a heart monitor at my side. My throat felt funny, and I realized I had a tube in it. I tried to move, but my body felt heavy. Panic welled inside me until I heard a soft, reassuring voice nearby.

"Easy, Fallon. You're in the hospital. You just had surgery."

My gaze settled on a kind-faced nurse standing beside my bed. Her words made sense as my groggy mind cleared. Surgery. Someone had shot me.

"Your family stepped out for a moment, but they'll be so happy you're awake. Let me remove the tube from your throat." She laid the bed back and then pulled out the tube. She had me cough as she slid it out, and it burned until it was free.

My throat was scratchy, and I croaked out, "Water?"

"You can't have water yet, but I can get you some ice chips to suck on." The nurse lifted the bed back upright and left. She returned a minute later with a cup of ice. "Open up. I'm sure your arms are heavy."

They were. Everything felt heavy.

She dropped a piece into my mouth, and the cool liquid soothed my throat as it melted.

"Thank you," I mumbled, my voice still raspy.

She smiled gently. "You're welcome. Just take it easy for now."

I nodded, my eyelids heavy. It was a struggle to keep them open, so I closed them.

The exhaustion from both the surgery and the ordeal before made me fall asleep again.

WHEN I WOKE AGAIN, I COULD HEAR MY MOTHER TALKING, AND I turned my head to face her. The moment she noticed I was awake, she rushed to my bedside.

"Fallon, sweetie. How do you feel?"

"Like I've been shot." That wasn't entirely true. Whatever drugs they had me on made it feel as though nothing had happened. I felt good.

A tear slid down her cheek. "Don't joke about it."

"Okay, but it's the truth."

"I know, but you almost died." She wiped her cheek. "Here. Suck on some ice."

Like before, the liquid soothed my throat as I swallowed it down. "I almost died?"

"Yes." She sniffed. "You coded on the way to the first hospital."

First hospital? "What happened?"

She stuck another piece of ice into my mouth. "You were airlifted here and rushed into surgery. They removed the bullet. Luckily, it hadn't hit anything vital."

"But I almost died?" Or had I died? If I coded, that meant my heart had stopped beating.

"You don't need to worry about the details." She waved her hand in front of her. "The important thing is you're alive."

"Yeah …" I breathed. "Where's everyone else?"

"Like who, sweetie?"

"My detail? Dad?" I glanced toward the door and couldn't see anyone standing outside. Where was Rhett?

"Agents are outside, and your father is dealing with Finn." She patted my hand gently, which had an IV stuck in it.

My eyes bounced back to hers. "Dad knows?"

"Who shot you?"

I nodded.

"Yes. The FBI are working on the case."

"Did they catch the guy?"

"Agent Day shot and killed him."

"And they know he was connected to the guy from Atlantic City?"

"Yes. You don't need to worry about any of that. Just get some rest."

"I want to see …" I hesitated. It was on the tip of my tongue to ask for Rhett, but I knew I couldn't. He wasn't at the wedding, and it would be suspicious if I wanted to see an agent who had nothing to do with the shooting or keeping me safe.

Before I could continue, there was a knock at the door. My gaze flicked toward it in hopes it would be Rhett. Instead, I found Tyler and Hayden.

"Hey, buddy," Tyler greeted and looked around the hospital room that resembled a hotel suite. It even had a kitchenette, as though I would cook meals while in the hospital. "Nice digs. How are you feeling?"

I opened my mouth to respond with the same answer as I had with my mother. Instead, I said, "Drugs are working."

"We're glad you're okay." Hayden frowned. At first, I didn't understand why he appeared sad, but then I realized it probably had to do with the boyfriend he'd lost in a car accident. Even though I wasn't his lover, we were still friends, and I couldn't imagine what he felt when he heard I'd been shot.

"Sorry I ruined your wedding." I hung my head.

"What? No!" Tyler moved closer. "You got shot. You didn't ruin anything."

"But it was at your wedding," I argued.

"We had already left," Hayden reminded me. "We actually didn't find out until this morning because we had our phones off. We feel horrible for not getting here sooner."

"How long has it been?" I asked, looking at my mom.

She took a seat in a chair in the sitting room portion of my hospital room. "It's been about twenty hours, sweetie."

"Shouldn't you two be on your honeymoon?" I questioned my friends.

"We leave in the morning," Tyler replied.

"Oh."

Tyler and Hayden were going to Anguilla for a week, where they would probably spend most of the time naked. That was all I wanted to do with Rhett instead of lying in a hospital room.

"We wanted to stop by and see how you were doing first. We received a text you were awake," Hayden said.

"From who?" I wondered. Would my parents let them know? Rhett, maybe?

Tyler glanced at my mom and then rubbed the back of his neck. "Your *friend*."

I stared at him for a moment as I tried to understand who he was referring to, and then it hit me. "Is he here?"

Tyler nodded. "Downstairs."

"Can you tell him to come up here?" I wanted to see Rhett so badly, and I didn't care if my mother would be watching.

"He ... ah ..." Tyler looked at my mom again.

"You're talking about Agent Davis?" she asked.

"Yes. I want to see him."

"That's not a good idea," she said.

"And why not?"

She took a deep breath. "Agent Davis was relieved of duty."

I blinked. "Relieved of duty?"

"Yes."

"Why?"

"Because he attacked your brother," she responded.

"Good. He's the fucking reason someone shot me, Mom! If I could, I would beat his ass too."

The machine next to me beeped annoyingly, and a nurse rushed in. "Your heart rate is too high."

"Yeah, well, it's because I'm pissed." I looked out the floor-to-ceiling windows, the harbor in the distance. I didn't want to meet anyone's stare. How dare my mother say I couldn't see Rhett!

"Maybe you need to take a little nap," the nurse suggested as she stopped the beeping.

"We should go," Tyler said.

I glanced at my friend. "Please tell Rhett to come up here."

"Fallon …" Mom warned.

"Mom," I replied sternly. "I want to see him. Now!"

The machine beeped again, and the nurse stopped it. "Only if you get your heart rate down."

I took a deep breath and begged my mother, "Please?"

She thought for a moment. "Fine, but make it fast. You need your rest."

"Thank you." I turned my attention to my friends. "Please send him up."

"We will," Hayden said and patted my leg.

"And have fun on your honeymoon. Have all the sex." I chuckled.

Tyler blushed and peeked at my mom. He backed up toward the door. "Yeah. I'll call you when we're back."

"Sounds good."

The couple turned on their heels and left.

"Is there something going on between you and Agent Davis?" Mom asked.

The nurse pushed the button on the blood pressure machine attached to me so she could check it.

"I …" I opened and closed my mouth. Lying to her was pointless when it had to be obvious why I was fighting so hard to see him. "Yes."

"I figured as much after last night."

"Is that why he was fired?" I asked.

"No, I don't think he was fired." She shook her head. "He was placed on leave because he attacked Finn."

"So, he won't get in trouble for dating me?"

"That I don't know."

Rhett had been removed from my detail, but what did that actually mean? Would he be transferred to another assignment? Or worse, no longer be a Secret Service agent?

"Will you give me privacy when Rhett gets up here?" I asked my mom.

"I don't know if that's a good idea."

"Why? What could possibly happen other than I get to see my boyfriend?"

She took a deep breath. "Okay, but you really need your rest. Make it fast."

I nodded. "Thank you."

It didn't take Rhett long to knock on the door. I smiled brightly at him as he stepped over the threshold.

"Hey," I greeted.

"Hey." He took a tentative step closer.

"You have five minutes," Mom stated. "Then Fallon needs to rest."

"Yes, ma'am," Rhett replied.

My mom kept the door open as she left. It didn't stop Rhett from rushing to me and engulfing me in a hug.

"Easy, handsome. I was shot."

"Shit. Sorry." He pulled back. "I was so worried about you."

"I'm sorry." I looked down at the pale blue blanket covering my lower body.

"Hey." He lifted my chin. "You did nothing wrong."

"I know, but I still feel bad you had to worry about me."

"It's my job to worry about you, baby boy."

"Is it still?"

He moved his hand back. "You heard?"

I nodded slightly. "Yeah. My mom told me, but what does that mean?"

"It means I lost control."

"But are you fired?"

Rhett lifted a shoulder. "I don't know. I'll have a meeting with the assistant director, and he'll decide my fate."

"But what about us? What will happen if you're transferred to Vice President Brooks' detail or his children? Or hell, someone else?"

"How I feel about you won't change because of where I'm stationed. We'll—"

A commotion erupted outside of my hospital room door. Two agents walked inside, followed by my father.

Rhett stood taller and nodded his head slightly. "Mr. President."

"I need the room," Dad stated.

"Wait!" I called out.

"It's okay." Rhett squeezed my hand gently. "I'll be in the waiting room. I'm not going anywhere."

"But I want you in here with me," I pleaded.

"Fallon," Dad clipped as though I was in trouble.

"What? I have nothing to hide from him and I want him to stay."

"It's fine." Rhett gave me a sad smile and then left. My father's agents followed him, and they shut the door behind them.

"So, it's true, then?" Dad asked as he stood at the foot of my bed.

"Is what true?"

"You're in a relationship with a member of your protection detail?"

"Yeah. Why is that such a problem?"

"This kind of situation is highly unprofessional. It compromises your safety."

I tried to sit up straighter, but it only caused a pain to shoot through my chest. "Dad, I get it. I really do. But love isn't something you can control. Rhett is damn good at what he does, and if he cares about me, it only makes him more determined to protect me."

Dad paced in front of the window. "It could cloud his judgment and put you in danger."

"Your other son did that," I spat. "Rhett wasn't even at the wedding. In fact, if he had been, I bet you I wouldn't have even been shot. He wouldn't have been across the room waiting for me to say I was ready to leave. He would have been at the bar with me. He would have been inches away, not feet. That guy wouldn't have even gotten close to me. That was what happened in Atlantic City the first time."

"Shit." Dad blew out a breath. "The first time. Fucking Finn."

"I trust Rhett with my life, and I believe in him. Love doesn't make you weak; it makes you stronger. It gives you a reason to fight harder, and I know deep in my heart, Rhett would do anything to protect me. Didn't he come to you after the state dinner? He could have easily let the information go up the chain of command or whatever, but instead, he went above and beyond to try to get ahead of it because he was worried about me. And for good reason, considering I was almost killed."

Dad sighed, his shoulders sagging with the weight of the situation. "I'll need to have a serious talk with Agent Davis and reevaluate his position on your detail."

I nodded, relieved my father was at least willing to consider my perspective. "Thank you, Dad. I know you have to do what's best, but please, don't take him away from me. I … I love him."

"You do?"

I didn't hesitate to reply, "With my entire heart."

My father gave me a small smile. "I'll do my best, Fallon, but I can't guarantee he'll be on your detail again. We have to do what's best for your safety."

"Rhett isn't the problem," I argued. "It's Finn."

"I know, and I'm dealing with him."

"How? I thought that was done when we were called into the Oval Office."

"So did I, but instead of paying his debts as promised, he gambled it all."

I rolled my eyes. "Of course, he did."

"It's being dealt with again, but this time, my team will make sure the debts are paid."

"And he gets off just like that?"

"No. We're selling his condo here in Boston, and he's moving into the White House. He'll get help for his addiction and will more or less be on house arrest for the foreseeable future."

"House arrest in the White House." I laughed sarcastically. "What a fucking joke."

"I'm doing the best I can, Fallon. The media are already looking into what happened and why I'm at St. Thomas."

"And you can't tell them the truth?"

"I could, but if I want to run again, it's probably not best they know my son was shot because his brother failed to pay off a loan shark."

"Yeah, well, don't expect me to be in the public eye pretending like everything is cool between me and Finn."

"I won't. He's going to be on a short leash for a very long time."

"Great." I rested my head against the mattress. "Now can you work on getting Rhett his job back?"

"I'll try, but I came here because you were shot, and I've been worried about you. Are you doing okay? Do you need anything?"

"Just Rhett," I wanted to say, but instead I shook my head and told him, "No. The nurses are doing an excellent job."

26

RHETT

WHILE I WAS DISAPPOINTED PRESIDENT DONNELLEY HAD INTERRUPTED my visit with his son, I walked out of Fallon's hospital room feeling as though the fear and anxiety I'd been carrying around for the last day were finally lifted. That didn't mean I wanted to continue being separated from him, but judging by Mrs. Donnelley's announcement that I could only stay for five minutes, it didn't appear I'd get to spend much time with him while his family was nearby.

Exiting the elevator on the first floor where the general waiting room was located, I walked along the bright white hallway that seemed to stretch endlessly. I'd been staying in the waiting room since Tanner took my badge.

Spending time alone in the hospital had given me time to think about the repercussions of my actions the night before. One thing I had been concerned about if my relationship with Fallon ever came to light was being removed from his team. Not only would it be difficult to keep dating him if I were assigned elsewhere, but I would live in a constant state of worry for his safety knowing I wouldn't be there by his side.

Dropping onto an uncomfortable gray plastic chair, I pulled out my phone to check my emails. My stomach sank when I saw one from the head of the Secret Service human resources department with the subject line: ***Administrative Leave and Mandatory Meeting***

I opened the email and read that I was expected to meet with Assistant Director Monroe at the Boston field office the following morning. The meeting wasn't unexpected because I knew my actions were going to be investigated.

While I believed whole-heartedly that Finnegan needed to be held accountable for putting his brother in danger, I was pissed at myself for losing my temper. If I'd played it cool, Tanner wouldn't have needed to remove me from duty in the first place.

I rested my head against the dingy white wall and closed my eyes. I tried to figure out a way to fix things. Unfortunately, my fate would be determined by others, and I couldn't force those in power to accept that I'd fallen in love with the man I was tasked with protecting.

"Agent Davis?" My eyes popped open, and I saw an agent I vaguely recognized standing in the doorway. "President Donnelley would like to speak with you."

"Okay. Is he still with his son?" I stood, ready to make my way to Fallon's room.

"No. I'll take you to him." I followed the agent into the elevator, and he pushed the button for the floor Fallon was on. When we stepped out of the lift, he led me down the hall to a closed door where two other agents stood guard. "He's waiting for you inside."

"Thank you." I swallowed hard, nervous about what Fallon's father wanted to say, and pushed the door open.

He sat on the edge of a desk in the center of the room. It appeared as though the space wasn't assigned to a specific hospital employee, but since it was on the VIP floor, I assumed it had been set up for family members to have a place to conduct business if needed.

"Agent Davis, thank you for meeting with me."

"Of course, Mr. President. I hoped I'd have the opportunity to apologize for my behavior last night."

He lifted his hand to halt my words. "Under the circumstances, I'm surprised you didn't haul off and hit Finn the moment you saw him."

My head jerked back. "I don't understand."

"I received a report earlier that you admitted to being in a relationship with Fallon, which raised several concerns for me regarding his safety."

While the Secret Service leadership would technically make the decision about my future with the agency, if the president didn't want me working with his son, then there was nothing I could do to save my job.

"With all due respect, sir, I care for your son very much, and if anything, that should make you confident in my dedication to keep him safe rather than give you any reason to worry."

I more than cared about him; I loved him, but I wanted Fallon to be the first to know how I felt.

A flicker of surprise passed over the president's face, and I wasn't sure if it was because I admitted my feelings or because I stood up for myself.

"I can appreciate that. However, as a parent, I need to make decisions based on more than emotions. Surely, you understand."

I nodded. "I do. I'm a father also, and if someone felt about my daughter when she is older the same way I do about Fallon, I would be grateful that she had a person willing to risk it all for her. I definitely wouldn't be looking for a reason to remove that person from her life."

"I don't want to remove you from Fallon's life." A mixture of resignation and understanding laced his tone. "Getting word that he had been shot was the most terrifying moment of my life. It made me question everything, but it's quite obvious your dedication to not only your job, but also to my son, isn't one of those things I need to question."

A small smile passed over my lips. "Thank you, sir."

There was a knock on the door, and one of the agents poked his head inside. "Mr. President, Marine One is ready for you."

President Donnelley stood and straightened his tie. "Thank you, Agent Hernandez. Give me one more minute." Hernandez nodded, then closed the door, and the president turned back toward me. "It's my understanding that your supervisors are conducting an investigation, and while they have their protocols to follow, you can rest assured I won't be pushing for you to be reassigned."

He offered his hand, and I reached out to shake it.

"I appreciate that. Thank you."

AFTER FALLON'S DAD LEFT, I WANTED TO RUSH OFF TO FALLON'S room, but given the icy reception his mother had given me before, I decided it would be best to head back to the waiting room instead and check on him once he'd had some time to rest.

An hour later, the sound of heels clicking against the linoleum floor pulled my attention from the TV, and I was surprised to see the First Lady entering the waiting room. Her face softened slightly when her gaze connected with mine.

"Fallon is awake again and would like to see you." My heart leapt as I rose from my chair. She stepped aside, gesturing for me to walk ahead of her. When we arrived at Fallon's door, she stopped and turned toward me with sincerity in her eyes. "Agent Davis, I want to apologize for my behavior earlier today. It's been a difficult twenty-four hours, and my emotions got the better of me."

I placed my hand on her arm. "You have no reason to apologize. Clearly, I haven't had the greatest hold on my emotions either."

"I'll give you two some privacy." She smiled and walked down the hall.

I stepped into the dimly lit room and saw Fallon propped up on a stack of pillows. His eyes were closed, and I thought he was asleep until he opened his eyes and said, "You better get your ass in here and finally kiss me."

I couldn't help but laugh at his demand for affection, especially since I was always willing to kiss him. When I reached his bedside, I bent down and brushed my hand over the top of his head before leaning forward and kissing him softly.

A grin spread across his face as we pulled apart. "God, I've been wanting to do that since I first woke up."

"Me too, baby boy. It's been hard not being in here with you."

"About that." He twisted the blanket in his hands. "I want you to stay with me tonight."

"I don't know ..."

"You don't want to stay?"

I pulled a chair over to sit next to the bed and laced our fingers together. "Of course, I want to stay with you, but will everyone be okay with that?"

"I don't care," he murmured. "I'm tired of people trying to keep us apart. In fact, I told my dad about us."

"Yeah." I rubbed my thumb across the back of his hand. "He pulled me aside for a little chat earlier."

"How'd that go?" He rested his head against the pillows.

"Actually, I think it went pretty well. He mentioned he had concerns about our relationship but seemed to feel a bit better about things after I told him how much I cared about you."

"Oh, really?" He quirked an eyebrow.

"Yep. Never thought I'd lie to the president."

Fallon's head snapped back. "What?"

I leaned forward and gave him another brief kiss. "The truth is, I don't just care about you."

He eyed me cautiously. "You don't?"

"Nope." I shook my head slightly. "I love you more than I thought was ever possible."

His eyes brightened, and he wrapped his IV-free hand around my neck, pulling me forward. "I love you too, handsome."

Our lips pressed together, and the warmth of his mouth sent a shiver down my spine. Time seemed to stand still while I deepened the kiss. Having come so close to losing him, I knew I wouldn't ever take a single moment with him for granted.

THE NEXT MORNING, FALLON'S EYES FLUTTERED OPEN, AND HE GAVE me a tight smile. "Good morning."

I pulled up a chair next to his bed. "Morning. How are you feeling?"

He let out a sigh. "Tired."

"Yeah," I agreed. It was hard to sleep when the nurses checked on Fallon multiple times a night, but I refused to leave his side and woke up with him every time someone came into his room.

I was about to ask him if he needed anything when a nurse walked into the room.

"Good morning, Mr. Donnelley. My name is Angie, and I'll be your nurse today." Her tone was entirely too cheery for the early hour.

While Angie began her assessment, I received a text from Tanner:

> Change of plans. Monroe is on his way to St. Thomas and will meet with you at the hospital

"Everything okay?" Fallon asked.

"Uh ... I'm not sure. I didn't want to worry you, but I have a meeting with my superior later this morning. It was supposed to be at the field office, but I just received a message saying he's coming here instead."

Angie typed a few notes into his chart and then headed out.

"Do you think they'll reinstate you?"

I shrugged. "I have no idea."

A few minutes later, Fallon's eyes grew heavy and he fell back asleep.

While waiting for Monroe, I quickly showered in Fallon's room and brushed my teeth with a toothbrush the hospital had placed in the room. I supposed things like that were expected on the VIP floor. Since I didn't have a change of clothes, I put the same ones on that I had been wearing for a few days and then checked my emails while sitting in the chair next to Fallon's bed. He was still sleeping when Tanner walked into his room.

"Davis, Monroe is ready for your meeting."

I stood to follow him, and he led me to the same room where I'd had my chat with the president the day before.

"Agent Davis, have a seat," Monroe greeted me from behind the desk.

I pulled out one of the chairs and sat.

"As you're aware, our investigation is ongoing regarding not only the shooting of Fallon Donnelley, but also your behavior and attack on Finnegan Donnelley."

"Yes, sir." My hands began to sweat. My future with the Secret Service possibly hinged on that one moment.

"I spoke with Agent Tanner, and he told me what happened two nights ago, but I would like to hear your side of the story."

For the next few minutes, I went over every detail with him, from rushing out of the command post, to confronting Finnegan, and finally confessing that Fallon and I had started a secret affair while I'd been assigned to his detail.

After a moment of silence from Monroe, he sighed. "The agency has decided you'll spend the next two weeks on leave without pay for your actions against Finnegan Donnelley."

That wasn't much of a surprise because I knew I'd face disciplinary action for my behavior. "And after two weeks?"

"A decision hasn't been made about your placement yet. President Donnelley has asked us to consider keeping you with Fallon, but we are still determining whether or not that's the best course of action."

I drew in a quick breath. Knowing the president had gone to the agency in support of me and his son gave me reason to believe everything would be fine despite what happened with my job.

Monroe continued. "If we do keep you on your current detail, you will need to understand that when you're off duty, you will have no say over the team's operations. You'll be a guest of Mr. Donnelley's during that time and nothing more."

"Of course, sir." That was something I could handle.

"Having said that, there is still a possibility we will assign you to another team."

"Understood."

Monroe explained I would receive the final decision regarding my employment before my administrative leave was over, and then I was dismissed.

When I returned to Fallon's room, he appeared to be asleep, and his mother, who had stayed at a hotel the night before, sat in a chair near the window.

She gave me a bright smile. "Good morning, Agent Davis."

"Ma'am, please call me Rhett."

She nodded. "He's been sleeping since I arrived."

I sat in the chair next to his bed. "He was awake for a little bit this morning, but he did say he was tired. I'm sure the pain medication is contributing to that."

A few seconds later, with his eyes still closed, Fallon asked, "How'd your meeting go? Are you still my sexy bodyguard?"

My eyes widened, and I peeked over at the First Lady and then said nervously to Fallon, "Um ... I'll find out in two weeks."

"What will we do if they move you?" His voice cracked.

I'd spent every moment since I had been relieved of duty asking myself that same question, and only one answer made sense.

"Then I'll turn in my resignation."

27

FALLON

"Do you have a three?" Rhett asked.

I checked the playing cards in my hand. "Go fish. Do you have a King?"

"Go fish," he said after he drew a card from the deck.

I drew a card too.

"Knock, knock."

I looked toward the door to see Declan saunter into my hospital room. "Hey."

"How are you feeling?" my friend asked.

"Like I live in a nursing home and am playing cards with my hot nurse." I winked at Rhett.

He rolled his eyes. "I'm not your nurse."

"No, but we could role-play." I smirked.

"So, I see you're doing well." Declan chuckled.

"As well as I can be."

"I can't believe you were shot." Declan pulled a chair closer.

Rhett and I filled Declan in on the shooting. In the last twenty-four hours, the FBI had arrested Joseph Hughes in connection with my attempted murder. I didn't know more than that.

"Wow. That's some crazy shit. I thought the Secret Service was supposed to keep you safe?" Declan questioned jokingly, then glanced at Rhett. "No offense."

Rhett held his hands up slightly. "Things would have been different if I had been there."

"How so?" Declan continued to ask questions.

Rhett reached over and grabbed my hand, Declan's eyes following and widening. Then Rhett told my friend, "Because I would have been the one shot."

"Wait …" Declan waved his hand between the two of us. "You two are—"

"Cat's out of the bag," I said and then glanced at my man. "Rhett and I are dating."

I expected Declan to keep grilling us about everything, but when I looked over at him again, his mouth was hanging open.

"Everyone knows, so we aren't hiding it anymore," I stated.

"Wow. Good for you two," my friend said. "I suspected something was up but wasn't ever sure."

"Apparently, we didn't hide it well," Rhett advised. "All my guys knew."

"That's crazy. How does it work with your job?"

Rhett lifted a shoulder. "Either I'll have one or I won't."

"You will." I turned to him.

"We don't know that."

"I'm not going to let you get fired or forced to resign because of me."

"What are you saying?"

"Either you'll still be on my detail, or I'll refuse to have one."

"Fallon …" Rhett cocked his head. "Don't do that."

"We can talk about it later." I wasn't going to let Rhett give up his career because of me. Being a Secret Service agent was what he was meant to do. He was good at his job, and us falling in love shouldn't change anything. I'd heard stories about other presidents' children having relationships with their details, so if they could do it, so could I.

Declan cleared his throat and waved his hand around. "How long are you in this place?"

I lifted a shoulder. "I don't know."

"What about school?" he asked.

Oh yeah. School. That was the least of my worries, considering I had almost died, but I couldn't miss school. "Shit, it's Monday. We had class today."

"Yeah, but everyone knows you're in the hospital."

Of course, they did. I sighed. "Great."

"But I was thinking I could video call you during the classes we share. That way, you won't miss anything."

"No matter what, I need to come up with a plan to stay caught up in all my classes." The last thing I wanted to do was attend classes from a hospital bed, but if I fell behind, I might not move on to my final year of law school. And I didn't want to delay becoming an attorney.

"Or." Rhett stood. "Give me a second."

He walked toward the door and spoke with Agent Day. There were a lot of head nods and glances at me and then a handshake.

Rhett walked back toward his chair. "Day is going to speak with Tanner about getting cameras put up in each classroom so you can attend remotely. An agent will bring you any materials you need, and we'll get your books and stuff brought over."

"You're the best." I beamed and had the urge to kiss him but refrained since Declan was so close.

"Don't forget to submit your internship applications," Declan reminded me.

The Boston area had only a handful of civil rights law firms, and I planned to apply to all of them and see which one I could get in with. Except, since I'd been shot and could possibly be a liability to anyone I was around, would I get hired? My phone was blowing up with my friends and the media talking about what had happened at Tyler and Hayden's wedding. Hiding that kind of story was impossible since I was the president's son, and I had to assume everyone in the world knew.

"Yeah." I blew out a breath. "I was worried before they wouldn't want me around because I had Secret Service with me, and now, it's obvious why I need my detail. No one is going to want to hire me."

"Hey." Rhett grabbed my hand. "You don't know that. It's the same situation as we talked about before."

"And what if a 'client'"—I used air quotes—"comes in and does the same thing as that guy at the wedding?"

"If that had been our wedding, the staff would have been thoroughly searched before starting their shifts. Sure, Agents Day and Bernard had done a sweep, but it's easier to keep you safe in a controlled environment. Like at school, you will have agents posted inside and outside of your work. We could search each person who walks into the building, if that would make you feel safer."

"Oh, great. That's exactly what clients want." I rolled my eyes. Rhett was trying to help, but having bodyguards still felt like a burden. Also, it didn't escape me that he'd said 'our wedding,' but I didn't draw attention to it.

"Let's see what happens." Rhett gave me a hopeful smile. "If anything, we can put a metal detector up at the doors to the building or the specific office you work from."

"Okay." I turned to Declan. "Where are you thinking of interning?"

"Well"—he grinned—"I'm going to apply to all criminal law offices, but I'm hoping to get into Ashford, Nolan & Torrance."

I blinked. "My dad's old firm?"

When my father was still practicing law, the firm was called Ashford, Donnelley & Nolan. Since he became a senator and more or less retired from being an attorney, my father's former partners added a new partner and changed the firm's name.

"Yeah. I figured if it was good enough for someone who became president, then it's a stellar law firm."

"You know my dad doesn't still work there, right?" I chuckled.

"I know, but a lot of other people at Hawkins Law want to intern there, so it has to be the firm to work at."

"I hope you get it." I smiled.

"Can you pull some strings?"

I barked out a laugh. "You mean, have the president call his old colleague?"

Sean Ashford was more than a former partner of my dad's; he was like an uncle to me. I always thought I would work for him, but my heart wasn't in criminal law.

"Yeah." Declan grinned.

"Sorry, buddy. Don't think I can make that happen, but I suppose I can give Uncle Sean a call and put in a good word for you."

SEVEN DAYS LATER, I WAS FINALLY RELEASED FROM THE HOSPITAL. IT had been a long ten days, and I was eager to go home and sleep in my own bed, and with Rhett. He never once left my side, and sometimes we cuddled in my small hospital bed, but he usually slept on the pull-out couch. I wanted to wake up next to him now that our relationship wasn't a secret anymore. He was still on leave from his duties, so there was no reason he couldn't stay the night.

"Why is it taking so long to get discharged?" I whined as I paced the room.

My doctor had taken me off the morphine the night before, but I wanted to be hooked up to it again. My chest hurt like a motherfucker, and the pain pills I was taking weren't even close to the liquid stuff, but the condition for going home was I needed to get off the IVs and see how I would do. I wasn't going to tell anyone how badly I really hurt; I knew I would heal eventually.

"I don't know, but I can go check," Rhett said and walked toward the door.

My cell rang, and I slid it out of the pocket of my jeans. Agent Day had brought me clothes to wear home, and I had no idea what happened to the tux I had been wearing the night of Tyler and Hayden's wedding.

Glancing at my screen, I saw it was my father. "Hey, Dad."

"How are you feeling?"

"Great. They're discharging me, and I can't wait to go home."

"About that." He paused for a second. "Your mother is getting ready to head to Boston on Air Force Two to bring you here."

I blinked. "Here? As in the White House?"

"Yes."

"Why?"

"Because we have doctors and staff to take care of you around the clock."

"I don't need them to take care of me."

"Fallon," my father groaned. "Don't argue with me."

"Look, Dad. I understand you're worried about me, but I'll be fine. I have Rhett and my team here if anything happens. What I need is to get back to my everyday life again. I'm tired of attending school through a computer screen, and I have to apply for internships and set one up for the summer. I can't do any of that in D.C. Plus," I continued, "I don't care how big the White House is, I refuse to be under the same roof as Finn."

Dad was silent on the other end. Then he finally said, "If I can't convince your mother, it's out of my hands."

"You should understand how important law school is," I argued. "Tell her I need to stay."

"I'll see what I can do, but you know she worries."

"I know." Rhett walked back into the room, followed by a nurse with a wheelchair for me. "I need to blow this popsicle stand now."

"All right. I love you, son."

"Love you too, and tell Mom I'll be fine." We hung up, and I asked the nurse. "Can I leave now?"

"Yep. I have your discharge papers right here."

"Great." She handed them to me, and I asked Rhett, "Meet you at my place?"

"I'll be right behind you."

28

RHETT

FALLON SAT ON HIS COUCH, SCROLLING FOR SOMETHING TO WATCH ON TV. Agent Day, who had been moved to my post while I was on administrative leave, had walked to the kitchen and sat at the island with his back to us when we arrived at the condo, trying to give us some semblance of privacy. We'd heard some murmurings that Day and Bernard would be transferred because of the shooting, but Fallon had also gone to bat for them and convinced the higher-ups to keep both agents on his detail.

"I can't believe I have to do online classes for another week," Fallon huffed.

"It's not like you had your appendix removed. It's going to take some time to heal from a gunshot wound," I said, dropping onto the seat next to him.

He sighed. "At least the press might have something else to report on by the time I go back to campus."

Even though it had been ten days since the shooting, it was all the news seemed to want to discuss, and it was hard to miss the media vans outside his building when I pulled into the parking garage.

I laced my fingers through his. "I know it's not easy, but I'll be here with you every day to keep you entertained when you aren't studying."

"And how exactly do you plan on entertaining me?" He turned his head to look at me with a mischievous gleam in his eye.

I shook my head. "Not like whatever you're thinking."

"Why not? I'll even let you do all the work," he whispered so Day couldn't hear us over the TV.

"You're ridiculous. You need to rest, not get riled up."

"Will you kiss me at least?" he pouted.

"I'll always do that without question."

I leaned in and did as he wanted. He palmed the back of my head as my tongue delved into his mouth. It was so easy to lose myself in him. I began trailing my hand up his thigh before I remembered we couldn't take things any further since he needed to focus on his recovery and we had company. As soon as I pulled back, the alarm on my phone went off.

"It's time for your pain meds. The pharmacist said they'll likely make you sleepy. Do you want to stay out here or lie down in bed?"

"I think I'll go to bed." He gritted his teeth and groaned in pain as I helped him up from the couch.

"Take your time."

"I'm fine," he snapped.

I couldn't imagine how much it hurt every time he moved, so him being grumpy didn't bother me. Instead, I walked alongside him to his room. "While you're sleeping, I'm going to head over to my apartment and pick up a few things."

"Okay."

He got into bed, and I gave him his pill and his water bottle. It didn't take long for him to fall asleep, likely worn out from coming home and still healing. Once I was sure he was settled, I slipped out of the room.

Wanting to let Day know I was leaving, I headed toward the kitchen.

"How's Fallon feeling?" he asked from where he sat at the island.

"He's in pain, but I gave him his meds, so he'll probably sleep for a bit. I'm going to pick up some stuff from my place, and then I'll be back."

"Okay." He picked at the label of his water bottle.

"Are you all right?" I asked and took a seat on the barstool across from him.

He shrugged. "Just wondering why I'm still a part of this team."

By his statement, I assumed he was harboring a massive amount of guilt because Fallon had been shot on his watch.

"Fallon wants you here," I explained.

He looked up at me. "I don't understand why. He almost died under my protection."

"Hey, you can't continue to beat yourself up about it. We all believed the threat was gone and Finnegan had handled his shit. Besides, it's likely you saved his life with your quick actions."

"I still let you down," he murmured.

Standing, I squeezed his shoulder. "Fallon is going to be okay. That's all that matters."

I hoped he realized neither Fallon nor I was upset with him. I knew firsthand how seriously Day took his job—we all did—and the only reason things would have been different with me there was because I would have been right next to Fallon—not because it was my job, but because I had a hard time being any sort of distance from him.

Day gave me a nod and then said, "Before you leave, Tanner wants you to swing by next door."

I cocked my head to the side. "Do you know why?"

"No." He shook his head. "He said to tell you after you got Fallon settled."

"Okay. I'll go over there now."

As I walked down the hall to the next condo, I began to feel anxious. Tanner likely wanted to speak to me about my future with the agency. Monroe had mentioned they were going to make a decision about my assignment before my two-week administrative leave was over. It was a moment I'd been dreading and ready to put behind me all at the same time. I was mentally prepared to resign if they wanted to transfer me, but I hoped it didn't come down to that.

When I stepped into the command post, Agent Jones was at his desk as usual.

"Hey, man. Good to see you finally," he said as I searched for our team leader.

"You too," I replied. "Is Tanner around?"

"I think he's in the dining room."

"Thanks." I patted him on the shoulder as I headed toward the back of the condo, where the kitchen and dining room were located.

"Agent Davis, have a seat," Tanner greeted. I pulled out the chair directly across from him and sat. "I've received official word from D.C. that you'll remain on your current detail as soon as your leave is completed."

I let out a long breath. "Thank you, sir."

"From what I hear, you have the president to thank. He's the one who requested you stay on his son's team."

I couldn't help the smile that passed over my face. "Still, I'm grateful for the opportunity to prove myself to you again."

Tanner folded his hands on the table in front of him. "You have nothing to prove to me. I know you're a damn good agent. The agency just needed to make sure there wouldn't be any issues with you remaining here with us."

"Understood."

"Having said that, it's my understanding Monroe explained to you what to expect if you stayed."

I nodded. "He did."

"Well, in case you need a reminder, when you are off duty, you are to defer to your colleagues. At those times, you're simply a guest of Mr. Donnelley's and not an agent. As long as we're clear, I want to welcome you back to the team." He stood and stuck his hand out.

We shook.

"Thank you again, sir."

AFTER PICKING UP MY STUFF FROM MY APARTMENT, I MADE MY WAY
back to Fallon's place. When I walked inside, he was on the couch in
the living room with Agent Bernard standing nearby since shift change
had happened while I'd been away.

"Hey, Bernard," I greeted and dropped my duffle bag next to the
door.

"Hey. I'll give you two some privacy," he said and turned toward
the kitchen.

A part of me had been concerned about running into my colleagues
after my relationship with Fallon became public knowledge, but so far,
no one had said anything negative to me.

I dropped a brief kiss on Fallon's lips before sitting next to him. "I
have some news."

"I'm hoping by your tone it's good news."

I couldn't stop the grin from spreading across my face. "It is."

"Well, spit it out already," he demanded when I didn't continue
right away.

"Looks like you're stuck with me on your protection detail."

His eyes widened. "Seriously?"

"I won't officially be back until my leave is done in four days, but
yeah, I'm here to stay."

Fallon wrapped his arms around my neck and then grimaced in
pain.

"I'm glad you're excited, but you need to take it easy."

He nodded. "Yeah. I'm just so happy things worked out."

"Me too, baby boy."

By the end of Fallon's first week back at school, I had rarely left his side. We'd settled back into a routine, and while the first couple of days of class had taken a toll on him, he seemed to be making a lot of progress physically. However, it didn't stop me from worrying.

Anytime he left the house, I was on high alert, not just looking for threats but also watching him to make sure he wasn't in too much pain, and checking that he had everything he needed.

When his final class of the day ended, I bent down and picked up his bag. Long gone were the days when I sat a row behind him. Since he'd returned to class, I sat right next to him.

"I got it." Fallon snatched the bag from my hands.

"I'm just trying to help." I frowned.

"But I don't want your help," he hissed angrily. "You're acting like I can't do anything on my own. It's irritating."

"That's not true," I replied as we stepped into the hall. "I know you're capable, but it's hard for me to watch you struggle when I can be there for you."

"Except that doesn't help me. I'm never going to get back to normal if you coddle me all the time."

Having an argument at school probably wasn't the best thing. The occasional journalist still popped up out of nowhere to ask questions about Fallon's recovery, and we didn't need a public squabble to become a part of the story. "Let's get back to your place, and we can talk more there."

"Fine," he mumbled and walked toward the SUV, where Leigh was waiting to drive us.

The doctor hadn't cleared Fallon to drive yet because he was still taking pain medication. And since we weren't trying to sneak in alone time because everyone knew we were together, it was easier for us to ride with the other agents.

Day hopped into the front seat, while Fallon and I sat in the back. The ride was silent, and I could tell he was still annoyed with my actions back in the classroom.

When we entered his condo, he went directly to his bedroom and slammed the door. Wanting to give him a few minutes to cool off, I walked to the kitchen and grabbed a bottle of water from the fridge.

A few minutes later, Fallon came back out, dressed in a tank top and sweatpants. "I'm going to the gym."

He'd been working with a physical therapist since he'd been discharged, and I knew he was allowed to do some basic exercises, but it felt as though he was trying to prove something at that moment because he was angry.

Knowing I needed to tread carefully to not piss him off further, I said, "Okay, give me a minute to change, and we can head downstairs."

I walked into his bedroom and grabbed my workout clothes from a drawer he'd cleaned out for me. Before changing, I called Day on the radio to let him know about our plans and allow him a chance to conduct a quick sweep of the onsite gym.

"All right, let's go," I said as I entered the living room.

Fallon gave me a curt nod and followed me into the hallway. We stepped into the elevator, and he punched the button for the second floor. When the doors opened, Day announced the area was clear.

"So, what are you planning on doing?" I asked as we walked inside the workout room.

Fallon's jaw tightened before answering tersely, "I know my limits, Rhett. I'm just going to walk on the treadmill."

He jumped onto the machine and pushed a couple of buttons before he started walking at a slow pace. I headed over to the stationary bike to start my own workout. I planned to keep it low key because I was afraid if I did anything strenuous, it might set Fallon off again, since he still had some restrictions.

I glanced in his direction a few times in awe of how toned he still looked despite not being able to keep up with his regular workout routine and rowing. He hadn't had much of an appetite either because of the pain meds, but given the way he was glaring at me through the reflection of the mirror, he must have taken my appraisal wrong because he finally snapped, "Why are you staring at me? I'm not over-doing it."

I climbed off my machine and walked over to him. "I know you're not. I was just thinking about how hot you are."

He rolled his eyes. "Sure, you were."

"It's true."

"I'm still mad at you," he grumbled, but I didn't miss the way his lips turned up in a faint smile.

"Bet I can get you to forget all about being mad." I smirked.

"How?"

"Finish your workout, and I'll show you when we get back upstairs."

29

FALLON

I WASN'T SURE WHY I WAS IRRITATED WITH RHETT. I KNEW HE HAD THE best of intentions, and it wasn't like being together for a long period of time was new for us, but for some reason, I was feeling smothered. Maybe it was the narcotics that caused my mood swings. Or it could have been because I was weaning off those drugs, so I hurt more.

After only ten minutes on the treadmill, I pressed the stop button. I wasn't used to activities being so difficult, but even the slow pace of three miles per hour was enough to make me winded. Rowing 2,000 meters with my rowing team would be impossible, so I had to tell my coach I was out for the spring. That pissed me off too.

I stepped off the machine and said to Rhett, "I'm ready to go."

He didn't question why we'd spent less than fifteen minutes working out. Instead, he said into his mic, "Windstorm is en route to the nest."

We stepped out into the hall, and Day gave us some room as we walked toward the elevator.

"I'm not usually one to turn down sex or anything, but I think I'm just going to go upstairs and take a shower. Can you order us pizza?" I asked Rhett.

"Of course."

"Then maybe we can watch a movie in bed before we pass out?"

"You're okay with me staying tonight?" He pressed the button to call the elevator.

"Yeah, but I can't promise I'll make it to the end of the movie."

My phone buzzed in my pocket, and with a quick glance at my watch, I saw it was Uncle Sean returning my call. I'd called him about Declan because I knew my friend would be an excellent intern at Ashford, Nolan & Torrance.

"I need to take this." I stepped back from the elevator and answered the call. "Hello?"

"Fallon, it's Uncle Sean. My assistant gave me a message you called. Is everything all right? I heard about you getting shot."

"Yeah, I'm on the mend, but I was calling because I need to ask you a favor."

"Oh? What's up?"

I looked out the window to the street one story below. It was getting dark, and rain was coming down hard. "A buddy I attend law school with applied for an internship at your firm. I know there are a lot of people who have, but please consider my friend Declan because I know he's a worthwhile candidate."

"I was hoping *you* would apply." Uncle Sean chuckled.

"You know criminal law really isn't my thing."

"I know, but I still dream of adding Donnelley back to the firm's name one day."

"Could still happen if I decide civil rights isn't my thing either." I smiled warmly at Rhett and Agent Day as they waited patiently for me.

"I would love that. So, what's your friend's name?"

"Declan Rivers."

"Okay. I still want to interview him, but I'll keep in mind that you've vouched for him."

"Thanks, Uncle Sean. I appreciate it."

"Of course. How are your mom and dad?"

"You know, busy running the country." I snorted.

"I'm surprised Mary isn't with you now."

"Oh, she wanted to be, but I refused and told Dad to keep her in D.C."

"And Finn?"

I took a deep breath. "He's in D.C. and supposedly getting treatment."

"If there's anything I can do, please tell your dad to call me."

"I'll tell him, but I'm staying out of anything that has to do with Finn."

"Should we expect a different kind of fireworks display this Fourth of July?"

I barked out a laugh. Since my parents would more than likely stay in D.C. or attend some presidential thing for America's birthday, my sister and I were hosting the annual party at our Cape Cod home. We had little to do except make sure the party planner was on top of things, and Faye was handling that. "Finn isn't invited."

"Understandable. Well, tell everyone hello when you speak with them, and I'll keep an eye out for your friend."

"Thanks again." We hung up, and I walked back toward the elevators. "Sorry about that."

"Everything good?" Rhett asked.

"Yep. Just trying to get Declan a job."

I sent a text to him about my call with Uncle Sean as Day pressed the button on the elevator again. The doors slid open, and the three of us stepped inside and then rode up to the eighth floor.

"We're ordering pizza," I said to Day. "You want in?"

"I'm good, thank you. I'm going home to my girl as soon as shift changes."

I stopped walking toward my condo and faced Agent Day. Speaking with my uncle about the upcoming party gave me an idea. "You know what? I want you both to request the Fourth of July off."

Rhett and Day shared a confused look, and then Rhett said, "Okay?"

"Bernard and Vance too."

"Why do you want all of us to take the day off?" Rhett asked.

I shrugged. "Because I want you all there as my guests and not my detail. You deserve a fun holiday, especially after the wedding."

"Thank you." Day gave me a small smile.

"Bring your girl also." I squeezed his upper arm. "There will be dancing, an open bar, and fireworks."

"We'll have to talk to Tanner," Rhett advised.

"Okay. If he gives you any problems, I'll talk to him," I stated.

We headed for my condo again, and once Rhett and I were inside, Agent Day stood outside or went to another post. I wasn't sure given he let Rhett be the man on the inside, even when Rhett wasn't on duty.

Even though I was aching and could tell I needed a pain pill soon, I found myself telling Rhett, "Order the pizza, then join me in the shower."

A slow smile slid across his face. "I knew you couldn't resist me."

I snorted a laugh. "It's true, but I don't want to fuck."

"Okay. I understand. You're still healing." He started for the kitchen, but I grabbed his arm.

"I'm not still mad," I told him.

"I know."

I took a step forward and placed my head against his chest. His arms went around my waist as he hugged me. "Really. I just want to feel better so we can do stuff again, especially sex."

"You'll get there."

"And coming off these pain meds is fucking with my emotions."

"That's understandable."

"Okay." I tilted my head up and kissed him softly. "I want pepperoni, green peppers, and extra cheese."

"You got it."

We broke apart, and I walked to my bathroom and stripped off my clothes. After turning on the shower, I stood in front of the mirror and looked at the small line that was starting to scar above my pec. The doctors had done an excellent job of sewing me back up and only had to open me enough to pull out the bullet. It was crazy something so small had almost killed me.

It only took a minute for the water to heat, and after I stepped inside, I heard Rhett come in and remove his clothes. With one arm braced against the cool, tiled wall, I rested my head against it, letting the warm water wash over me.

"Are you okay?" Rhett asked as he stepped inside.

"Yeah," I replied, not moving my head. "Would you mind washing my back?"

He squirted my soap into his hand and then started to wash my back. Even though his touch was gentle, it stirred things inside of me. Maybe it was the talk a few minutes before about sex, but at that moment, I needed to feel his hand on more than my back.

Reaching behind me, I grabbed his wrist as it moved lower and pulled his hand to my front.

"Fallon," he whispered, his voice laced with desire and caution.

"Make me come," I urged, guiding his hand to my growing erection.

Rhett hesitated for a moment but then moved his fist with an expert touch. I couldn't help but groan as my body responded eagerly. It had been two long weeks with no form of release, and I hadn't even felt the need to take care of myself. I knew it wouldn't be long before I was left weak in the knees.

He positioned his free hand against the wall beside my head, while his lips planted soft kisses across my shoulders. His soapy palm glided effortlessly as it worked me closer to the edge.

"Fuck," I hissed, my breath hitching. "I've missed this."

I turned my head, keeping it propped on my arm, and he stepped closer, his own arousal pressing into my ass cheek. I longed for him to slide inside me, but I knew it was too soon. If I couldn't manage more than ten minutes on a treadmill, how could I handle making love to him?

His lips moved along my wet skin, and the slippery hand jerked me at an increasing tempo, pushing me closer to coming apart.

"God," I groaned. "Don't stop."

Leaning forward, he took my mouth in a passionate kiss, and it didn't take long for my body to tense and the pleasure to intensify until

I released my pent-up load against the shower tiles and into his skillful hand.

"Better?" he asked.

I straightened, no longer needing the support of the wall, and then dropped to my knees. "Yeah."

"Fallon," he warned, but I didn't respond. I might not have been ready for vigorous sex yet, but my smart mouth was still useful.

Rhett leaned against the shower wall where I had been standing, but now facing me.

Without hesitation, I took him into my mouth, teasing the tip before engulfing his shaft. His hands pressed flat against the wall, his hips shifting slightly, as I devoured him until he was shooting down my throat.

30

RHETT

FALLON LAY ON HIS SIDE IN BED WHILE HE WATCHED ME PACK MY BAG. "You should have Poppy stay here tonight."

I turned to look at him. "What?"

He grinned. "You've basically been living here for the last two months. Don't you think it's time we make things official?"

He wasn't wrong about me practically moving in. The other agents had started staying in the hall next to his front door, which made it feel as though we were in a little bubble just for us. The only time I left his place was when I had Poppy. Sometimes the three of us would spend the day together, but Poppy and I always headed back to my apartment alone at night. I hadn't wanted to impose by forcing him to make a space for my daughter in his condo if he wasn't ready for that step in our relationship.

"Official? Are you saying you want us to live together?"

"Well, I thought we already were, but if you need me to give you a formal invite, I can." He winked.

I set my bag on the floor and walked over to him, kneeling next to the bed. "I would love to live with you, as long as you're sure."

He answered with a passionate kiss, and there was no doubt left in my mind he wanted me to move in. That he wanted the same future I could so clearly see for us.

I couldn't get enough of kissing him as I ran my hand down his side to his perfect ass. My movement elicited a groan from his throat before he nipped at my bottom lip.

"Why are you wearing clothes," he grumbled.

"Because I'm an idiot and thought I was leaving." I gave him a cheeky grin, and then undressed in record time.

"That's so much better." He pulled me onto the bed and went back to attacking my lips with his.

We spent several minutes kissing until my lips were swollen and I could barely catch my breath.

I pulled back and stared into his eyes as they darkened with need. "Let me take care of you."

I trailed kisses down his neck and abs until I knelt between his outstretched legs. His cock was hard and begging for attention. I ran my tongue up his thighs, then along the underside of his dick until I reached the tip and licked the bead of pre-cum I found there.

Fallon hummed with satisfaction, and I smiled before wrapping my lips around his length and taking him to the back of my throat.

His hand tugged at my neck and guided me up and down his shaft. "I love the way you suck me," he managed to breathe.

Knowing how much he liked it when I used my hand while giving him a blowjob, I reached between his legs and gently massaged his balls.

"I'm so close," he moaned after a few minutes and pushed me away. "But I want to come with you buried inside me."

Crawling up his body, I whispered against his lips, "I want that too."

Grabbing the lube from the nightstand, I poured some onto my fingers and slid them down to his hole. While I stretched him, Fallon ripped open a condom and rolled it down my length.

"Are you ready for me?" I asked after slipping a third finger inside him.

"Yes," he breathed.

Kneeling between his legs once again, I slowly eased into him, and Fallon pulled me down for another kiss. Our tongues tangled together as I started rocking my hips.

I'd never felt a connection so intense with anyone before, and I thanked my lucky stars for that morning six months before when I was assigned to protect the son of the president. At the time, it felt as though my dream was being ripped away from me. Little did I know I would soon be living an even greater one.

Fallon wrapped his legs around my waist and angled his hips so I could go deeper. I could feel his ass squeezing my dick like a vice, and I knew I wouldn't last much longer.

Gripping his shaft, I stroked him in time with my thrusts. His eyes slammed shut as he moaned, and hot spurts of cum exploded onto his stomach.

Rocking into him a few more times, I spilled my release into the condom. With one hand braced on the bed, I cupped his face with the other and whispered, "I love you."

He gave me the brightest smile I'd ever seen and said, "I love you too, handsome."

STANDING ON ALEXIS' PORCH UNDER THE MIDDAY SUN, I RANG THE doorbell and waited for her to answer.

"Hi, Daddy!" Poppy shrieked as she appeared in the doorway with her mom.

"Hey, there, sweet pea." My heart filled with joy like it did every time I saw my daughter. "Are you excited to go to the park today?"

"Yes." She nodded enthusiastically, her blonde curls swinging with the motion.

"She's been bouncing off the walls since breakfast." Alexis

laughed. "The park will be a great way for her to burn off some of that energy. Let me grab her bag, and then you guys can go."

"Actually, do you think we can talk for a minute?" I asked.

"Sure." She turned to Poppy. "Why don't you go pick out a couple of books to take with you?"

"Okay." Poppy ran off toward her bedroom.

Once she was out of earshot, Alexis asked, "What's up? Everything okay?"

I took a deep breath. "Yeah, but I wanted to let you know that I'm moving in with Fallon, and I'd like Poppy to stay there with us during my nights."

Alexis had found out Fallon and I were together a few days after he was shot when I'd called her to explain what had happened and why I'd needed her to pick up Poppy that night. She'd been supportive of our relationship since then, so I didn't expect any pushback from her.

She considered my words for a few seconds before responding, "As long as Poppy is happy and taken care of, which I know she is when she's with you, then I think it's great."

"Thank you." I smiled, relieved that things were so easy between us.

"I'm happy for you." She squeezed my shoulder. "Now let me go make sure our child isn't grabbing every single book off her shelf."

A minute later, Poppy came bounding down the hallway. "I'm ready, Daddy."

"Here's her bag." Alexis handed me the small pink suitcase decorated with hearts. "We narrowed it down to two books."

"All right, let's go."

After hugging and kissing her mother goodbye, Poppy's small hand latched onto mine and we walked toward my car.

"I've got a surprise for you."

Her eyes lit up. "Really? What is it?"

I lifted her into the vehicle and buckled her in. "We're going to have lunch with Fallon in the park."

Fallon and I had decided he would go buy sandwiches at the deli while I picked up Poppy. It would also give me a chance to explain to her in terms she could understand that I was moving in with my boyfriend.

"Yay!" she squealed. "I like Fallon."

"I'm happy to hear that." I closed her door and then rounded the front of the car and slipped into the driver's seat. "I like Fallon, too. In fact, I like him so much I'm going to live at his home with him."

I glanced in the rearview mirror to see her eyebrows knitted in confusion. "You're going to stay there forever?"

"I hope so, and when you come to visit, you'll stay there with us. How does that sound?"

"Can I still bring my books?"

"Of course, you can, sweet pea." I started the engine and pulled away from the curb. "You can bring as many books as you'd like."

"Okay, Daddy."

I couldn't help but chuckle. Accepting my new relationship was likely easier at her young age, versus if she were older and fully understood about relationships.

Her happy chatter filled the car as we drove to our destination. When we arrived at the park, I opened the car door and lifted her from her car seat. I held her hand as my eyes searched the grassy area, and I saw Fallon lounging on a picnic blanket under a tree. Agents Vance and Shea stood a few yards away.

"Fallon!" Poppy shouted, tugging at my hand as she pulled me toward him.

He stood and caught Poppy when she jumped into his arms. "Hey, princess!"

His recovery from the gunshot had been remarkable, but I still checked his face for any signs of discomfort as he spun my daughter around. He seemed fine.

Poppy giggled as she hugged him. "Daddy said I get to stay at your house."

Fallon smiled warmly. "Yeah. In fact, when we're done here, we're going shopping so you can pick out a few things for your room."

Poppy turned to me. "Can I get a stuffed animal?"

I brushed her hair out of her face. "Absolutely. Now let's eat."

We all sat down on the blanket, and Fallon passed out our sand-wiches and bags of chips. As we ate, I felt a sense of contentment wash over me. This was how things should be. My daughter, my boyfriend, and me.

Our own little family.

LATER THAT NIGHT, THE THREE OF US WERE WATCHING A MOVIE IN Fallon's living room. After her bath, Poppy had asked him to read the bedtime story she'd picked out before we started the film. She only watched the first fifteen minutes of the princess cartoon before she fell asleep, her head resting against Fallon's side and her feet in my lap.

I turned toward Fallon, admiring the way he looked with Poppy sleeping on him. He caught my gaze and smiled, reaching over to take my hand in his.

"I love you," he whispered.

"I love you too," I replied softly, and leaned over to kiss him.

EPILOGUE

FALLON

As the door to my en suite bathroom at my parents' Cape Cod house opened, I stayed still as I lay on my stomach in the king-sized bed. I heard Rhett's footsteps as he neared the bed, and a moment later, the sheet around my waist slid down my body. The cool breeze from the air-conditioning blew across my skin, leaving me with goose bumps, but I didn't move. I knew what my boyfriend was doing, and I wasn't going to stop him.

I spread my legs, and Rhett chuckled. "You're awake?"

"No," I lied. "Keep going, though."

His hands slid up the back of my thighs as he climbed onto the foot of the bed. "Do you think you can stay quiet? People are probably awake."

"No. Keep going, though." I smiled as I repeated the same line.

Rhett grunted a laugh but didn't stop, his hands moving to my ass and spreading my cheeks wide. "You might have to push your face into the pillow because I'm so fucking hard right now, and I'm not going to be gentle."

My erection swelled against the mattress. I fought to not move my hips to get some sort of relief because I wanted Rhett to be balls deep in me when I came. "I don't want gentle."

He placed a soft kiss on my ass cheek before walking to the nightstand for the lube. Since moving in together, we'd given up condoms, and I'd learned that taking him bareback deep inside of me was one of the best feelings in the world. I loved knowing he was moving inside of me with no barrier and we were feeling all of each other.

"Damn. You have the nicest ass I've ever seen."

"Can you shut up and fuck it already?" I groaned.

The cap to the lube bottle flicked open, and then I heard Rhett squirt some into his hand. A moment later, his fingers moved to my crack and rubbed my puckered rim. "You're lucky I love your sassy mouth."

"And you're lucky I love your ginormous dick."

Rhett groaned, and I heard more lube being squirted from the bottle. He tossed it onto the bed next to me and then crawled up my backside. Gripping his cock, he ran it along my seam and leaned over to whisper into my ear, "Try to be quiet, baby boy."

I sucked in a deep breath, clutching the sheets as he filled me to the hilt. I wanted to moan, but with agents, my sister, and some friends in the rooms nearby, I didn't. Instead, I buried my face in the pillow, biting down hard as Rhett rocked into me.

His pounding increased, and with each delicious thrust, I gripped the sheets harder, my cock rubbing against the bed and begging for more.

"I want to come with you," I said, turning my head.

Rhett stilled and pulled out. I quickly flipped onto my back, and he pushed my bent legs into the air.

"While I love watching my dick slide into your tight hole, I love watching you come even more." He kissed me feverishly, and at the same time, his hard steel slid back inside of me.

Our mouths moved together as his hips rocked and I fisted my shaft. My hand glided easily over my cock with each thrust, and it was as though we were both in a race to see who could finish first.

The headboard hit the wall in rapid thuds, and it didn't take long before our eyes locked and he shot his hot jizz into me. Rhett swatted my hand away a second later and jacked me a few times until I erupted all over my stomach. He pulled out of me and bent down, licking the cum off my stomach.

I watched him gather every last drop.

"Jesus. Watching you do that is going to make me hard again."

"I know. Let's go shower."

AFTER TAKING A *LONG* SHOWER, WE WENT DOWNSTAIRS FOR A LATE breakfast. Faye was at the table with what I presumed to be an egg white omelet in front of her.

"Morning," I greeted my sister.

"Don't talk so loud," she whined.

I shared a confused look with Rhett and then replied, "I'm not talking loud. Are you hungover?"

"Yeah. After you went to bed last night, your friends got me wasted."

I chuckled and began piling scrambled eggs, bacon, and fruit onto my plate that our chef had prepared. Rhett followed behind me and made himself a plate too.

"Can't hang with college kids?" I teased Faye.

Dylan and Jase were staying at the house for the holiday. Since my parents were no longer the official hosts of our annual Fourth of July party (at least until my dad was no longer president), my sister and I added some new people to the guest list. Declan was coming, and, of course, Tyler and Hayden. The newlyweds were still in their honeymoon bliss phase, and since we had the room, and I'd gotten to know Tyler's brothers, I had offered for them to stay at the house to give Tyler and Hayden their privacy. It seemed Dylan and Jase were taking advantage of being on vacation and had partied with my sister after Rhett and I had called it a night. Okay, we went back to my room for our own private party, but it seemed the others had stayed up and drank.

"I *did* hang with them. That's the problem." She grabbed the bottle of ibuprofen in front of her and downed a few.

"You need the hair of the dog," Rhett said. "Want me to get you a beer or something?"

"Oh god, don't mention alcohol," she moaned.

I grinned and sat across from her. "Are you going to make it through the party?"

"I just need to eat."

Rhett sat next to me. "Did you add avocado to your omelet?"

"Yeah, why?" my sister questioned.

"It should help." Rhett stuck a bite of egg into his mouth.

"Handsome and smart." I winked at him.

My sister's new party buddies sauntered into the kitchen.

"Morning!" Jase beamed.

"Who's ready to party today?" Dylan boomed.

"Jesus. How are you both smiling and chipper?" Faye asked them.

"What's the matter, sunshine?" Dylan questioned with a smile.

"She's hungover." I smirked.

"Well, we can't have that," Jase stated. "You promised us dancing tonight."

Faye stood and grabbed her plate. "I'm going back to bed."

"Sleep it off," Dylan said. "Then we'll see you on the dance floor."

ONCE WE WERE DONE EATING, RHETT AND I RETURNED TO MY ROOM TO get ready for the party. Not only was it a national holiday, but we were also celebrating my boyfriend's recent promotion to team leader on my protection detail. He'd assumed he wouldn't get the job after facing disciplinary action, but Tanner had pushed for Rhett to still be considered for the job.

The house was in full chaos as the party planner directed her staff and the caterer on what to do before everyone arrived.

While in my bathroom fixing my hair, there was a knock on the door. Rhett turned to answer it, and I peeked around the corner. He cracked it open, spoke to whoever was on the other side, and then closed his eyes and took a deep breath.

"Thank you. I'll let him know," Rhett said to the person who I assumed was Agent Shea. He was the lead agent while we were in Cape Cod because Rhett, Day, Bernard, and Vance were guests. Rhett closed the door and turned to me.

"What's going on?" I asked.

"Finnegan is on his way."

I balked, not expecting those words to come out of his mouth. Finn wasn't invited to the party and was supposed to be in D.C. with my folks. "What? Why?"

"He wants to talk to you."

I began pacing. "Talk to me? There's nothing to talk about."

"Hey." Rhett reached out and grabbed my wrist to stop me. "When someone is in recovery, one of the steps is usually to make amends with the people they hurt—"

"He almost got me killed," I clipped, as though Rhett didn't know that.

"I know, baby boy, but this is part of the process to help him get better."

"So, I'm supposed to pretend I'm okay with getting shot because of him?"

Rhett let go of my wrist. "No, of course not, but since he's your brother, you might feel better if you hear him out."

It wasn't like I never wanted to speak to my brother again, but it had only been a little over three months since I'd almost died. Everything was too fresh and too raw still. "Yeah, well, he doesn't need to come all this way to do it. He's trying to ruin the party he wasn't invited to."

"I know," Rhett agreed. "I'm not going to force you to speak with him. I was only saying it's probably part of his steps to recovery. If you want, we'll have agents turn him away."

I let out a long groan and paced again. Fuck my brother. He may have been born first, but that didn't mean he was the boss of me.

My phone buzzed with a text, and I glanced at my watch to see it was from Finn.

> Please talk to me

Was it some sort of ESP? Did he know what I was feeling because we were identical? Good. Maybe he felt my pain when I'd almost died.

"I'll go tell Shea to turn him away." Rhett took a step toward the door.

"Wait!" I called out and groaned again. I looked up at the white ceiling and then said to my boyfriend, "No. If I don't talk to him, I'll be thinking about it all night, and I don't want him to ruin another party for me."

"Are you sure?"

"Yes, but I want you with me."

"Absolutely."

Sliding my phone out of my pocket, I shot my brother a text:

> You have 5 minutes

I strode to the door and opened it, Rhett a step behind me. When I saw Agent Shea, I ordered, "Have Finn meet me in my father's office."

"Yes, sir," Shea responded.

My heart was pounding in my chest, and my palms were sweaty. I wasn't nervous but pissed. Of all the times Finn could try to meet with me, the day of the first party I was hosting without my parents' involvement wasn't the right one. Finn probably thought by telling me he was sorry that I would tell him all was forgiven and he could stay for the party.

Hell. No.

I headed to where my father kept his alcohol in his office and poured myself two fingers of his expensive scotch then tossed it back. It burned as it slid down, and ironically, it reminded me of how it felt after the nurse pulled the tube from my throat when I'd woken after surgery. It was another reminder of the shit Finn pulled.

"Hey." Rhett stepped closer. "Just hear him out. If you have nothing to say, then don't say anything."

I glared at my boyfriend. "When have you known me to keep my mouth shut?"

"Okay, fair point." He grinned. "But what I mean is, let him say whatever he needs to, and then you can leave. No need to say something you don't mean or even forgive him."

"I can tell you I'm absofuckinglutely not forgiving him."

"I don't blame you, and as soon as you want to leave, I'm right behind you."

"I love it when you're behind me." I smirked.

"Jesus." Rhett chuckled. "Always twisting things to be sexual."

"Only with you, handsome." I cupped his cheek. "I can't help it."

"One reason I fell in love with you."

"Because of my innuendos?"

"Because you're funny as hell."

My hand slid from his cheek to the back of his neck, and I pulled him to me. Capturing his lips, I kissed him hard. "If you keep telling me why you love me, I'm not going to talk to my brother at all. I'll just take you back up to my room and let you fuck me."

Before any more was said, Shea knocked on the open door. "Your brother just pulled up, sir."

"Thank you." I stepped back from Rhett and took a long breath.

A few minutes later, Finn and one of his agents walked into the room, and my mood shifted again to seeing red.

"Hey," my brother greeted, then eyed Rhett. He probably wondered if Rhett was going to attack him again.

"Don't *hey* me. Just spit it out," I growled.

"Okay, you're still mad."

"Of course, I'm still mad," I snapped. "I'm never going to forget what happened."

"I know, and I'm sorry." He held up his hands.

"Are you?" I sneered.

Finn blinked and dropped his arms. "Yes, I am."

"We tried to warn you something would happen. Instead of paying off your debts and making things right, you used the money to gamble some more. What the hell did you think would happen?"

"I know I fucked up, and all I can say is I'm sorry."

"Okay. Is that all?"

"I don't blame you for being mad, Fallon, but I'm trying."

"Yeah, well, it's going to take more than a few months for me to be okay with the fact my brother's stupidity almost got me killed."

"I understand, and again, I'm sorry."

"You can go now." I waved my arm toward the door.

"Fallon—"

"I said leave!" I shouted.

"I have a right to be here too."

I quickly glanced at Rhett. The glare on his face told me he was itching for a reason to forcibly remove Finn from the house.

"You're not on the guest list, and everyone has orders to only let those in who are on the list." I headed toward the door because I was done with the conversation. "Goodbye, Finn."

"Fallon, wait!"

"If you don't leave, Agent Shea will make you." I rounded the corner, Rhett right behind me. Knowing I needed a few minutes to cool off before guests arrived, I hurried up the stairs to my room.

Once inside, I closed the door and pushed Rhett up against it. I attacked him with my mouth and worked on the buckle of his belt.

"Baby," Rhett said against my lips.

"Shut up and take your pants off."

A stiff drink would probably help me calm down, but so would my boyfriend's dick.

PEOPLE HAD STARTED TO ARRIVE BY THE TIME RHETT AND I WERE ready for the party again. In a few hours, the sun would set and the fireworks would begin. They were always my favorite part.

We walked outside, and I greeted the people I knew. I figured the ones I didn't recognize were on Faye's guest list. Getting past all the Secret Service agents surrounding the property or the ones posted at the gate would have been impossible otherwise.

Walking toward the bar, I spotted Declan, who had brought Luca with him. The two were throwing back a shot, and I headed their way to say hello.

"Sup, guys? Having a good time?"

"Always," Declan replied, and each of them gave me a bro hug then shook Rhett's hand.

"I'm going to go talk to Day and his girlfriend." Rhett kissed me on the cheek and then walked away.

"If you get too wasted, don't drive back. We have plenty of spare rooms here," I advised.

"Thanks. We're working on it." Luca held up his shot glass for the bartender to refill.

"How's Ashford, Nolan & Torrance treating you?" I asked Declan.

"It's good. Drafting a bunch of briefs mostly, but that's to be expected until I'm hired as an attorney there."

"Even then you'll only be a junior associate, so I bet you'll be doing the same thing."

"Maybe, but at least I'll have eye candy."

I tilted my head slightly and tried to think of who Declan could be talking about. Since my father wasn't working there anymore, I had no clue who was on their staff. "Oh, really?"

"Yeah." Declan squeezed my shoulder. "You didn't tell me your uncle was hot as fuck."

I shuddered. "He's my uncle, bro. I don't see him like that. Plus, he's straight."

"I know, but he's still nice to look at." Declan's stare moved to the other side of the pool, and I turned to see Uncle Sean talking to a woman I didn't know.

"And he's your boss," I reminded him.

"I know, but damn." Declan bit his lip. "I wouldn't mind calling him Daddy."

"I'm going to leave before I throw up in my mouth." I shook my head and moved toward where Rhett was talking to Day.

Day handed Rhett something, and Rhett quickly stuck it into the pocket of his shorts. If I didn't know any better, I'd think they'd just done a drug deal.

Before I got closer, I saw Tyler and Hayden walking across the lawn. I changed my path and headed toward them.

"You guys made it." I greeted them both with a hug.

"We had so much fun last year, we wouldn't miss it," Hayden said.

"But ..." Tyler looked at his husband. "We might miss next year."

"Oh?" I arched a brow.

"Can I tell him?" Tyler asked Hayden.

Hayden snorted a laugh. "You might as well now."

Tyler turned back to me, a huge grin on his face. "We're thinking of adopting."

"A cat or a dog?" I grinned.

Both Tyler and Hayden chuckled and Hayden said, "Neither. We'll probably go with a human."

My eyes widened. "A kid? You're thinking of adopting a kid?"

"Yeah." Tyler kissed Hayden. "This guy isn't getting any younger, so we figured we should start thinking about it."

"But you just got married," I reminded them.

"We know," Hayden agreed. "But the adoption process takes at least eight months, if not much, much, much longer. Depends on the age of the child we will adopt. Newborns can take two to seven years."

"Holy shit." I was stunned, to say the least. "Here I thought I'd be the first one with a kid if Rhett and I got married."

"When Poppy is older, she can be our babysitter," Tyler said.

"Already pawning off your kid before you even have it?" I teased.

"You know what I mean." He punched me playfully on the arm.

"I do, and congrats, guys. I truly mean it. You two will be great fathers."

I hugged them again and then went over to Rhett. He was getting food from the buffet, and I stepped in line behind him and grabbed a plate too. "Just caught up with my friends and got all the gossip."

"Yeah?"

"Rundown is Declan is hot for his straight boss, and Tyler and Hayden are going to adopt a kid." Rhett's mouth dropped open. "I know. I'm as shocked as you."

"And those three"—Rhett pointed at Faye, Dylan, and Jase—"I'm pretty sure are about to have some fun of their own."

I watched as the three hurried into the house.

"Jesus. Can this night get any more interesting?"

Rhett continued down the line of food. "Guess we'll see."

WE ATE, WE DRANK, AND WE DANCED. THE SUN HAD SET AND THE fireworks show would start soon.

"I'll be right back," Rhett said and headed toward the house.

I sipped my vodka soda until he came back a minute later. "Everything okay?"

He held out a box of sparklers. "Come with me."

"Oh … kay," I replied skeptically. We were about to watch a massive fireworks show, and he wanted to do kiddie sparklers?

I fell into step with him as we walked toward the beach. Rhett led me down the stairs, and we kicked off our sandals and strolled along the shoreline.

"I just need a break from all the people," he stated.

It was a gigantic party, and each year it seemed only to grow, but I loved it. Hell, it was a way for me apparently to find out what my friends were all up to since I didn't see them as often as I'd like. I was busy interning at a civil rights law firm during the week, and the weekends I spent with Rhett and Poppy. We would go to the park or a movie or hang out at the condo and have tea parties. My life wasn't at all like it was before Rhett came into it. Back then, a lot of my free time was spent at Chrome looking for someone to hook up with, or spending my Fridays fooling around with Declan. I didn't need any of that anymore, and I wouldn't change a damn thing about it.

"That's cool. Back when I was younger, I would come down here with my brother, sister, and our cousins. We would drink the beer we stole from the party and watch the fireworks."

"Oh yeah?" Rhett opened the box of sparklers and started to stick them into the sand in a circle around us. "You have a lot of memories here, huh?"

"I do."

"And it was the first place you and I ever spoke to each other," he reminded me.

"How could I forget? It was the first place you called me Fallon."

"And the first place I realized you were going to be trouble."

I clutched at my chest playfully. "Me? Trouble?"

Rhett chuckled and pulled two lighters from his pocket. "Yeah, you. Can you light the ones on your side while I take care of the ones over here?"

I took a lighter from him, and we both quickly got to work lighting them. When I finished my last one, I turned, and my breath caught in my throat.

He held open a velvet box, and once again, my hand went over my heart as I ogled the silver band with diamonds wrapped around it.

"From the moment we met, I knew there was something special about you. I had a hard time denying the attraction I felt for you, and since fate has a wicked way of making things happen, she made it so I would get to know the man you are on the inside and not just the sassy-talking flirt I assumed you were. You've brought so much light into my world, and I can't imagine a day without you by my side. So, Fallon, who makes me laugh every day, I was wondering if you'd make me the happiest man alive by marrying me?"

A lump formed in my throat, and I tried to hold back the tears, but it was no use. Rhett assumed marrying me would make him the happiest man, but him becoming my husband would make me the luckiest man in the world. He was everything to me.

"Only on one condition," I stated and wiped a tear from my cheek.

"And what's that?"

"Neither of us goes to Atlantic City for our bachelor parties."

Rhett laughed. "Deal."

"Then yes, I'll marry you, handsome."

He stood, the fire from the sparklers fizzling out, and he crashed his lips to mine just as fireworks exploded in the dark sky.

Cheers erupted behind me, and when we pulled apart, I could see all our friends on the small cliff above us. Tyler and Hayden had cameras around their necks, and I realized my fiancé had planned the whole thing.

"How did you pull this off?"

"I'm Secret Service, baby boy. I can make anything happen."

The End.

Declan Rivers and Sean Ashford's story is told in Boss of Attraction. Grab BOA today!

Also, Emmett Cooper and Ford Mahoney's story is told in Hooking the Captain. Grab that today too!

ACKNOWLEDGMENTS

We'd like to thank our husbands, Ben and Wayne, who help make sure everything is running smoothly when we are locked away writing. Stacy Nickelson, Julia Goda, Laura Hull, Margaret Neal, Lynann Adams, and Magan Vernon, thank you for the time you took to help us with this story. We are grateful to each of you.

To Enticing Journey Book Promotions, Tracy Ann, all the bloggers, and authors who participated in our coming soon promo, review tour, and our release day blitz: thank you! We appreciate you helping us spread the word about Secrets We Fight.

And to all of our readers: thank you for the support you continually show us. Because of you, we are able to pursue our writing dreams.

ALSO BY KIMBERLY KNIGHT AND RACHEL LYN ADAMS

Off the Field Duet – A MM Baseball Romance

Dibs - A MM Friends to Lovers Romance Standalone

Forbidden Series - A MM Forbidden Romance Series

Off the Bench Duet - A MM Hockey Romance

Butcher - A MMF Hockey Romance

ALSO BY KIMBERLY KNIGHT

Club 24 Series – Romantic Suspense

The Chase Duet - Spin off duet from Club 24 - Contemporary Romance

Halo Series – Contemporary Romance

Saddles & Racks Series – Romantic Suspense

Ex-Rated Gigolo – Spin off standalone for Saddles & Racks Series - Romantic Suspense

Sensation Series – Erotic Romance

Reburn – Spin off standalone for Sensation Series - Romantic Suspense

Amore – Spin off standalone for Sensation Series - Romantic Suspense

Dangerously Intertwined Series – Romantic Suspense

Burn Falls – Paranormal Romance Standalone

Lock – Mafia Style retelling of Rapunzel

Deliverance – Spin off standalone for Lock - Mafia Romance

Off the Field Duet – A MM Baseball Romance

Dibs - A MM Friends to Lovers Romance Standalone

Forbidden Series - A MM Forbidden Series

Off the Bench Duet - A MM Hockey Romance

Butcher - A MMF Hockey Romance (Coming Soon)

Audio Books

ALSO BY RACHEL LYN ADAMS

Desert Sinners MC Series

Mac

Colt

Off the Field Duet

Traded

Outed

Forbidden Series

After Hours Lectures

Secrets We Fight

Boss of Attraction

Taste of Surrender

Off the Bench Duet

Hooking the Captain

Retaking the Shot

Standalone

Dibs

Falling for the Unexpected

Butcher (Coming Soon)

ABOUT KIMBERLY KNIGHT

Kimberly Knight is a USA Today Bestselling author who lives in the Central Valley of California with her loving husband, who is a great *research* assistant, and young daughter, who keeps Kimberly on her toes. Kimberly writes in a variety of genres, including romantic suspense, contemporary romance, erotic romance, and paranormal romance. Her books will make you laugh, cry, swoon, and fall in love before she throws you curve balls you never see coming.

When Kimberly isn't writing, you can find her watching her favorite reality TV shows, including cooking competitions, binge-watching true crime documentaries, and going to San Francisco Giants games. She's also a two-time desmoid tumor/cancer fighter, which has made her stronger and an inspiration to her fans.

www.authorkimberlyknight.com

ABOUT RACHEL LYN ADAMS

Rachel Lyn Adams is a USA Today bestselling author who lives in the San Francisco Bay Area with her husband, five children, and a crazy number of fur babies. She writes contemporary and MC romance.

She loves to travel and spend time with her family. Whenever she has some free time, which is rare, you'll find her with a book in her hands or watching reruns of Friends.

www.rachellynadams.com

68982118R00149